Mom in the City

Mom in the City

Kausalya Saptharishi

RANDOM HOUSE INDIA

Published by Random House India in 2013

1

Random House Publishers India Private Limited
Windsor IT Park, 7th Floor
Tower-B, A-1, Sector-125
Noida 201301, UP

Random House Group Limited
20 Vauxhall Bridge Road
London SW1V 2SA
United Kingdom

978 81 8400 315 4

Typeset in Sabon by R. Ajith Kumar

Printed and bound in India by Replika Press Private Limited

With all my love and gratitude to my dearest Amma and Appa—the best parents in the world from whom I am still learning the meaning of sacrifice, faith, and unconditional love.

My darling son Antariksh—you are the best gift God has given me. Thanks for lighting up my world and making the beautiful journey called Motherhood immensely enjoyable and enriching.

One

'Ammmaaa!' shrieks Abhi, almost making me swerve the car dangerously close to the road divider. I meet his twinkling eyes in the rear-view mirror and shake my head seriously. His chubby fingers are back to meddling with the toddler car seat harness, his tongue sticking out as he desperately tries to break free from the navy blue Graco. I drive on, hoping he won't succeed in unlocking the triple-locked, Made in Taiwan contraption that serves as a constant reminder of the suburban mom's life in New Jersey I'd recently swapped for a vastly different one in New Delhi.

'Abhi, no screaming when Amma is driving,' I say in my firm mommy tone but he sees the hint of a smile twitching at my mouth corners and giggles like a spring brook. The morning sun casts a honey glow on Abhi's face, colouring his curls a deep bronze and gold. I catch my breath and marvel at this cherubic wonder for the millionth time. He is wearing his favourite red Mickey Mouse T-shirt and shorts after rejecting, with an ear-piercing tantrum, my more staid choice of a blue corduroy shirt and pants.

I give in to his sartorial demands, as I often do with most other things these days. It's the orientation programme at his playschool this morning and I want everything to go without a glitch. I wake up earlier than usual, shower, reply to emails, get Abhi ready, prepare his lunch, chase after him coaxing him to eat breakfast, go trigger-happy like the paparazzi for first-day-at-school photos, and finally wrestle him into the car seat for the ride to Bumblebees.

Vinnie Warsi, my slightly intimidating boss, who had recently brought in her sixtieth birthday at Bali with her girlfriends, was bemused that I would be so excited about Abhi starting playschool. 'Been there, done that, honey,' she'd flicked her Virginia Slims and shrugged. 'It's far more thrilling when you pack your kid off to college; that's when you get to hog the television,' she'd chortled, while I could only think as far ahead as training my almost two-and-a-half-year-old to aim his pee inside the commode.

I honk furiously at the black Innova in front for abruptly braking to a halt. After twelve years of driving on American roads, I am rapidly learning Delhi's roadside etiquette that also permits cussing till you are blue in the face, skipping red lights, and speeding like a tipsy, sleep-deprived maniac on the loose. I dismally wonder if I would ever get accustomed to driving here. Or stop comparing, ad nauseam, India's evils with America's virtues. It used to be the reverse when I was in the US.

'Beep beep,' yawns Abhi, gazing at the clogged-up traffic around us. He has momentarily forgotten his battle with the harness. The dashboard flashes 9 am in red. I crave for the cappuccino and velvety blueberry muffin that used to be my morning Starbucks staple when I was a single working girl in Washington, DC. Ah, those were the days when I still had a waistline and stayed up nights watching *Saturday Night Live* instead of changing soiled diapers. A rising cacophony of horns from behind makes me slam the pedal with such force that I startle Abhi. 'Sorry!' I say to his wide-eyed expression in the mirror. Damn! I missed three seconds of the blessed green light. Two more traffic junctions to cross in this never-ending rush hour nightmare.

I zoom into the parking lot in front of Abhi's playschool. Bumblebees is located in a tony and genteel neighbourhood of Lutyens' Delhi where the lawns are always manicured and its residents are mostly elderly people who walk their pedigreed dogs in the mornings, read the day's papers at their apartment clubhouse and go to the nearby park for a leisurely stroll at sundown. Churchill Lane has an old-world charm to it, cocooned in a life cycle of its own and enviably cut off from the rushed existence plaguing less fortunate Delhiites. The ancient red brick apartment buildings look refreshingly quaint and mercifully untouched by the city's real estate developers who seem to have gone into a ruthless overdrive giving a broad-brushed 'facelift' to the homes of Delhi's nouveau rich. Wherever I go, there is no escaping the tacky beige exteriors and cookie-cutter-style architecture dotting the crammed South Delhi landscape. In contrast, though desperately crying for a coat of paint, Churchill Lane's red brick façade, high arched entrances, and large white-framed windows tell stories of old money and a glorious colonial past. Tales abound of the famous personalities who have lived and died in these apartments with their cavernous rooms and high-ceilinged bathrooms that are double the size of your average Delhi living room. A recent article on Churchill Lane in *Architecture Digest* mentioned that some of its oldest residents are the descendants of an erstwhile royal family from Rajasthan and that the granddaughter of a renowned female playback singer from the golden era of Bollywood (who lives by herself in the complex) is grappling with early signs of dementia. A frail old lady with a mop of snow-white hair fixes her gaze on me from a window on the second floor. I can't help but wonder if she leads a lonely and miserable existence. I remember reading somewhere that not all of Churchill Lane's geriatric community lead *the* charmed life as described in books chronicling the city. There are those who have been abandoned by their children and left to age, along with the peeling walls and stately Ashoka trees that border the property like silent sentinels.

The minute I unstrap Abhi, he sprints towards the lawn glistening with morning dew. His face lights up on seeing the swings and slides next to a jacaranda tree in full bloom. They lie in a state of neglect, their paint chipped, with one of the swings broken. I would later learn that these had been thoughtfully installed by Churchill Lane's residents, anticipating visits from their grandchildren. However, they are now mostly used by the children from Bumblebees or by servants' kids. I grab Abhi's hand and purposefully march across the lawn towards Bumblebees; his blue Snoopy schoolbag, his football-shaped water bottle, and my overstuffed handbag weighing on my shoulders.

'Amma! Want shwinggg!' Abhi shouts, his face scrunched with determination. Oh lord! I know that look. His large black eyes threaten to spill tears. I bend down and kiss him. The smell of baby soap mingled with that of freshly cut grass adds to the redolence in the July air, pregnant with the promise of rain.

'Not now, sweetie. Later. Don't you want to have fun in your new school today?' I say in my most placating tone, 'fun' being the operative word. Abhi considers this for a moment and nods. I am relieved when he takes my outstretched hand without further protest. The last thing I want to deal with right now is a full-blown tantrum. From the corner of one eye, I see a swarm of well-dressed parents and their toddlers spilling out of their vehicles and making their way towards Bumblebees. The scene appears straight out of a TV soap commercial where everybody looks incredibly fresh and chirpy—attractive moms in chic Western wear and dapper dads who look ready to take on any boardroom in their pinstripe shirts and carefully pleated trousers. Abhi looks with interest at the spiffily attired children who are trying to wriggle out of their parents' grasp to make a dash in the direction of the school gate. Had I known my generation of parents resembles Page 3 people, I would have paid more attention to my appearance. My faded kurti—that had once been a great Lajpat Nagar find—pales in comparison to the trendy capris, skinny legging jeans, tight tees, and well-cut body-hugging dresses that make these women look as if straight out of a Zara catalogue. I am tempted to go home, curl up with my child and read *101 Dalmatians* to him.

But despite the super-thin and super-hot mommas around me, I'm all knotted up inside with excitement and anticipation. After three gruelling months of scouting for a playschool 'with a difference' for Abhi, I instinctively knew I had found the perfect one when I first stepped foot in Bumblebees. It is one of those rare finds in Delhi where escalating real estate prices make it next to impossible to run a school in as enchanting and classy a neighbourhood as Churchill Lane.

Bumblebees is a haven unto itself. It occupies the farthest corner in Churchill Lane and is fronted by an understated black wrought-iron gate with a stylish 'B' looped around it. The school is a duplex-style, red brick structure that squats right in the middle of the property, looking bright and cheerful like a house out of a fairytale book. Bumblebees is the only stand-alone apartment, fashioned like a mini bungalow, in the entire Churchill Lane complex that is otherwise a series of blocks segregated by dark passageways.

According to the grist mill, the school property belongs to a renowned artist. His great-grandfather, an influential post-Independence-era statesman, had bamboozled the builders of

Churchill Lane into constructing for him this corner apartment in exchange for certain underhand government favours. The artist, a diehard bachelor, leased out his inheritance to the Bumblebees management twelve years ago before retiring to his Himalayan mountain cabin at Almora. His vivid oil landscapes of the school, mounted in the principal's office, stunningly capture the property's open green space and the happy faces of frolicking children.

A long colonial-style veranda, flanked at both ends by teak columns, wraps itself around the front porch like a satin bow. Designer terracotta pots are neatly lined up along the veranda from which the wispy leaves of ferns, ground orchids and money plants spill onto the red earth outside.

The Bumblebees classrooms are independent clusters, enclosed by cane walls and topped by thatched bamboo rooftops. All around, giant leathery trees with gnarled branches look on like wizened elders, while tiny human beings make the most of their time in this Xanadu. This is just the kind of natural ambience I'd wanted Abhi to experience, not a run-of-the-mill structured classroom facing a busy road. A passerby or pedestrian, a rarity in these parts, might never guess that over a hundred preschoolers are screaming and playing in this sedate neighbourhood. And unlike other 'chain' playschools in the city, there is no splashy signboard shouting out a welcome to prospective parents. I recall feeling confused about the exact location of Bumblebees when I had come for an introductory tour of the school in February. Bumblebees is probably Churchill Lane's second best kept secret, the first being its geriatric residents' cobwebbed stories, stubbornly clinging to its dank apartment walls.

Lilting piano notes of *Pat-a-Cake* float towards us as Abhi and I approach the gate. Parents and children are milling around a man who is belting out popular nursery rhymes from his electronic synthesizer. The trees are festooned with balloons and there are smiling faces everywhere. Chatter and squealing rent the air and it feels like we are in the midst of a summer carnival. I catch the eye of the Bumblebees principal, the elegant fifty-something Mrs Sippy, who has her hair done up in the same impossibly complicated French coif as the last time when we'd met. I must have called her at least half-a-dozen times to inquire about Abhi's chances of getting into the school. From my personal experience, it wouldn't be an exaggeration to state that making the cut at a reputed Delhi playschool is far more challenging and nerve-wracking than cracking the IIT-JEE. While the latter has an entrance exam, the former tests your place in the Delhi social hierarchy: it's all about Whom You Know. But to be fair to Mrs Sippy, this unwritten rule didn't apply in my case. I guess the constant nagging helped.

It had been an agonizing moment to see Mrs Sippy's fuchsia-painted finger-nail nimbly travel down the admissions list till it halted at 'Abhishek'. 'Well,' she had smiled beatifically, gingerly taking off her tortoiseshell reading glasses, 'he's in.' I had grinned maniacally like a kid in a candy store, and could only imagine how I'd feel if Abhi joins an Ivy League college some day. She slid a form across the table. 'Forty-five thousand rupees for the first quarter, dear. The fee break-up and other details are on the sheet.' I balked at the mini fortune I'd be spending on my preschooler's education. I don't think my parents spent so much even annually on fees for my sister and me when we were studying at a prominent Delhi school about two decades ago. But then again, this isn't the same India I had grown up in. The country, this city in particular, has undergone a sea change in the decade I have been away. People in the newly botoxed capital now speak in a Manhattan accent, dine at pricey Mediterranean restaurants, watch movies at multiplexes and splurge on 'Made in China' products in the ubiquitous malls. Playschools have become coveted brand names that are as fiercely desired as high-end couture labels by my generation of parents. And it's my fault, really. I could have settled for the no-frills playschool in my neighbourhood instead of Bumblebees. So why crib about the price tag? A fancy playschool translates into fancy fees.

Mrs Sippy acknowledges my presence with a bright smile and a slight wave of her toned arm. She is wearing a sleeveless white top and khakis, her enviably svelte figure giving stiff competition to the young mothers flitting about. These women are bloody fashionistas, I grimace. I should have at least applied lipstick. But despite my years abroad, I have yet to become a fashion victim and obsess over my appearance. I mean, I love *People*, *Hello!* and their ilk—I'm a self-confessed celebrity news junkie— but honestly, why wear clothes that only Size 2 women can pull off? The effort and time required to shrink to my pre-baby size seems too daunting. Besides, these days, I have a one-word excuse for all pending (read overwhelming) tasks, such as exercise: Motherhood.

Abhi's gaze is fixed on the synthesizer player's fingers as they fly over the keys. He loves music. While in my womb, he would react to music with swift liquid kicks. When he was a baby, he would wail each time the Baby Mozart CD ended; I used to play it in a loop till I fell asleep exhausted, only to wake up zombie-like for his early morning feed.

Abhi claps cheerily to *Old MacDonald*. I smile indulgently. The Alpha Mom in me can't wait to have him start learning an instrument. Maybe the piano or the violin. Or perhaps both? It's quite possible he has the makings of an A.R. Rahman, if I were to believe the words of our family astrologer. But then again, he had also 'predicted' that I would have twins. Bah!

'Excuse me?' a soft voice asks me from behind.

I spin around to see a petite woman, her hair neatly pulled back in a high ponytail. She is wearing blue capris topped by a white linen shirt and looks young enough to be in college.

'Hi, I am Shelly, a teacher here.'

'Hi, I am Iravati,' I return her warm smile.

'I gather from Mrs Sippy that your son is in my class…is that him?' She smiles at Abhi.

'Yes, this is my son, Abhishek—Abhi.'

Shelly kneels down to Abhi's level. 'Hi, Abhi, I am Shelly Aunty. How are we doing today?' Abhi flashes a toothy grin.

Shelly checks the class list on her notepad. 'Have you registered him as only Abhishek or is there a surname too?' she asks. I cringe, not wanting to go down that road.

'Only Abhishek. Registration number 105?' I reply a bit too hastily.

Shelly scans her list again. 'Yep, got it.' She ruffles Abhi's hair and gets on her feet. 'I promise you're going to love it here. Welcome to Bumblebees, buddy!' Abhi considers her words solemnly and returns his gaze to the synthesizer player.

I like Shelly instantly. She has an open and friendly demeanour that encourages conversation. There are two things that first-time moms want from teachers and paediatricians—a willingness to talk and patience. I changed Abhi's first paediatrician only because the man wouldn't open his mouth and whenever he did, was as snappy as a crocodile. He had a long list of accomplishments and degrees but no patience. Then, one day, when he snapped at Abhi for howling after an inoculation, I grabbed my son's medical folder and marched out of the clinic, seeing red everywhere.

'Come on over for a meet-and-greet session with the other parents in the classroom,' Shelly says, pointing in the general direction of the six classroom clusters. 'Mine is the one with the purple fish wind chime in front.' That's when I notice the different wind chimes dangling in front of the classrooms: ladybird, snowman, bird house, sun, fish, and kite.

'Thanks,' I wave to Shelly as she makes her way to the classrooms. Abhi and I join the sea of parents who seem as caught up as me in the moment. Amid the commotion, I spot twin girls in identical red frocks walking hand in hand with an elderly couple whom I presume to be their grandparents. I feel a catch in my throat thinking of my parents who would have loved to be present for Abhi's big day. They are currently in London helping my younger sister get through her difficult pregnancy.

'Amma?' Abhi's high-pitched, little-boy voice cuts into my thoughts. 'Want otter.'

I hand him his water bottle and run my fingers through his hair. 'We are now going to your class, baby. Ready for some fun?' Abhi might not understand what a 'class' is but the idea is to keep talking to the child, to build his vocabulary and enhance his awareness of his surroundings. This is not me, but my new best friends on the block—some insanely optimistic American child care experts—speaking. Catching up on my ever-growing reading list, like, *Manners Time* and *I Use a Potty*! rank even higher on my to-do list than remembering to pay the electricity bill.

Abhi makes loud slurping sounds with the straw in the bottle and races ahead of me to his new classroom.

The minute I enter the classroom, I can sense where the power centre is going to lie in the group of mothers who are chatting animatedly. Anyone who has experienced high school girls' politics would know that power almost always rests with the one who acts as if she is interested in you but actually cares more about her zits; who loves flirting with only the popular boys (and detests the popular girls for being, well, popular); who believes she is way too beautiful for the Miss Universe pageant; and who has a smile so fake that she will win, hands down, the Tupperware Queen title. And yet, surprisingly, these are the girls who wield power everywhere—be it in the classroom, the boardroom, or the bedroom. Everything remains the same in Mommydom politics except that Miss Plastic is now Mrs Plastic and at liberty to slap on more make-up than a Kathakali dancer, keeping her 'real' looks hidden under layers of foundation, blusher and concealer.

I get the queasy feeling that the tall woman in a see-through white kurti and slacks might have been such a girl in school. The first thing that strikes me about her is her dark brown lipstick, that's almost black, and the ridiculous amount of rouge on her cheeks. She is someone my friend, Priya, would intuitively classify as a Class-A bitch.

'Thanks. You are a pet, Riya,' she trills to the petite woman standing next to her as I approach them.

'No seriously, Avantika, you've got a supermodel's height,' gushes the petite woman, Riya. She is clad in skinny jeans and a pink Lacoste T-shirt. Her pink-tipped fingers dance on her pink Nokia slider that she has just pulled out from her pink handbag. Pink candy floss will complete the picture, I silently smirk. 'Gimme your number, babe. I'll give you a missed call,' she adds. Avantika languidly runs her bejewelled fingers through her ironed-to-perfection shoulder-length hair and tilts her head just enough so everyone can see the platinum hoops in her ears. Oh yeah, I have seen enough of chick flicks to know her type.

'Store me as Avantika Sen, darling. That will remind you of my fashion label,' she winks. Wow, some people don't waste any time in marketing tactics.

'You are a fashion designer?' asks a stout woman in the group. She has sad brown eyes that droop at the corners and a tinny mirthless voice. The clingy kaftan-style purple top and black Lycra churidar don't exactly flatter her flabby figure.

'Yep, darling. "The Avantika Sen Collection". Sexy saris and cholis are my specialty.' There she does it again. The thirty-degree head tilt and the brand promotion for recall value.

'Why don't we do introductions?' suggests the stout woman. 'I am Hutoxi and this is my daughter, Jhanvi.' She adjusts the hairclip in her daughter's hair. I notice Jhanvi has the same melancholic eyes as her mother.

'I am Riya and my son's name is Kunal. He is with his dad over there,' says Miss Pink, pointing to a clean-shaven man in crisp formals.

All eyes are on me now.

'Um, hi everyone. I am Ira, and the boy in the red Mickey Mouse T-shirt is my son, Abhi.'

Abhi is seated on a tiny green chair, piling up the wooden blocks scattered on the long turquoise blue table. A girl with two curving pigtails is seated beside him, twisting the arms of a half-naked doll. The classroom is getting noisier as it fills with more people. A few kids are crying, quite bewildered by the change in their daily routine. Shelly is consoling a boy who is whimpering uncontrollably. A man cuddles his weeping daughter and bribes her with a chocolate. I am relieved that Abhi is quietly soaking in his new environment, sans any meltdowns. I knock on my head, not wanting to jinx the moment.

A statuesque woman joins our group. 'Hi, everybody, I am Carol,' she says. Her voice is husky and confident, like she is used to addressing large gatherings. I am sure she must have been a debater or the Head Girl at school. Her hair falls in angular steps over her shoulders, like some pop star whose name I can't remember. The copper highlights in Carol's hair perfectly match her tan-coloured tote. How do these women look so put together, I shake my head in wonderment. I am lucky if I remember to run a comb through my hair in the mornings.

'My daughter, Anna, is in this class,' adds Carol. 'She is the pigtailed girl tearing apart her doll.' She points to the girl sitting next to Abhi, the doll's pink taffeta frock lying forlorn at his feet.

Carol laughs. It's throaty and flecked with mirth. 'Anna does that to all her dolls. But I let her be, for these childhood years won't come back. I mean, do we women ever go around ripping things apart—besides our husbands, of course?' We concur with laughter. I recall being like Anna once. By the time I outgrew Betty, the flaxen-haired plastic beauty was left with only one eye and half a limb.

'Jhanvi knows better than to break her dolls,' says Hutoxi dryly. 'Once when she chopped off her Barbie's ponytail, I shut her in her room for half an hour. It's all right to be Tiger Mom once in a while,' she winks. That explains Jhanvi's sad eyes. I sigh.

Carol frowns and is about to respond when Shelly calls out, 'Parents, please come and collect your child's orientation folder. It contains all the information you'll need about Bumblebees, our syllabus for this quarter and the class telephone list.'

Our group of mothers instantly disintegrates, abandoning chit-chat for parenting duties.

'Ta-dah, ladies. Promod is getting antsy,' says Avantika. Our eyes briefly lock as she turns on her five-inch stilettos. Is it my imagination or is she looking reprovingly at me? No, her mascara-laden eyes are clearly giving me a disdainful once-over, as if I were a sack of onions. She flashes a withering smile before click-clocking away. I flinch. Yes, she *is* a Class-A bitch.

A heavyset bearded man, wearing horrendously large yellow-tinted glares, links his arm around Avantika. They collect the folder from Shelly and exit the classroom, their daughter frolicking behind them in an elaborate net-and-lace magenta party gown. Oh, that would be so apt for the Queen's debutantes' ball, I think wickedly.

Shelly instructs the children to remove their lunch boxes from their bags. My son takes out his lunch box but chooses to ignore the idlis and the smiley faces on them I've made with jam. I wait and watch, but his eyes are fixed on the multistorey structure he is building—he is a committed architect, my son. I take matters in my hand and begin my signature 'Six Stages to Making Your Child Eat: Requesting-Pleading-Begging-Coaxing-Threatening-Shouting'. I'll, of course, have to omit the last two steps to avoid coming off as another Tiger Mom. But our man stubbornly refuses to nibble more than half an idli. I grimace, casting envious glances at those children wolfing down their food. How do their mothers make them eat?

'It's okay,' Shelly's gentle voice interrupts my thoughts. 'Don't get hassled. Trust me, even the fussiest of eaters will start eating by the end of the year.'

I nod feebly, a bit sceptical of someone so young spouting assured words of wisdom.

'My son was an extremely picky eater at this age. Now he is fastidious even about his greens,' she adds, her large hazel eyes dancing.

'Wow, you have kids?' I almost yelp. 'I…I mean, you look incredibly young.'

'I guess a decade of being in such youthful company at Bumblebees has paid off,' she laughs and hands me the folder. 'I have a twelve-year-old boy and a daughter who is seven. Don't worry. Your child is in experienced hands.'

I flush and thank her for everything. The wind chimes tinkle melodiously in the cool pre-monsoon breeze. I call out to Abhi, but he is nowhere to be seen. I panic. My eyes frantically scan the crowd. I run helter-skelter before finally finding him squatted in the sand pit, shovelling sand into a red bucket. I am about to admonish him, but stop myself short seeing his butter-smooth face, glowing with the sort of supreme contentment that only children are capable of. His tiny fingers impatiently play with the sand, as if searching for hidden treasure. When he finally turns his face and smiles at me, I do what every parent has been doing the entire morning: I train my camera on him to capture the purity of the moment. As I do so, I can't help but register the impressive turnout of fathers at the orientation. The new and improved version of the Indian dad has finally arrived. He is mostly an unabashed metrosexual man and a hands-on parent, completely involved in raising his children. I am touched to see dads twirling their kids around, carrying them on their shoulders, helping them climb the monkey bar, hugging them close after a fall and wiping snot off their noses. The dads are busy capturing their children's special moments in the playground and classroom—recording their little ones' squeals, giggles, wails, and tantrums for posterity. I can imagine them indulgently running these movies over and over again for family and friends. I can imagine them posting today's pictures on Facebook and inviting a wave of congratulatory comments.

The New Age dads also seem to be doting husbands. I observe them unobtrusively trailing behind their wives, allowing their better halves to take the lead in mingling with fellow parents and teachers. They seem to be in perfect sync with the rhythm of marriage and parenting—these are men who will make great magazine feature stories. It's hard not to feel envious of the many acts of tenderness displayed among the couples walking around me. But it's especially hard to ignore a tall bespectacled man, who has been protectively chaperoning his heavily pregnant wife, while also tending to their toddler daughter.

I try to blink back the tears prickling behind my eyelids. This is the first time since my divorce that I acutely feel the absence of a man standing beside Abhi and me to complete the family picture. Seeing this man lavish attention on his wife takes me back to the days when I would often ask my ex-husband, Arun, to place his hands on my own enormous tummy to feel our unborn child's movements. (Only later did I realize that not once did he do so on his own.) Even so, I was the picture of married contentment until the third trimester of my pregnancy: hosting dinner parties for my ex's boss and colleagues in our New Jersey apartment and leading the charmed suburban life to which Indian–Americans grow accustomed. I now recall a friend, who was a mother of two, prophetically remark, 'Enjoy this phase, Ira. Everything changes once the baby arrives.'

Well, everything did change in my case. *Everything*. One balmy August evening in New Jersey, when I returned home with Abhi after an invigorating walk around the apartment complex, I found a handwritten note from my husband pasted on the refrigerator door, next to the Sears studio photo of the three of us in colour-coordinated denim and white outfits. Arun's neat handwriting, which looped gracefully to the right, read: *'Can't do this any more. I'm leaving you both for a new life. On my way to California. Will initiate divorce proceedings soon.'* Abhi was fast asleep in his stroller, unaware of his father's betrayal, while I felt numb and stood frozen like a statue. Thus my life changed in a snap—just like it happens in the movies. Only, minus the background violin score. I had no choice in becoming a single mom—it was unexpectedly thrust on me.

The residual pain and anger against my ex-husband rises to my throat like bitter bile. But more than any other emotion, I feel a deep-rooted sense of shame at what happened. Unlike the women around me, who seem to have their husbands wrapped around their perfectly French-manicured fingers, I had failed to hold on to mine. In the last six months since I relocated to India, I have been so caught up in carving a new life for Abhi and me that I have never had the time to pause and consider the ramifications of being a single parent in a country where, surprisingly, societal prejudices against divorced women are still hard to shed. Maybe I should have heeded my sister's advice and moved to London instead.

I suddenly feel fatigued and want to go home. Even as grey clouds glide across the sky to unleash the season's first rains, my throat feels parched with a queer sensation that I'll later recognize as fear. Within minutes, the drizzle turns into a downpour and has everyone running for cover. Since the orientation is over, I see no point in hanging around. I wave a quick goodbye to Mrs Sippy who waves back while unfurling a lemon green umbrella.

Abhi is immersed in making squiggly patterns in the wet earth with his fingers. His face is upturned in the anticipation of tasting the sweetness of fresh rain. As I grab his hand and make a dash across the lawn to where my white Swift is parked, it suddenly strikes me that there is a unifying factor linking the women I've seen today. The Bumblebees Mothers Uniform (BMU): large Aviator sunglasses perched on top of the forehead, oversized branded handbags, groovy footwear that Carrie Bradshaw would totally approve of and discreet solitaires twinkling on various parts of their anatomy. If truth be told, I feel rather intimidated by these women. They are pretty, perky, waxed, toned supermodels on the loose. Not my idea of what mothers should look like. As my car's wipers criss-cross the windshield, I am gripped with the uneasy sensation that I might possibly be the only single mom in Bumblebees; a pariah in this fairytale setting. I see a very frightened woman reflected in the car mirror. Not the committed wife who flew to California with her child, trying every tactic in the book to convince her husband to give the marriage a chance. Not the courageous woman who lived out the remainder of the lease in the New Jersey apartment with just her hard-earned personal savings and freelance income to dip into. Not the strong-willed woman who utilized that period to hunt for a job in India, believing in her abilities.

'Did you like your school, baby?' I ask, five minutes into our journey back home. 'Abhi?' But my son is fast asleep in his car seat, emitting gentle snores from behind. I am filled with a rush of maternal love that is the closest feeling to divinity that I have experienced. I send a silent prayer of gratitude to the heavens for blessing me with Abhi.

The rain has stopped and a clear white light takes over

the gloomy skies. I roll down my window to get a whiff of the delicious wet-earth fragrance that reminds me of my childhood days. Every time it rained, my sister and I would run to our garden and grab fistfuls of the wet earth and store them in empty jam bottles. We would seal the lids with Sellotape and brag to friends that we had permanently trapped this heavenly after-the-rains scent. Those were the days when I had believed I could do anything—even steal Nature's perfume from her.

I turn around and see a smile playing on Abhi's lips. He does that while dreaming. I have a long road ahead to make our combined dreams a reality. 'We'll make it, kiddo,' I say with resolve. 'It's all good, we'll make it.'

Two

My name is Iravati Krishna and I am a senior editor at a renowned publishing house. I head World Ink's to-be-launched non-fiction imprint for women that will soon bring out relationship titles, like *How to Live Happily Ever After*, *Have the Most Besotted Hubby in Town* and *Banish 'Divorce' from Your Marital Dictionary*. Yeah. I know. Prior to this, I had been an editor at Hepworth Allen, a prominent American publishing house synonymous with its range of chick lit books, including *A Vodka and a Man to Go* and *The Perfect Couple in Suburbia* that stayed for weeks on the *New York Times* bestseller list. My first job after grad school was at a popular teen magazine in Washington where I had assisted their Agony Aunt columnist (a twenty-something redhead who was seeing a shrink due to her commitment phobia) in coming up with snappy solutions for readers' relationship problems. An example of my expertise:

Q: I don't think my boyfriend is interested in me. What should I do?'

A: Dump him before you get dumped, girl! Get a new man and get on with life.

So, my life has been full of ironies and my work, far removed from my reality. But I do get the best perk a working mother in any part of the world could ask for. I work from home and report to office only when required. Email and phone take care of the bulk of my work; thank God I'm not a gynaecologist! In essence, I get to be as dedicated a professional as any, fingers stuck to my laptop, but in the comfort of my PJs. I am what the mommy mafia calls a SAHWM (Stay at Home Working Mom). However, as my job contract says—in bold, underlined and 14-point font—this arrangement is only for one year. The time I've bargained to get Abhi and me acclimatized to a completely new life. But seeing the ill-kept neighbourhood parks, the unnerving lawlessness on the roads, the blatant red-tapism for everything (from opening a bank account to parking tickets), and the general rudeness of people (as opposed to cheery 'hellos' from passersby in America), I often wonder if I made the wrong decision in relocating. Don't get me wrong. I don't want to sound like a stuck-up NRI returnee but, after having been away for so many years, this is what I am beginning to believe. I guess once we Indians spend a considerable amount of time in pristine foreign locales, our memory goes into selective mode—remembering only the best of what the West has to offer and being quick to criticize everything about our own country. We tend to forget the shabby parks we played in as kids, the potholed roads our family car zipped through on countless occasions, the Diwali 'bakshish' doled out to MTNL linewallahs to ensure the good health of our phone lines, and dour-faced neighbours, like Mrs Saluja, who smiled only when she sought favours from my father: 'O ji, aap Bittu ke job ke liye kisise baat kar sakte hain?'

Oh well, like they say, no pain, no gain. But what really made me lug my American Tourister to India was the proximity to my parents who are a short flight away in Chennai—more for Abhi's sake than mine. I surmised, in the absence of a father, he needed the semblance of a family unit, something that only his doting grandparents could provide us with. Besides, it was getting quite lonely for me in America—I couldn't see myself spending a lifetime there. Even while pregnant, I would often tell Arun, 'We should go back to India when Abhi turns five.' But I wasn't able to predict back then that the homecoming run would occur much sooner, and under such circumstances.

After the divorce, it only made sense to move back to India rather than 'live like ghosts' (as my father likes saying) in an eerily quiet part of American suburbia. It's true. In all the years I lived alone in the US before my marriage, I would hardly hear even birds' chirps in apartment communities. The only constants were the refrigerator's hum and the heater's drone. Weeks would pass without hearing my neighbour's voice, even though his television regularly blared through the thin wall separating our apartments.

But I almost didn't relocate to India. Convincing my publishing house, World Ink, to let me work flexi-hours sapped me of all my negotiating skills. On second thoughts, being mom to a toddler has taught me Negotiation 101 like no fancy B-School would ever be able to. After three months of dithering over my stipulation of wanting to be a SAHWM, World Ink was on the verge of withdrawing its offer and I had started filling out apps for a PhD programme at a top-tier university in upstate New York. At least, family housing, student hours, a crèche and a modest income would be assured. Not to mention the added bonus of intellectual growth to distract me from wallowing in self-pity over my divorce. Hell, I was determined to reclaim my life. The morning I was to courier the apps, I received an email from Vinnie Warsie that read more like a telegram:

> 'The water is infested with foreign sharks. Need someone of your calibre. Can negotiate on your terms. Hop aboard!'

Wow, I was humbled. And thrilled enough to scoop up my dazed one-year-old boy from his high chair and waltz him around to a groovy piano jazz number that was playing on the National Public Radio. While it felt good to be acknowledged by a distinguished Indian publisher, it was *the* Vinnie Warsie, for God's sake! Vinnie Warsie—the feisty prima donna of the Indian publishing scene; the fearless female warrior who had fought all odds over a three-decade-long career and nurtured a home-grown publishing house from being a nondescript player to scaling enviable peaks in the publishing firmament; whose intuitive editorial skill was every author's nightmare and dream; whose razor-sharp insight had turned the fortunes of World Ink from a sinking entity to reincarnate itself as a thriving market leader; and whose redoubtable verve and passion for quality publishing had earned her the respect of every rival publisher—had chosen to hire me *despite* my condition of working from home. I guess it reflects the twenty-first-century India we're living in. Just as thirty-plus married actresses are finally getting their due in Bollywood, corporate India has also finally woken up to the harried working mother's travails by offering her flexible working practices. I mean it's not as if the arrival of a child strips us of our competitive edge. Rather, we become adept multi-taskers and can strike that killer book deal on the phone while sterilizing bottles, folding laundry, and burping baby Balaji.

Even before Abhi was born, the one thing I was clear about was that working full-time away from home was non-negotiable. I was willing to take a pay cut but not cut short the time I would spend with my child. I didn't want a nanny to witness the milestones or expend phone-parenting from my office cubicle. In my mind, I had already become a mother who sang syrupy lullabies and massaged her baby's bottom with Shea buttercream. Arun was bringing home a handsome six-figure-dollar income, so we wouldn't exactly be on the streets, I surmised. Besides, I could always rejoin the workforce once our child was older. Or, who knew, turn into a sassy millionaire mom entrepreneur who worked from home? The idea of being a stay-at-home mom planted itself in my mind when my increasing girth—in the third trimester of my pregnancy—made it physically taxing for me to do the New Jersey–New York commute that involved a car ride to the nearest metro station, a forty-five-minute train ride to Penn Station and the bus ride that would drop me one block from my steel-and-glass office building on Lexington Avenue. It became daunting to walk even that measly one block as a gasping and panting pregnant woman, when normally I used to sprint that distance in high heels.

The tempestuous maternal hormones raging in my system urged me to quit my beloved job three months before the baby came along. But I was worried about how my husband would react. He was a typical desi techie who worshipped everything American. Besides American soccer, his other obsession was the American dollar. According to him, the steady multiplication of the dollar was ensured only when both spouses earned. Come to think of it, he even befriended only those couples who were both working and always reserved generous words of praise for W3 (Wives Who Worked). The words 'lay-off', 'outsourcing' and the US Citizenship and Immigration Services (USCIS) were enough to make him perspire during a blizzard. A good chunk of his online time was spent tracking the tedious movement of his Green Card processing and the quixotic USD–INR exchange rate. Every headline about the US–India partnership (or face-off) mattered more to him than if a psychotic killer were to be at our door. Good bi-lateral ties boded well for the dollar-to-rupee conversion that reflected in greater savings in his NRI bank account. For him, the very reason for our stay in the US—rather, our very *existence* on earth—was the US dollar. So when I told him about my decision to be a stay-at-home mom, his cool reaction baffled me. He briefly turned his gaze away from CSI, solemnly smiled at me, nodded his acquiescence, and returned to watching guns being fired in a casino. I had braced myself for a full-blown argument but he didn't even whimper. I tried to have a conversation the following morning when there was no crime drama competing for his attention and I got the same reaction, except that this time he looked up from his breakfast cereal and wordlessly nodded his consent. When, after a few more failed attempts at pinning him down for a discussion, his reaction remained status quo, I made up my mind to quit. Only later, did I realize the import of his callous silence: 'Do what you want, woman. I am leaving you anyway.' *And our baby.*

I turned in my papers at Hepworth Allen on the day New York recorded its coldest temperature in thirty years and my baby performed Olympic-worthy triple loops in my small intestine. As the stations whizzed past me on the train ride home, I managed a small smile through my tears. I had fiercely loved my job, where I had climbed the ranks from being a coffee-serving intern to a full-fledged editor. Reading scores of manuscripts that delved into the psyche of the New Age American woman had taught me many things about her. For instance, however bumbling and clumsy she might be, she would always, *always*, triumph Cinderella-style in the end.

This is exactly what I hope to accomplish at World Ink. But it wasn't all win-win for me from the get-go. When we closed the deal, I realized that if I had followed to the letter the three Cs—Cooperation, Compromise and Concession—to a good negotiation, so had Vinnie Warsie. She had cooperated and I had conceded to foregoing perks, like earned leave and representing World Ink at prestigious international book fairs for the first year of my employment. So we had both compromised in our own ways. But, like I mentioned: I've still got the best perk a working mother could ask for.

Three

Abhi and I got home after spending a lazy Sunday at Lodi Gardens. I'd packed sandwiches, cheese rolls, and fruit salad for a picnic lunch. Abhi befriended a few toddlers from the rambunctious Punjabi family picnicking near us. While the children played, I managed to skim through the day's newspapers and read a few back issues of *Filmfare* and *People*. It's unbelievable just how much news escapes your attention when you become a mother. By the time you learn the new Italian prime minister's name, the government has toppled; when you think inflation is at 7.43 percent, it has jumped to 8.56 percent; and when you argue with friends that Branjelina have only three kids, they scream: 'Don't you read *People*, woman?'

I sip my ginger tea contentedly, reminiscing about the relaxing afternoon Abhi and I had had at Lodi Gardens. I propose to do this more often with him; maybe organize play dates with his friends from Bumblebees. Yes, that would be a great way to get to know the other moms. Abhi is furiously pedalling his red tricycle all around the spacious L-shaped drawing-cum-dining room, almost toppling over the three-foot porcelain Laughing Buddha. The little guy is full of beans despite the energy-packed day. I look around the tastefully furnished room done up in a palette of warm colours—the maple green couch, the dazzling Rajasthani mirror-work cushions, the six-seater dining table in deep mahogany, and the sleek curio cases containing exquisite baubles; they add so much elegance and character to the room. The setting sun is a melting ball behind the sheer olive curtains. The darkening evening shadows jut out angularly on the butterscotch walls, reminding me of the Ramayana shadow puppet theatre I'd seen in my father's native village in Tamil Nadu many years ago. It would be lovely to see that again with Abhi, I muse.

I am staying at my aunt's fully furnished apartment that's fortunately tucked into one of the quieter lanes of Greater Kailash 1 (GK-1). She lives in Abu Dhabi and is a distant cousin of my mother's. Her husband is in the oil business, and buying premium real estate is his idea of money well spent. This spacious three-bedroom, three-bath, first-floor apartment had been lying vacant for a few years on account of all the hassles associated with handling tenants long distance. The previous occupant had refused to vacate and the matter almost went to court. That's when my aunt decided to lock up the flat and hire a caretaker for its basic maintenance. Before I moved to Delhi, she had insisted that I stay here for free. But I wouldn't hear of it. 'Delhi is very unsafe, Ira,' she would say every time she called me in New Jersey. 'I'll feel better if you and Abhi stay at my place. It'll be in safe hands—good for you, good for me.' Since I stood my ground about paying rent, my aunt, after much persuasion from my mother, agreed to let me pay quarter of what she would have normally charged a tenant. GK-1 is extremely congested and too chaotic for my taste, but I know better than to complain. I realize how lucky I am to have got a fully furnished flat for a piddly rent at a gilded South Delhi address. And thankfully, there are no pesky neighbours to contend with. The ground floor is vacant and the floor above mine is occupied by a middle-aged German man, a travelling pharma executive. I have seen him only a couple of times when he emerged travel-weary from his company sedan.

I know I have a lot to be grateful for about this accommodation. When I walked through the apartment door the first time, I was blown away with how well appointed it was. Everything was there—from furniture, linen, kitchen appliances, cutlery, washing machine down to the balcony chairs and bathroom rugs. Only the hand-woven durries which I had picked up at Dilli Haat, the three bookshelves crammed with my books, and the family photographs hanging on the walls, are my flourishes.

Abhi finally abandons his tricycle and comes running to me. He raises his arms. I know what that means. I lift him and perch him, legs akimbo, on my hips. 'I lurve you, Amma,' he tiredly coos and plants a wet kiss on my cheek. It is spontaneous moments like these that make me forget all the heartache and tears of the last one year, and revel in the privileges of single-parenting. I rub my nose against his and make a funny face. He starts giggling. 'I love you so much, baby,' I whisper into his sweet breath.

Abhi falls asleep soon after dinner. Just as I settle down with a bound manuscript, which Vinnie has marked 'Urgent', the phone rings.

'Hello, chellum.' Only my mother calls me 'sweetheart' in Tamil.

'Hello, Amma! How are you and Appa? How is Anusha doing?' The words tumble from my mouth.

'Anusha is in fine form. But first tell me about our darling Abhi. Give him the phone.'

'He is sleeping. We went to Lodi Gardens –'

'Oh no! We are so eager to talk to him.'

'Sorry, Amma. We had a long day at Lodi Gardens and he has just fallen asleep. The monkey was super-active till twenty minutes ago.'

My mother laughs. 'Your father and I miss him a lot...'

I smile, knowing how attached my parents are to Abhi. I bring my mother up to speed on Abhi's adventures. From her end I learn how pleasant London is in July, about my brother-in-law's culinary adventures in the kitchen and the banal shows on British television.

'Hey, Ira.' It's my sister, Anusha.

'So, how is it going, Anu?' I ask. 'I hope the bleeding has stopped?'

'Yes, touch wood. My second trimester started yesterday. I'll mail you all the sordid details,' she says. 'But I'm still advised bed rest. Thank God for Amma, otherwise I would've been a nervous wreck.'

My father comes on the line and instructs me to remain indoors after 6 pm.

'Appa, I'm not caught in a curfew in Srinagar!' I protest.

'Keep a pepper spray handy at all times, and feed Abhi almonds, dates, and cashew nuts every morning. The boy is looking thin in the photographs—make sure you feed him well,' he says. I smile at the constant concern he has for us.

Anusha comes back on the line and launches into her pet topic. 'Why do you want to be in Delhi, Ira? I'm sure you'll find a good job in London too. Our kids can grow up together and we can all live like one big happy family.' I smile at her choice of words. My sister, younger than me by two years, was the one who believed in princes and fairytale endings. Though she became a genetic engineer, and was steeped in the practical world of pure sciences, I now realize that a little bit of the fairy dust lives on in her.

'Yeah, Anu's right. You and Abhi should come here,' my brother-in-law's voice booms into the phone. I hold the phone a little away from my ear. I teasingly call the hefty, six-foot-two, swarthy-complexioned Venkat, 'the gentle giant'. According to Anusha, he has a beer belly that competes with her swelling baby bump. When my extremely fair sister, blessed with fragile, Dresden china doll features started dating Venkat in college, my father was a little taken aback by his imposing frame. He had uncharitably remarked that Venkat looked less like an engineer and more like a bodybuilder. But over a period of time, my parents and I have come to dote on Venkat. We now know a marshmallow heart resides within his tough exterior. When Arun walked out on me, it was Venkat who flew to California (even before I could) to counsel my ex and try to din sense into him. I had half-hoped that Arun would be beaten to pulp by Venkat's steely arms and thrown into the strong Pacific currents. But what is most endearing about my brother-in-law is his devotion to my sister. He is your typical modern-day husband, who cooks, vacuums the house, and does the weekly groceries without forgetting to plan a romantic getaway with his wife. I am glad that at least one of us sisters ended up with Mr Right.

'Ira? You there?' Venkat interrupts my reverie.

'Hmm...I don't know, Venkat,' I reply, reaching for a kettle to make tea. 'London weather is too gloomy. Besides, Appa and Amma are here. It's good for Abhi.'

'No arguments there. Anyway, take your time to think it over,' he says.

I can't believe that he and Anusha are still hopeful that I would consider relocating to the UK, so soon after my epic relocation to India!

After hanging up, I tune in to an FM station playing old Hindi movie songs and ponder over Anusha and Venkat's words. This is not the first time they have advised me to move to London. Post my divorce, there has been a subtle role reversal in our relationship. My sister and her husband have assumed the role of my older siblings and love parenting me at every opportunity. Not that I mind, I think, stretching back on the couch and watching the steam rise from my ceramic cup. While it would be wonderful to live near my sister, I believe that my returning to India happened for the best. For one, the timing couldn't have been better. The publishing industry is booming, with MNC publishing houses—or 'foreign sharks' as Vinnie puts it—entering the fray. I love my challenging role at World Ink and have so much to learn from Vinnie. I close my eyes and savour the hot liquid coursing down my throat. The tulsi-flavoured tea and a peppy Kishore Kumar number lift my spirits. With a new job, new surroundings and all the new friends I am going to make, I want to believe that life will come up smelling of roses again. For starters, I want Abhi to settle down in his playschool, and me to leave behind the baggage of my failed marriage. Anusha's lips curl with contempt whenever I say 'failed marriage'. '*He* failed as a husband and father. You're stupid to shed tears over the coward,' she never tires of chiding me. But I have cried myself to sleep on countless nights, trying to fathom why Arun deserted us. He never did offer a convincing explanation, only kept repeating like a zombie that he wanted out. 'Cheat,' my mother wept. 'Rascal!' my father exploded. 'Why, Arun? *Why*?' I lamented. We had been married for five years and I was certain we'd waltz into the silver, golden, and platinum years with a sprint in our steps and grandkids in tow. I can't say our marriage was the most romantic and perfect, but there was a patina of tranquillity and stability to our marital routine—similar to the fabric binding most Indian arranged marriages. When my parents had brought Arun's proposal from one of the marriage bureaus where they had registered my profile, I had agreed to the match since it had seemed the right thing to do at the time—get married to an educated 'good' boy from a 'good' family and settle down. Arun may not have been a trophy husband, but neither was he a wife-beater or an alcoholic. In the five years we had been married, I could never figure out the man. 'Still waters run deep' is an expression aptly coined for people like Arun.

My lips twist with bitterness. I smooth my hand over my hair that is no longer lush and black as it once was. The weekend after Arun left, I'd driven eight miles to the nearest suburban mall and had my hair chopped off in a fit of fury. It has now grown back to almost waist length. This morning I discovered two more strands of grey in my comb. Post my divorce, anxiety, self-pity, depression and comfort food have taken their toll on my skin, hair and weight. There is a reason why pizzas, French fries, and pastries are called comfort food. They know how to pamper you with extra calories when you are down in the dumps. On most days I feel older than my thirty-four years. Though I am not stunningly beautiful like my mother or sister, I have seen better days in front of the mirror. Just a week before my ex left, he had taken pictures of Abhi and me in our apartment complex. The sun was slipping behind the grey-shingled roofs and had bathed the undulating grass in front of our door a mellow gold. Whenever I see those photos, even I am struck by the stunning mother–son moments Arun had captured with his new camera, purchased during the manic Thanksgiving (Black Friday) sale before Abhi was born. My favourite one is of Abhi—in a blue onesie and cap—and me looking into each other's eyes and laughing. The sun is bouncing off my hair, colouring my black eyes a liquid brown. What I see on my face is H.A.P.P.I.N.E.S.S. I long to be that person again.

A honey-tinged female voice from the radio fills the room. The time is 10 pm, she purrs in Hindi, and urges listeners to curl up and leave the fatigue of their long day behind them. She promises to play soulful ghazals for the next one hour that would transport us to the era of romance, courtesans, and nobility. I am in the mood for gentle Urdu poetry and carry the portable player to my room. I kiss my sleeping child and settle down on my recliner with the bound manuscript that requires 'urgent' evaluation.

It has been years since I have listened to late-night radio. I feel like I am back in college when Gulzar, Talat Aziz, and Asha Bhonsle would keep me company on excruciatingly long pre-exam nights. As a plaintive baritone bursts into song about healing his battered soul and coming to terms with the blow dealt by destiny, I know he is speaking for me too. I moved across continents to re-map my life and have no intention of rocking the boat again. This time I want to be the captain of my ship—of my destiny.

Four

Abhi and I reach Bumblebees forty minutes early. The school gate is still closed so we amble over to the lawns facing the school. Bird calls greet us as we step on the moist grass. Churchill Lane is slowly stirring awake to what promises to be a sultry day. Drivers are cleaning the Benzes, Fords, and Škodas parked on the tree-lined roads framing the lawn. Rising dust particles glimmer in the morning light as a bent woman briskly sweeps dry leaves into a corner. I sit on a bench near the swings while Abhi flings his school bag and runs around with gay abandon. He makes a swooping motion with his outstretched arms and cries, 'Pwaane! Pwaane!'

Suddenly, a plump black Labrador bounds across the lawn, startling Abhi into running in the opposite direction. 'Come 'ere, Bonny boy!' a shrill voice commands from behind me. I swirl around; it's the same old woman whom I had seen at her window last week. A faded salwar kameez, a size too large, hangs over her skeletal frame. She flashes me a gummy smile. The few teeth that remain are tiny and stained like brown rice grains.

Abhi forgets his initial fear and inches closer to Bonny who seems to be enjoying a dollop of sunshine.

'Does he bite, Aunty?' I ask, rising from the bench.

'Oh no, he is harmless. Quite foolish, really,' she cackles into a cough, her parchment-paper-like skin crinkling at the eyes. 'Your child studies at Bumblebees, eh?'

'Yes, joined last week.'

Abhi tentatively pats Bonny's raven coat. The dog gratefully sinks on all fours and licks his front legs with his bubblegum pink tongue.

'Amma, look. Doggie!' my son cheerfully shouts.

'Careful, Abhi. Don't touch him,' I admonish, never one to completely believe people's perception of their beloved pets.

'No, really. Bonny *is* a harmless soul,' insists the old woman, patting my hand reassuringly. She sighs. 'Bumblebees is a lovely school. My grandson attended it seven years ago.'

'Which school is he in now?' I ask, assuming it must be either of the two well-regarded schools in the five-kilometre radius from Churchill Lane.

She shakes her head in a defeated manner. 'No idea, dear. Never can remember his school's name in Dublin. My son and his wife—she is Irish, you know— left India after Siddy completed playschool.' Her small, greyish-black eyes, half-eaten by glaucoma, stare wistfully into the distance. 'In those days, Siddy and I would be on these lawns for hours and hours...'

I feel guilty for reminding her of saddening thoughts. But I am strangely filled with curiosity about this old lady. I wonder why I'm drawn to her world. For some reason, I intuitively feel she and I have something in common: perhaps, we are battling emotional angst over something we have no control over.

I want to barrage her with questions: 'Do you live alone?' 'Do you have other children?' 'Why did your son leave you to fend for yourself?' 'Are you in touch with Siddy?'

'I am Iravati,' I say, instead. Abhi waves to me from the swing that wobbles dangerously to the left. 'And that's my son, Abhi.'

'I am Hiroo Zardari. Nice meeting you,' the old woman extends a bony hand to me.

I am relieved to see her earlier vitality return.

She waves the red leash at her dog. 'Bo-ho-nnyy! Let's go, my boy.' The Lab trundles through the lawns' narrow exit and proceeds to pee on a car tyre. Mrs Zardari follows him, her soiled white sneakers squelching when she steps in the puddle of water created by a gushing hosepipe.

Children and adults have started trickling in; the air is buzzing with voices. A teacher is at the gate, her thin lips stretched in a tight welcoming smile. A line of vehicles, dropping off the children, clogs the road in front of Bumblebees. Toddlers, saddled with their school bags and water bottles, come into my line of vision. Parents gently goad their children to walk to their classrooms. After a week of hand-holding, I decide to let Abhi go to class on his own today. Besides, Mrs Sippy has been dissuading parents of well-adjusted kids from coming inside. 'Let the children sprout wings! Make them more independent,' she untiringly repeats to parents.

I reluctantly release Abhi from my bear hug and wait for his reaction. My son wears the look of a martyr and bores an accusatory look into me. 'Why me?' he seems to ask. For a moment I fear he is going to cry. Is this the first sign of separation anxiety? We have always been together, mother and son, and I'm not sure who will cry first. A group of didis—uniformed nannies—hovers around, assisting the parents. The middle-aged woman allotted to Abhi's class smilingly leads him away. I hastily shout out a litany of instructions: 'Didi, please take him to the bathroom, he is not fully toilet-trained... he should eat his snack...watch him at the swings, he is very naughty...he could get hurt...' A lump forms in my throat seeing Abhi's retreating back. I almost wish he *had* made a fuss of wanting his mommy. I keep waving till he turns the corner and vanishes into the blinding greenery. I will not cry. I will not cry. Motherhood is fraught with so many emotional moments.

There is a small commotion brewing at the gate. A prim-faced little girl is howling, fiercely tugging at her mother's chiffon sleeves. A didi tries lifting her but is met with stiff resistance and violent leg stomping. Another didi appears, but is equally rebuffed by Miss Moppet.

'Bhaiya, baby ko uthao,' the mother orders the guard.

'Nooo!' the girl glowers at her mother and the guard backs off.

The teacher on gate duty remains aloof, not straining a muscle to console the child. She stands transfixed like a wax statue, daintily scratching the tip of her nose, running her fingers over her perfectly streaked auburn hair.

Finally, the mother takes charge. She adjusts her fitted denim skirt that shows off her shapely legs, deposits her leather tote with her maid (who looks suspiciously underage), pushes down her glares to the bridge of her nose and carries her screaming daughter inside with the same determination as that of an army general at war.

'Phew, what tantrums!' mutters the teacher, her thread-thin eyebrows raised in consternation. Her stony presence is not exactly helpful. I wonder why schools hire such surly women to teach preschoolers. In my opinion, more than any fancy Nursery Teachers' Training or the Montessori versus Playway brouhaha, playschool and nursery teachers should be primarily equipped in the joviality, patience, and kindness departments. I suddenly feel blessed that Abhi is in gentle Shelly's class. I am so engrossed in my thoughts that I walk past a posse of mothers clustered behind a black Scorpio.

'Ira!'

I turn to see the Formidable Fashion Police—Carol, Riya and Avantika—waving at me with only their fingertips. It's like they are playing piano notes in the air. While they resemble the *Desperate Housewives*, I look...er...just desperate. The women give me the same languorous once-over that seems to be the de rigueur greeting of Bumblebees moms. I feel their X-ray eyes upon me and quickly check my green kurta—nope, no Bournvita or puke stains—and join them.

'Sorry, didn't see you guys,' I chirp, self-consciously tucking a strand of hair behind my ear.

Before I realize what's happening, I get grabbed for cheek kisses. This, I will soon learn, is the standard greeting protocol among Bumblebees moms. Mwah, mwah, like those Page 3 socialites one loves to ridicule. Those who are compulsive cheek kissers, like Avantika, will kiss even those whom they consider unworthy of their time. For them cheek kissing is a compulsion that's second nature to their personalities.

The women are in standard BMU, their glares exaggeratedly reflecting my features. In all the chaos of my transcontinental packing and unpacking, I had misplaced my only pair of sunglasses that I had impulsively bought for $19.99 at a J.C. Penney summer clearance sale. Arun had called it an 'unnecessary expense' we could live without.

I squint my eyes against the sun glowering in the pasty sky. Sweat is trickling down my back and dampening my kurta. Carol looks dew-fresh in a lavender T-shirt and white trousers. Riya is in distressed jeans and has left her freshly shampooed hair loose. Avantika is in a sleeveless red top and black jeans, her lips painted a flaming scarlet. I think I am getting used to her pancake Geisha make-up.

'We are headed to Java Beans for coffee,' says Carol. 'Why don't you come along?'

Vinnie has often raved about Java Beans and its Jumbo Lava Tava, whatever that is.

I glance at my watch. It is 9.50. I had planned to return home and evaluate a hefty manuscript. Vinnie will go beserk if I don't turn in my detailed assessment by tomorrow. A media moghul's wife has penned her first novel and World Ink might have to acquire it even if it's complete crap. Such favours are part of the publishing business—we publish your crappy novel and you give us free advertising space in the numerous media channels you own.

'Coming?' Carol asks again. I notice for the first time the mustard-seed-sized mole that sits just below her lower lip, like a well-placed beauty spot.

'I'm not sure…' I waver, though terribly tempted to mingle with adults for a change. I mean, I love my son, but it's been a long time since I've talked about anything other than potty, Barney, and Chhota Bheem. I quickly size up the women. An expensive playschool makes for strange bedfellows. Riya looks like a confused wannabe. Avantika is certainly not my type but Carol looks like someone I might like to be friends with.

'Don't worry, the kids need to be picked up only at 12.30,' Carol urges, grabbing my hand. 'Come on, it's just City Market, round the corner.'

I decide to tag along, suddenly feeling adventurous, like a schoolgirl bunking classes. The four of us proceed towards the main road.

'Darlings, did I mention that I'm having a summer sale

on Facebook?' Avantika announces breezily, pushing up her rhinestone-encrusted sunglasses.

God, I wish I were more forgiving of her type.

'Wow, Avantika, you are amazing!' Riya exclaims, wrapping her arm around Avantika's waist.' Avantika winks and links her arm with Riya's. I try not to roll my eyes too much.

Carol and I are two steps behind on the narrow footpath. The roads have been dug up for the new Metro line and we try to walk single file through the mess and dust of urban construction.

'Was this get-together planned in advance?' I ask.

'Nothing formal-shormal, yaar. Just we mothers getting to know each other,' Riya says, waving her Rolexed wrist. 'We decided, like, ten minutes ago.'

'I have spread word to the other moms in our class that we will be at Java Beans,' adds Carol, gingerly side-stepping an uncovered manhole in the nick of time.

'Can't wait to have something cooold,' shouts Riya happily, above the din of the traffic.

As we wait at the stop light, I am filled with quiet anticipation. It is, indeed, going to be a new life for me.

Five

City Market is, without doubt, the most expensive shopping centre in South Delhi. It is compact, snooty, and exclusive. Foreign brands unabashedly merchandise their products from shop windows, and unpronounceable Indian couture labels display slinky creations that come with hefty price tags. In the years I have been away, a host of trendy boutiques, cosmetic shops, coffee joints, delicatessens, and restaurants has mushroomed in every available square inch of this precious real-estate space.

From top-level diplomats to tattooed hippie tourists, foreigners are a regular fixture in City Market—the driving force behind the snootiness of these shopkeepers whose ancestors were, in another lifetime, humble post-Partition immigrants.

We enter Java Beans through a quiet side lane. A mehendi artist is squatted across the street, drawing squiggly patterns on a blonde woman's outstretched palm. The Java Beans interior is very Art Deco—stark black-and-white geometric artworks hang on the stucco walls, which are painted a deep orange. The leather seating is done in shades of cocoa, and sultry Spanish music is playing in the background. The crowd is sparse, just a smattering of people reading or working on their laptops. This place looks insanely expensive. I wince, wondering if I can slink away without these women noticing. But it's not as if I'm going to hang out with them every day, I tell myself. I am sure they have other things to do after dropping their kids—which I would later learn, include herbal mani-pedis, colouring their hair and…um…shopping for lingerie.

We pick a well-lit corner near the opaque glass windows. A waiter arrives and hands us the brown-and-gold menu cards.

'How are you, ma'am?' he asks Avantika, rushing to push in her chair.

Avantika smiles and bats her eyelashes coquettishly. 'Very well. I'll have my usual, Karim,' she says, without glancing at the menu. 'Low-fat Grilled Chicken and a Vegetable Wrap with sundried tomato paste on the side.'

'Right, ma'am.'

'Do you come here often?' Riya asks in a slightly awed tone. This girl's Avantika fixation is starting to get on my nerves.

'Promod loves this place, sweetie,' replies Avantika, with a careless shrug.

That's when I notice her unruly eyebrows that look like they haven't been threaded in weeks. My mouth twitches and I want to double up with laughter.

My gaze slides away when Avantika's cold glance falls on me.

'A Kiwi Slush and a Three-Cheese Panini for me, thank you,' says Carol.

'I'll have a Banana Milkshake and a Spinach Croissant,' says Riya.

The waiter smiles at them and turns his imperious gaze on me.

'Umm, just a sec,' I say, blindly flipping the pages, searching for the cheapest item on the menu.

'Looking for something in particular, ma'am?' the waiter asks with a veneer of politeness. Going by the way her pout is swelling, Avantika seems to be enjoying my confused expression. Ah! I finally find a regular cup of tea listed as Té Masala Blasto (High-grade zesty traditional Indian tea flavoured with authentic spices). Though I would have loved to try the other exotic-sounding teas, like Moroccan Chai and Ultimate Detox Tea, I settle for the cheapest, which is really quite pricey at Rs 125 without tax. Okay, there have got to be other ways to befriend Bumblebees mothers that don't result in a depleting bank account.

'One Té Masala Blasto,' I say.

'Anything to eat, ma'am?' the waiter inquires in a phony foreign accent that does nothing to conceal his sadda Punjabi roots.

'No thanks,' I smile brightly, snapping shut the menu card.

'So ladies, let's get to know each other better. We barely had time at the orientation,' says Riya, folding her sunglasses and putting them inside her bag. 'Okay, I'll start. As you all know, my son, Kunal, studies with your kids. My husband, Rahul, runs two call centres.'

'Do you work, Riya?' asks Carol.

'No. I used to work in a travel agency but I quit when I got pregnant. I'm now just a housewife, happy to splurge my husband's money.' Riya grins.

I marvel at the honesty of her statement. As Arun's wife, such breezy marital references to money had never come easily to me.

Avantika flicks her ironed mane and clears her throat. 'Well, I am a fashion designer and own a fashion label called the "Avantika Sen Collection". Sexy saris and cholis are my specialty.' *Tell us something new.* 'I operate my business through Facebook. Check me out, girls!' She hands each of us her business card that has her mugshot on top.

'You have a daughter, right?' asks Carol. The waiter places our orders on the table.

'Yep, Rimli.'

'What does your husband do?' asks Riya.

'Promod owns a gym,' says Avantika, biting into her wrap.

'Oooh, where?' cries Riya.

'In Green Park. It's called "Fit 4 Life".'

'Wow, two entrepreneurs in the family,' gushes Riya, the besotted fan. Maybe now is the time she will ask for Avantika's autograph. For someone who is in the fitness business, this Promod guy looks quite unfit, I think. I see him every afternoon when he comes to pick up Rimli.

'Now your turn, Carol,' smiles Avantika, coolly ignoring me.

Carol sips her Kiwi Slush that looks an inviting peppermint green. 'I am the proud mother of two girls. You all know Anna; Saira, my older one, is in Class Five at Loreto Convent. My husband, George, is a vice-president at American Express.'

We all coo in appreciation.

'What do you do?' Riya asks, expertly slicing her croissant into four pieces.

'I, too, used to work at American Express but I quit my job when my second baby came along.'

'You've done an MBA?' asks Riya.

'Yep, from IIM Bangalore.'

This time the appreciative murmers are louder. So my first impression about Carol on orientation day had not been too far off the mark. She gives off the confident vibe that is a trait of high-achieving women.

'Oh, but the joys of motherhood are far greater than those of banking,' Carol waves her hands dismissively. 'Never knew I would get burnt up so fast in my career. But luckily, George just lets me be. Says he will support me even if I decide to become a governess.' She giggles. 'I guess I have all the skills necessary to become one.'

'How about you, Ira?' asks Riya.

'My bundle of joy is Abhi. I work in the publishing industry.'

'Wow, with which publisher?' asks Carol.

'World Ink. I head their non-fiction imprint.'

'Super-cool,' says Carol, playing with her hair. 'I've always wanted to write a book.'

'And your husband? What does he do?' Avantika inquires in a patronizing tone.

Think quickly. Make the bitch jealous. I don't know why, but this is what my brain instructs me to do. I stare at Avantika, taking in her mocking expression. I am not sure whether what I see is a mischievous glint in her eyes, perhaps egging me on to wax eloquent about my husband being better than any of the other husbands in this group. I rise to her challenge.

'Arun is a chip designer at Intel,' I blurt out. Wow, that was smooth. Besides, I just gave my ex a more impressive job profile. Arun was a mid-level developer at Vatni Computers, a desi sub-contractor who had a shack of an office in Edison, New Jersey. Vatni used to bid for projects and place Arun at various client sites. That is why Arun was constantly travelling when we were married.

Avantika doesn't look so smug any more. Lying certainly has its advantages.

'Is Intel in Gurgaon?' asks Carol.

'Oh no, he is still in Santa Clara,' I say. 'I was in the US and recently moved back with Abhi.'

Riya looks at me with newfound respect. After all, her hubby's call centre operations and the number of diamond bracelets she owns depend on Uncle Sam's generosity.

'Oh, you must miss him so much!' she says. 'I can't live without Rahul for even a day.'

'Why is your husband still in America and not with you?' Avantika asks in an excessively polite tone. I debate whether I should tell her that she has a smidgen of tomato paste on her chin and her lipstick has smudged. And that her eyebrows could do with some efficient threading. My jaw hardens but I manage a small smile.

'He is trying to get transferred to India. Such things take time, you know.' I shrug and sip my tea.

'Once when George was away on training in London, he sent me red roses every week through a local flower service,' pipes Carol, her expressive eyes sparkling at the memory.

'Oh, yeah, even Arun does such things all the time,' I say. *Moron. Don't overdo it.*

Maybe it's the achingly romantic voice of Enrique Iglesias or the complacency of these happily married women who seem so besotted with their husbands, but the lies keep rolling off my tongue like butter scones. I never realized my alter ego was so in denial of her divorce. I had wanted to be called someone's sweetheart, someone's wife, but never a...a divorcee!

Divorce was almost a cuss word when I was growing up in the 1980s. I remember there was a divorced woman in our housing society who always remained cooped up in her apartment. The aunties used to gossip about her in hushed tones while sipping their 4 pm adrak chai. Now *I* have become that woman and fodder for people's gossip.

Regardless, I still want to play along. I straighten my back and put on a moony grin. 'Just last week, Arun couriered me a parcel of my favourite perfumes.' I try to look modest about being a pampered long-distance wife. The truth was Arun believed women's perfumes were a waste of money. ('2 oz Gucci for $85? Are you nuts? We can put that in the NRI bank account. Just use Pond's talcum powder instead.')

'Awww!' says Carol, squeezing my hand. 'You probably weep with joy at his romantic gestures.'

'Oh yeah, my husband is like that. Makes me cry a lot.' I am itching to change the subject.

'Shoot, Facebook needs me!' says Avantika, rising from her chair. 'I gotta go now, ladies. I'll settle my account at the counter. Ta-dah, see you later.' She blows us kisses. Did I mention a variant of the cheek kiss is the air kiss?

I grin to myself. Perhaps it was too much for her to expect US connections and a loving hubby from me. But her withering smile directed at me promptly wipes off my grin. Has she caught on to my yarn? A small voice dins into my head that I have invited trouble by upstaging her today. At what cost have I won this round?

The gravity of my lie suddenly hits me. Oh God, what have I done? How long will it be before the truth unravels? Should I just backtrack and say, 'Hey, it was an honest slip of tongue. What I meant was that I am a pathetic divorcee and a single mom. And my ex would rather shoot himself in his eyes than buy me perfume.'

I look at Riya and Carol cracking up over a husband joke that's gone viral on all social networking sites. I inhale sharply to stave off the panic building up within me. I so don't belong with these smug married women. But I feel too ashamed to openly call myself a divorcee. I still can't say the word without feeling like I've just confessed to being a kleptomaniac. I drain my fancy tea and grip the armrests with my clammy palms. Even Abhi's school doesn't know of my single-parent status. I didn't provide Arun's details on the admission form. 'Giving sperm doesn't make a father' is what I have come to believe—years of watching Oprah is finally making my latent feminist tendencies surface. This is also the reason Abhi is without a surname. It's there on his birth certificate but not in the Bumblebees records. Besides, since Mrs Sippy didn't seek further clarification about Abhi's father, I didn't volunteer any. I try to banish thoughts of how this one lie could ruin my reputation at Bumblebees and inadvertently jeopardize Abhi too. Darn. I wish I had not come to City Market in the first place.

Six

Thank God for friends like Priya!

'Try power yoga, babe,' she says between deep breaths, her lissome five-foot frame doing an expert headstand. I consider her advice, leaning back in the beige Lazyboy that's the only piece of furniture in Priya's spare bedroom that has been converted into her yoga den. *Om Namah Shivaya,* set to world music by a Nigerian blues-singer-turned-Iskon-devotee, has me in a trance. I am glad I decided to visit Priya after dropping Abhi at school—even if it means having to drink her sugar-free, Chinese, organic green tea served with asparagus sticks. Eugh!

'Easy for you to say that, Size Zero. Too much work,' I retort, tossing aside the asparagus. 'Have you seen the tyres around my waist? And please give me something that normal people eat.' My friend's 'no transfats, no artificial flavouring, no food additives' mantra is tough to emulate.

Priya nimbly slides off the wall and assumes the erect Padmasana posture. She closes her eyes and takes in hungry gulps of air. The cymbals and drum beats of *Om Namah*

Shivaya have reached their crescendo and the singer rasps the Sanskrit words before the music peters out.

Priya rolls up her yoga mat and switches off the music player. Her naturally frizzy hair is bunched into a tight bun and held back with a fluorescent headband. Her face is flushed pink, her lush knitted eyebrows furrowed with concern.

'Just look at you, Ira,' she says exasperatedly, her dark brown eyes holding mine. 'You are letting yourself go due to that loony bin Arun. Forget the bastard and begin afresh. Isn't that why you returned to India?'

I choose not to respond because my otherwise worldly-wise friend wouldn't understand the aftermath of a break-up.

'And *please* start getting out and meeting men. What you need is a hot man and hot, steamy sex—'

God, I hate it when she goes on this man trip. 'Don't start already,' I thwack her with a magazine. 'What I really need is a cup of hot tea, not this awful green yucky concoction.'

Priya pats my waist and dryly adds, 'As for these tyres, they'll have to be punctured, my dear.'

We start giggling and it feels like college days again when Priya and I used to bond over chai and samosas. This is why I love Priya: her absolute loyalty to me. No questions asked. Nothing much about her has changed: her positive and feisty spirit, her straight-talking manner or her passion for fitness. It's remarkable that she cashed in on the fitness wave at the right time and is now one of the most sought-after yoga professionals in the country. She has authored three bestselling books on yoga, hosts a wellness show on television and extensively tours the country for workshops and seminars. More importantly, she is also my 4 am or anytime-anywhere shrink. Priya is the kind of friend that every woman wishes she had on her speed dial. She is so much wiser and self-assured than me. There has never been a time in the fourteen years since we graduated that we haven't been in touch. My mind flashes back to all the secrets we have shared, all the milestones we have celebrated, and all the bittersweet growing up we have done together. I knew about her Syrian Christian boyfriend (now husband) Jonathan, long before her orthodox Tamil Brahmin parents got wind of it and threw a Bollywood-style fit. I called her as soon as our family astrologer (now a redoubtable voice of the future) pronounced Arun's horoscope as tailor-made, 'like Shiva–Parvati', for me. I call Priya my soul sister, making Anusha good-humouredly crib about this.

'But how is power yoga going to bail me out of this fake husband mess?' I throw up my hands in despair. I had called her last night to bring her up to speed on my self-created trouble.

'You suffer from low self-esteem and denial, which is why you lied,' replies Priya sagely. It's sometimes spooky how much she gets me. I close my eyes, trying to shut out the image of Arun's note on the refrigerator. Priya continues, 'It's all in the mind, which affects the body and the soul. Power yoga will help you de-stress and heal you mentally and physically. Join my class and you'll see its nurturing benefits.'

I throw up my hands again. 'That's fine but how is it going to solve my present problem? Do I just confess to these women that I am a single parent with no besotted hubby sending me roses by the truckload?'

'Eventually, yes. But not immediately, as this would create unnecessary prejudice towards you. Befriend them and take things one at a time. I'm sure this will get resolved,' says Priya with the calm assuredness of a Brahmakumari.

'But—' I begin, not entirely convinced.

'Just relax, yaar. It's no big deal! How is this one lie going to harm you?'

'I'm not sure—'

Priya hugs me. 'Ira, as courageous as you are, you are also vulnerable and scared. Let the Universe take its course.' Her lithe arms gesticulate in the air. It's been her favourite phrase ever since I can remember—even when she got severely reprimanded by Sister Abigal for wearing low-cut necklines in the Catholic women's hostel she stayed in during our Delhi University days.

I grimace and don't argue my case any further. Besides, I am too tired to make her see my point of view.

'Come on, cheer up. I'll make you some piping hot chai,' she says and leads me by the hand to the kitchen.

Jonathan and Priya's is a match made in organic/herbal/fitness heaven. If she is the yoga guru, he is an exercise fiend and never misses his daily one-hour power walk on the treadmill. It's no surprise that their kitchen counter is crammed with an assortment of protein powders, digestive mixes and herbal tablets of every conceivable variety and for every imaginable dietary purpose. But something else catches my eye today.

'What's this?' I ask, holding a plastic container labelled 'Bee Pollen Fertility Superfood'. It's strange that this should find shelf space in my friend's kitchen. Priya and her husband had long ago decided not to have children. She simply sighs and puts the kettle on.

I wait for her to respond. Finally, she meets my gaze squarely. 'After seven years of marriage—seven!—Jonathan has caught the parent bug,' she says in a low voice. 'At forty-two, he wants to try every concoction in the market to better his sperm count. He has been begging me to have a baby.'

'But you don't want to,' I surmise, noticing her sullen face.

Priya leans back against the spotless kitchen counter. 'I am too set in my ways, Ira. I mean, I love children, but with no strings attached, thank you. Motherhood is hard work; I know because I grew up seeing my mother raise five boys and a girl. She never *ever* had any time for herself.'

'But look at you now!' I gush. 'A celebrity with clients like corporate tycoons, society women, and dashing young ministers. Your brothers are VPs, doctors, and scientists. Your mom's hard work has more than paid off.'

Priya shakes her head exasperatedly. 'That's not the point. It's simple: either you're born with a mothering instinct or you are not. You know I fly with my iPod glued to my ears and ask for a seat at least fifteen rows away from babies and toddlers. So, how self-sacrificing a mother can I be?' I smile, recollecting the four-hour flight during which a sick child had puked all over Priya's hot pink Bebe tank top.

'Trust me, babies become adults one day,' I say, trying to imagine a six-foot moustached Abhi.

We take our teacups and move to her cosy living room. Priya's three-BHK apartment in the leafy Asiad Village is a tribute to India's artisans. Jonathan is an executive with a UN organization and his travels to the country's interiors is reflected everywhere. The house is a potpourri of handmade woven baskets, terracotta pots, papier-mâché lanterns, Madhubani paintings, and colourful floor mats. I admire the good taste and simplistic design values that have gone into creating this homely ambience. A crawling baby will complete the look, I smile to myself.

'What you smiling about, smug cat?' Priya asks, catching me off guard.

'Nothing, just thinking about babies and you,' I say, resting my feet on an ottoman. We sip our tea in silence.

'I'm not sure if I am prepared for motherhood after living life on my own terms,' Priya finally ventures. 'I am worried I will make a lousy mom. I am not exactly Mother Hen tending to her chicks. More like the self-obsessed lady who forgot her kids in the mall. And what if Jonathan doesn't share in the parenting duties after all the trouble I go through for nine fricking months? What will happen to my career? I refuse to give up all that I have achieved.' For someone who believes in the Universe's secret powers of resolution and Girl Power,

Priya appears on the verge of a meltdown. I reach out and squeeze her arm.

'Hey, Pri,' I say softly. 'Wake up, this is the twenty-first century; you can be a career woman *and* a mother too. You can be a supermom. The best part is, *you* are your boss, so you don't have to stealthily pump breast milk or abscond from office for parent–teacher meetings. No woman is a born Mother Hen. Those who say so are lying to the high heavens. You will see how beautifully you'll transform into a loving mother once the baby arrives. You are so great with Abhi, in fact, your next book should be on yoga for babies—commissioned by me, of course!'

Priya smiles feebly. 'You seem to be enjoying motherhood.'

I shrug. 'I have my banshee moments, though it's mostly good. But clichéd as it may sound, motherhood is the most soul-enriching job on earth. I really wish I could have more kids.'

'Of course you can, honey. Once you remarry.' Priya's tone is direct and matter-of-fact. I make a face though I know she means well. My faith in men is at an all-time low. I would much rather focus on my career and raising Abhi than remarry.

'I am done with men. Why does everyone presume I need a man to make my life complete?' I snap.

'Of course you do, Ira,' says Priya, ignoring my dark tone.

'I. Do. Not.'

'Better still, you could have a love child out of wedlock.'

Priya's eyes sparkle. 'A one-night stand and, voilà, you get pregnant.'

'I'm game if George Clooney is,' I grin. 'There must be a reason why God has kept him childless.' We laugh.

Priya frowns. 'While I have never bothered with the biological-clock mumbo jumbo, I am suddenly racing against it now.' She looks tense again. 'I don't know how to handle Jonathan who is behaving like *he* has got to worry about ovulation and what-else-you-have-got-to-do-to-get-pregnant. It's quite unfair he is going back on the 'no kids' policy we'd agreed on. If I didn't love him to bits, I would have dumped him in the nearest garbage bin.'

'It's okay, Priya,' I say, rising from the sofa. 'Take your time and talk it out with him. Remember, whatever your decision, *you* must be happy with it. I'm sure Jonathan will come around.'

We both descend the stairs and make our way to my car. 'Thank you,' Priya half-whispers, holding me in a tight embrace. 'And keep the fake husband story going for a while, babe. You are not on the CIA's most-wanted terrorist list.'

'Er...not yet,' I say morosely, my insides once again tormented by my Big Lie.

'You are just a heartbroken woman who lied,' shrugs Priya. 'If you were to scratch the surface of these hip Bumblebees moms, there would be far graver lies in their lives than what you have concocted. Believe me, I have an insider's peep into Delhi's society queens. They are shiny outside but crusty inside.'

I yell out above the engine's din, 'I refuse to visit you if you serve me any more of this asparagus baloney.'

'Next time it will be karela juice. Promise,' Priya grins and waves out to me.

Seven

I mull over Priya's dilemma en route to Bumblebees. She and Jonathan had radical views on having children even when they were dating. They were one of those free-spirit folks who didn't want baby spittle and report cards to get in the way of their bohemian lifestyle. Globe-trotting, whitewater rafting and scuba diving figured high in their life's ambitions—not creating a Little League team from their genetic pool. Of course, they had fought tooth and nail with their families who vehemently opposed their decision. But heck, this is what they wanted from life. And this is what they had worked determinedly towards. So Jonathan's sudden turnaround comes as quite a shocker, even to me. I wonder if age blunts one's idealistic views on life and propels one towards joining the herd.

I look at a family of five squeezed on the two-wheeler next to me. It's a couple and their children, their bodies pressed together like assorted vegetable chunks on a BBQ stick. They look like they might collapse in a heap any minute, but seem happy nonetheless. Then I think of privileged people like

Priya and Jonathan who revel in their DINK (Double Income No Kids) status. They represent a thin slice of India's social strata who are finally making bold to speak their minds and deviate from the conventional path of marrying and having kids. I had always admired their courage to stick to their guns, despite the stigma that comes with being childless in India. It is one thing to remain childless due to fertility issues, but quite another due to one's own belief system. In a country where children are revered as God's avatar, opting to remain issueless for lifestyle pleasures is considered an audacious, selfish act. Oh well, we divorcees face similar flak. Just as DINKS are labelled 'cold and selfish', divorcees are perceived to be 'difficult and non-adjusting'. The world is quick to pass judgement.

I hastily pull into the Churchill Lane car park and run towards the school gate worried that Abhi might be crying for me. I am relieved to see that the gate is still locked. A smattering of moms, dads, grandparents and maids are clustered in their respective groups, braving the hot sun. By now, some faces have become familiar and we exchange polite smiles. There is the tall wiry mom with the perky boobs; the sophisticated fortyish mom who is always impeccably turned out in designer fusion wear; the giggling group of twenty-something moms in BMU; the eternally harried-looking mom (though unfailingly put together in colour-coordinated accessories) with her baby slung in a stylish Ergo baby carrier; a balding dad poring over pink papers; and a stern-looking grandfather in crisp formal wear, cap and suspenders—

whatever be the weather. If you enjoy celebrity-spotting like I do, swing by the Bumblebees gate some day. You'll find the chic bespectacled lady who is the Indian bureau chief of a reputed US weekly magazine; the alabaster-complexioned aloof wife of a dashing young industrialist (a plainclothes bodyguard always discreetly hovering around her); a young poet who has just won a $25,000 coveted literary award for his esoteric poetry on world peace; and a glamorous, well-known newspaper columnist who prefers standing in the shade, scanning the crowd with disdainful interest.

In this mélange are the maids in their Lycra churidars, jeans, ethnic kurtis, and fashionable footwear. Gone are the generations of maids who wore torn saris and tattered chappals. Today's New Age maids wear French plaits and fringe cuts. Initially, I was a little taken aback to see well-turned out maids confidently stepping out of their employers' expensive cars, unfurling their frilly umbrellas, swinging their handbags (Gucci rip-offs from Sarojini Nagar) and rattling off instructions to their ward in pidgin English: 'Baby, drink pani. Baby, no cry.' They greet each other with a 'Hi', and chat on their cell phones that have Bollywood item numbers downloaded as ringtones. But what astonishes me the most is that some of these maids appear underage—as young as fourteen or fifteen—barely out of their teens. It feels grossly irresponsible on the parents' part to entrust the care of their children to young girls who are barely out of their childhood themselves.

I realize that somewhere in the chaos of juggling a

demanding career and managing the home front, the child falls by the wayside. Modern-day parenting in India is a stressful affair that operates with the clockwork precision of a battle strategy: office commuting time should synchronize with the child's school commute, and this should align with the driver's punctuality, the maid's efficiency, and the traffic signals' functionality. Which is the reason why the average mom is manically dependent on her household help. I know a woman whose Facebook updates show more gratitude for her driver and cook than for anyone else in her life. 'Cook back from vacation, couldn't have been happier even if I'd won a lottery,' was her latest post. Even so, it bothers me that a sizeable percentage of Bumblebees parents have left their children almost entirely in the care of their domestics. Though it is completely understandable in the case of busy career mothers with no extended family support, I cringe seeing non-working mothers also delegate the daily drop and pick-up to their maids and drivers. Dropping and picking up Abhi are my favourite parts of the day. Soon Abhi will be a big boy and might start using the school bus. I am a selfish, selfish mother. I want to make the most of his toddler years and eternally stamp on my mind the memory of seeing his short sturdy legs sprint towards his class in the mornings and the giddy delight with which he greets me at the gate in the afternoon. These are cherished moments from my *Mommy Memory Book* that I will take with me to my grave.

The gate opens and the children are handed over class-wise. In the ensuing din and commotion, Abhi comes charging out of the gate, waving a fancy-looking toy in one hand and a big multicoloured lollipop in the other. 'Amma, look! Pober Langers!' he gleefully shouts. The electronic price scanner that my mommy mind is gasps at the expensive items: Robot: Rs 400? Lollipop (the one I had denied Abhi in the mall last weekend): Rs 100? A tall, taut woman in a coral halter-neck dress approaches me with a simpering smile. She's the mom from Abhi's class who stands out for her high-end fashion sense.

'Hi!' she says, extending a hand. 'I am Nikki. My daughter, Bianca, is in Abhi's class. You are his mom, right?'

'Yes,' I smile, trying not to stare at her exquisite rhinestone-encrusted Rolex watch. A little girl in an identical dress creeps up behind Nikki. Her hair is done up in African-style braids with multicoloured beads dangling at the ends. She has the same shy smile and slanting eyes as her mother. 'Hi, Bianca,' I give her a small wave.

'Pober Langers!' Abhi waves the robot at Bianca who flinches.

'We are celebrating Bianca's third birthday on Friday and I would love to have you and Abhi at the party.' Nikki hands me an invitation rolled like a mini calendar. 'Bianca cut a cake in class today and I gave the children some gifts,' she explains.

I nod. 'Thanks so much, we will be there.'

The mother–daughter duo gets admiring glances from other moms.

'Rockin' jaan,' shouts Avantika, blowing her a kiss before roaring away in her car.

'Will call you, babe,' mouths Riya.

'Very pretty, Nikki,' yells someone else from afar.

Nikki beams at the compliments and flicks back her burgundy-streaked bangs with élan.

'Do bring your husband along too,' she trills, before sashaying away in her six-inch-high scarlet Gladiators. *Yeah, sure.*

I strap a hot and sweaty Abhi into his car seat and open the pink- and-gold birthday invite, dazzling with fairy glitter. It opens up as a scroll with satin tassels at the ends.

Our Princess turns 3 on September 15!
You are invited to
rub shoulders with Her Royal Highness
Bianca Vadhera
at
Vadhera Villa
1000 Paschimi Marg
Vasant Vihar
Time: 5 pm onwards
Come and Enjoy the Royal Carnival!

(RSVP on Facebook Group: Bianca Vadhera Turns 3)

I put away the invite and wonder how these *Princess Diaries* will unfold.

Eight

So I had thought I would be a supermom, impeccably turned out like the nothing-can-ruffle-me TV mothers, cheerfully flipping omelettes for my family, not a hair out of place, not a crease in my clothes. This was around the time Abhi was still a speck of an embryo and I had visions of me walking down the motherhood ramp with élan. Fast forward to today—here I am in my faded nightie that's missing two buttons, groggily stirring Bournvita in Abhi's sippy cup and willing my eyelids to pop open.

Vinnie has this incredible manic energy that prods her to call me at all odd hours to discuss book ideas that are either 'huge' or 'HUUGEE'. But yesterday's midnight call was to gripe about bestselling authors who give her hell once they are raking in the moolah and fame. Svetlana Swaroop, World Ink's golden girl who shot to fame writing erotica novels, was, not so long ago, a largely anonymous, pampered rich housewife from Pune. This was before the sales of her debut erotica novel, *Lips*, went through the roof and catapulted her into publishing superstardom. India's very own bestselling erotica novelist, a desi E.L. James, was launched by World Ink. Thereafter, she wrote two more bestsellers as part of the *Lips* trilogy, and each has sold lakhs and lakhs of copies. Being aware that she brings in the cream of the revenues for the company, Svetlana now believes that World Ink's employees are her bonded labour and Vinnie, her bank. When the time came to bid for her fourth erotica novel—the shenanigans of smutty air hostesses and a horny pilot—Svetlana hired an international literary agent to do the math for her. And boy, did the agent drum up an astronomical number as her asking advance and marketing spend for the book! Ever since then, Svetlana has been threatening to sign up with a rival publisher if Vinnie doesn't match the numbers, which run into a crore plus.

'I can't take it any more, Ira,' Vinnie had rasped down the phone line last night. 'This woman is being grossly unreasonable, but we can't afford to let her go. Her three books are constant revenue churners for the company.' Vinnie had droned on and on last night, cursing Svetlana, the agent, the publishing industry, Obama, the weather, her tailor and Svetlana's dog that makes an appearance in all her book acknowledgements. Vinnie hung up after an hour, thanking modern medicine for the gift of Valium.

The morning light filters through the sheer curtains in the living room. I yawn and stretch my limbs. I sometimes wonder if the formidable Vinnie Warsi is now only an old warhorse battling post-menopausal blues. She does seem to be extra prickly these days.

I drearily take in my surroundings. The house is a mess: scattered with blocks, toys, puzzle pieces, story books and magazines. Play-Doh is smeared on my aunt's prized Persian rugs and crayon doodles decorate the walls. I start the vacuum cleaner that determinedly probes and unearths Abhi's beloved soft toy, a ragged Dalmatian puppy from behind the curtains. I have lost count of the number of times Fido has gone missing.

The part-time maid seems to be on full-time leave—viral attack, conjunctivitis, niece's wedding—and any effort to look for a replacement appears more daunting than the infamous Delhi Nursery school admissions process that I constantly hear horror stories about.

My search for a full-time maid has not yielded any results though I did interview a number of candidates sent by the agencies. Candidate One was a pious twenty-five-year-old who wanted Friday (Mata ka Jagran) and Sunday (Church) off. She was the face of secularism: a practising Hindu who had converted to Christianity. She also made it clear that cleaning baby poop or puke was not her scene. 'I am allergic to all this,' she said, twitching her button-like nose. Candidate Two, a middle-aged tribal woman, boasted of having raised seven grandchildren all by herself but claimed her arthritic knees wouldn't permit her to run after Abhi. 'I can sit and keep an eye on him,' she said magnanimously, popping a piece of betel nut into her mouth. How am I to trust a nanny who can't keep pace with an active two-and-a-half-year-old's antics? Of what use is she if I send him to the park with her and he runs in the direction of traffic? Candidate Three was heavily made up like a TV sitcom diva and her opening line was that I should install a cooler and a TV in her quarters. It seems she had earlier worked as a nanny in a well-known industrialist's family in Sainik Farm.

In addition to the extravagant salary she quoted, she also wanted a separate 'expense' account for her cell phone recharge coupons and beauty parlour visits. After interviewing a few more 'interesting' characters, I decided to freeze my search temporarily. As it turns out, finding responsible and safe child care in Delhi is an unbearable hassle. Since Abhi and I live alone, I would rather tread carefully down this path than rush into anything half-heartedly. While I am not looking for the elusive, kind-hearted 'Ramu Kaka' of Bollywood lore, I would certainly want someone who is good with children and has reasonable demands. Since I am in the process of expanding World Ink's non-fiction line, my working hours are only going to lengthen. A responsible and good-natured nanny who can play with Abhi—and match his energy levels—would be helpful. I ache for my parents. Even though they live in Chennai, they would have gladly visited us in Delhi to take care of Abhi, whenever help was required.

So I am currently maidless in Delhi and, frankly, it's not too bad. Cooking, cleaning, mopping, and washing were chores I had mastered in my years abroad, so what was the big brouhaha about? In fact, cooking and cleaning are extremely therapeutic for me.

I run through the chores for the day noted in my diary:

- pack upama for abhi's lunchbox: check
- sort the laundry for washing and ironing: pending
- put away toys and books: check
- water the plants: pending
- pay electricity bill: pending
- email parents abhi's pics: check
- fix paediatrician appointment: pending

I wrap my hands gratefully around my mug of filter coffee. I have fifteen glorious minutes to spare for the newspapers before Abhi wakes up. I glance through the headlines: Minister caught in sex scandal; Infosys earnings dip; popular godman is a conman. Yawn, so what's new? I move on to the tabloids: Goldie Hawn is in Jaipur; Shah Rukh Khan is in Los Angeles; Star couple on tonight's *Koffee with Karan* (must watch, at any cost, come what may); and former Bollywood actress-turned-mom reveals her beauty secrets. Ah, finally some worthwhile news.

Reporter: How do you stay so fit? What is your fitness mantra?

Actress: I am a hands-on mom. I burn my calories running behind my child.

Liar. Your trainer works on your shapely derrière. I know, Priya told me so.

Reporter: What is the secret of your glowing complexion?

Actress: Thinking happy thoughts and staying positive.

Yeah, like thoughts of luxury spas and Louis Vuitton handbags.

Reporter: What tips do you have for young mothers like you?

Actress: Ladies, please bond with your child.

Eh?

Reporter: How do you deal with stress?

Actress: Children are the greatest stress-busters. One look at my daughter's face takes away my stress.

Does your Botox give way when your child throws the devil of a tantrum?

I am itching to tell Priya about my Freudian interpretation of Ms Yummy Mummy. But far more important things await me, like bathing and getting Abhi ready for school.

When I emerge from my shower, Abhi is rifling through the contents of my handbag. I watch him as he jangles my car keys, flings them on the floor, stares intently at Mahatma Gandhi on the Rs 100-note, drops it, and digs deeper into the bag to unearth more treasures: my comb, a pink scrunchie, my purse, face tissues, toffee wrappers, cheque books, two pens with missing caps, and crumpled petrol receipts. He picks up a tissue and dabs his face like he has seen me doing. A piece of the tissue sticks to his long lashes like a snowflake and I burst out laughing. I grab my camera from my study desk and click away. Abhi looks up, startled, and grins mischievously. I suppose this is why baby Krishna is so beloved to Indian mothers. I smother him with kisses. We play peekaboo with the bedsheet for a few minutes before I pick him up in one sweeping motion and deposit him in the bathtub for his bath. Thereafter, it is yet another roller coaster of a morning till I see him off at his school gate with a huge sigh of relief.

'Where are you going?' accosts Riya, as I almost ram into her in my rush to get home. I have a telecon scheduled with Vinnie this morning to discuss my non-fiction imprint. We want to bring out edgy and fun titles for thirty-plus women, and I want to brainstorm with her about the possible authors we could approach to write these books.

'Hey, Riya! So good to see you,' I smile exaggeratedly and return her cheek kiss.

'Long time no talk, yaar,' she says in a complaining voice, thumb-dancing on her iPod. It occurs to me that she seems to own a number of phones. I remember seeing a pink Nokia Slider in her hands on the orientation day at Bumblebees. She pauses to read a text message and laughs. 'Rahul is always sending me the cutest jokes from office.' She jabs a few more buttons on her iPod and finally looks up at me.

'So?' I ask, not sure what else to say.

'I am going with Nikki to Silhouettes for a pedicure. They give the most awesome avocado and tea tree oil foot massage. Want to come?'

I steal a look at her beautifully manicured feet encased in

kolhapuris. Her toenails are painted a baby pink, and thin silver anklets adorn her delicate feet. I try to figure out why she needs a mani-pedi. I self-consciously shuffle my feet, relieved to be wearing jootis that conceal the chipped nail polish on my toes.

'Sorry, yaar. Today is tough, too much work to catch up with,' I say, trying to wear a regretful expression. 'Maybe next time?'

Riya gives me a pitiful look. 'Sure. But you should step out more often with us. You are always working, Ira,' She gives me a hug and leaves. I sigh. Riya can't be closer to the truth. I can't remember the last time when I had a 'real' outing where I actually dressed like a lady: wore party clothes, sprayed on perfume, and applied make-up. Maybe, at the company Christmas party hosted by Arun's firm. That sounds like from some faraway land now.

As I sprint across the lawns, I spot Hiroo Zardari sitting forlorn on a bench. Bonny, her Lab, is nowhere in sight. I run into her and Bonny almost every morning when I drop Abhi at school. Sometimes, we exchange pleasantries, but mostly, wave from afar. She seems to be fond of Abhi and often gives him éclairs and mints. Abhi now views her with renewed respect for she is the kind lady who gives him goodies his mother is not so generous in doling out.

Mrs Zardari's hunched frame and the usual baggy salwar kameez, gives her the appearance of a crumpled brown paper bag. She looks so dejected that I can't help approaching her out of concern.

'Good morning, Aunty,' I say cheerfully, sitting next to her.

She slowly turns her weathered face in my direction. 'Morning,' she says listlessly. Her tiny world-weary eyes are unfathomable puddles of melancholy and loneliness.

'Where is Bonny?' I ask.

'At home; the poor boy's eczema has worsened.'

'Is...everything all right?' I ask. I barely know her and don't want to appear too nosy. A chorus of sirens slices the tranquil morning air. VIP vehicles zipping past Churchill Lane is a daily occurrence since MP bungalows are in the vicinity. A child dawdles past us, his mother sternly ordering him to walk faster. They are obviously late for school. The hum of chatter from a group of maids sitting in a circle at the other end of the park floats towards us.

'I miss my Siddy,' Mrs Zardari says, her voice quivering. 'Today is his tenth birthday. When I was in better health, I used to mark the occasion by baking his favourite chocolate plum cake. But now—' she breaks down, her petite body convulsed in sobs. I clasp her palm, her bony fingers cold and hard, like autumn twigs, against mine. I rub her back and wait for her to continue.

From the corner of one eye I see the mother carrying her son in exasperation.

'I send Siddy a birthday card every year but never receive a response from my son,' she says at last, dabbing her eyes with her kurta sleeves. 'Not even a phone call.'

'How many children do you have, Aunty?' I ask quietly.

'Jay is my only son, my only child. He hardly keeps in

touch with me. He used to be a very affectionate boy, always sensitive to his old Mama's needs. But he has changed after marriage…' She snorts a short, brittle laugh. 'I had no issues when he chose an Irish wife—we are a liberal family—and I welcomed Janice into the family like a daughter. But she is so cold and aloof towards me. I don't know why. I even gave her my jewellery, family heirlooms from my grandmother. Of what use would they be to me when I am dead and gone?'

Mrs Zardari looks about ninety, older than Churchill Lane. She must have had her son very late in life.

'Does your son call you?' I ask, remembering the frequent phone calls I would make to my parents from the US.

Mrs Zardari shakes her head. 'Maybe three or four times a year. I booked trunk calls a couple of times but the conversations were so hurried and abrupt. I have repeatedly told Jay to send me photos of Siddy through post but I suppose he is too busy to oblige.'

'Do you use a cell phone?'

'Oh, no, I hate this technology mumbo jumbo. Besides, it will be a hassle paying cell phone bills. I have one servant, and am lucky if the boy remembers even to buy eggs for breakfast.'

I smile. 'When did you last speak to Siddy?'

'Last Christmas,' she says, brightening at the memory. 'He sounded so grown-up and mature! Not the little boy who would pester his grandma to tell him stories…'

I don't know what to say. I wish I could help her in some way. Suddenly, a thought crosses my mind. 'Aunty, why don't you try and get your son's email address next time he calls?

Or maybe you could book a trunk call? I will create an email ID for you and you could dictate a letter to your son asking for Siddy's photos and I'll key it in. Maybe he will send them via email!'

Mrs Zardari smiles for the first time this morning. She pats my hands and nods. 'I will. Thank you, my dear,' she says, rising from the bench. 'Thanks for listening to a mad old woman's rants.' She slowly walks away in the direction of her apartment. My gaze sweeps Churchill Lane's chipped brick buildings, bathed a warm ruby by the early September sunshine. I wonder how many more Hiroo Zardaris are trapped inside these ancient walls.

Nine

At 10 am on a Wednesday morning, as I am about to enter City Market's Brew, I see Riya and Nikki coming out of Curvy Secrets from two doors away. They are giggling and carrying the spoils of their retail therapy in two overflowing bags each. Nikki says something and Riya almost collapses with laughter on the sidewalk. Nikki has opted for a classic white shirt and blue jeans teamed with a tan sequinned belt. Riya is wearing an electric blue cotton jumpsuit that is all the rage among Delhi's young moneyed crowd. I slide through Brew's glass doors before they can see me. Of course, it will be only a matter of minutes before we come face to face.

The last time I hung out with Abhi's friends' mothers was two months ago at Java Beans. After politely declining many more such invitations from Carol, Riya and Nikki—never Avantika—to 'do coffee' with them in a variety of hip eateries across South Delhi, I have finally agreed to join them today. Work, home and all the added responsibilities of single-parenting leave me with no time to simply 'hang out', a privilege that can be exercised only by these well-heeled 'Ladies Who Lunch'. I am impressed with the amount of money they blow up every day on food, shopping, and beauty treatments. This swish set includes Carol, Riya, Nikki, Avantika, and a few moms from other classes. I bitchily think Avantika's sole purpose of hanging out with them is to promote her business.

But I digress. I want to set aside my everyday humdrum life for the next two hours. I am here for some fun girl talk before it is time to pick up our children. I catch a fleeting reflection of myself in the scalloped mirrors on the wall as I make my way up the narrow wooden staircase leading to the café. My sky blue cotton salwar kameez seems a sensible choice for an inordinately sticky day. The word 'sensible' has come to define my very existence since I became a mother. Everything should be sensible: what I wear; how much I spend; the people I befriend; the hours I keep; what Abhi eats; the TV time I dole out to him; and the kind of toys I buy him. I tighten the scrunchie on my ponytail, and spot the table where the ladies are seated. Carol waves at me, Hutoxi's sad eyes acknowledge me with rapid blinks and, two others, who belong to the hip twenty-something mommy gang—the other mommy mafia at Bumblebees—carefully part their matted lips just enough to smile at me coolly. They check me out as covertly as possible. These two women look so alike that they could be mistaken for sisters. They both have silky shoulder-length hair, high foreheads and the same baby-doll eyes made up with frosted mauve eye shadow. They even seem to covet the same Italian brand for their handbags. It is hard to believe that a nine-pound and a twelve-pound baby emerged, respectively—as they would later recount their labour stories with breathless theatrics—from these petite child-woman frames.

'Ladies, this is Iravati,' Carol gets up to cheek kiss me.

'Hi, I am Tina,' says the slightly taller of the two women.

'And I am Jasmine,' says the other, blinking at me several times.

'Hi, it's great to meet you guys,' I smile. 'I've seen you with your sons at the gate.'

Hutoxi gives me a tepid hug as I sit down.

Just then Nikki and Riya sashay into the room, drop their shopping bags on the floor, and plonk themselves in the two empty chairs awaiting them.

'Lingerie-shopping, are we?' asks Hutoxi, perking up at the sight of the Curvy Secrets bags.

'This place has the best underwired and lace négligées in the world,' says Riya.

'In the hottest colours!' adds Nikki, flipping her hair, which is streaked light claret today. 'I bought everything in teal since it is *so in* this season.'

Carol rolls her eyes. 'Really, Nikki. You truly believe in all that crap about which colours are in and out? It's all marketing hogwash.' Thank God there is someone here who thinks like me.

'Whatever, darling. When your husband loves seeing you in teal, you'd better give him what he wants.' Nikki tilts her long oval face to the side and hi-fives Hutoxi.

I join in the laughter and feel like I am in the midst of a *Sex and the City* shoot.

'Shall we order?' Carol asks, signalling a waiter to our table.

We place our orders. I stick to the mantra that what fits my budget fits my tummy and place my order quickly.

Brew is filling up with couples, corporate folks, and a smattering of foreigners. It was the first trendy coffee chain of its kind to open shop in India, around the time the country became an outsourcing hub. It instantly connected with the growing surge of young men and women who worked at call centres and had disposable income to splurge on Café Mochas and all-American donuts. Compared to other over-priced newfangled eateries that offer Mediterranean, Lebanese and Japanese tongue-twisters on the menu, Brew, with its unfussy décor and standard snack bar fare is far more appealing. At least, to me.

'Brew is so boooring,' whines Tina. 'We should have gone to Penne instead.'

Jasmine blinks rapidly. 'Yeah, it's a way cooler place.'

'But we went to Penne just last weekend with the kids,' says Nikki, examining her blue acrylic nails that resemble a witch's talons dipped in poison. It beats me why otherwise-genetically blessed women want ugly fake nails.

'Oh?' Tina says, her smooth forehead knit in a frown. 'Who all?'

'Carol, Hutoxi, Riya, Avantika and I. The kids had a blast in the play area.'

I feel a stab of jealousy that I was not invited to Penne. Then I shrug it off. Whom am I kidding? There is hardly anything in common between these women and me. Except motherhood, perhaps? So why crib? I look from one exfoliated, toned and moisturized woman to another and realize what a misfit I am in this group of fashionable mothers. I feel like a country bumpkin compared to these glam dolls, notwithstanding my education and job. Their obsession with clothes and make-up, their Godzilla-sized shopping allowances, their posh cars, and their perfect husbands don't exactly tally with my more humble world. More fool me for thinking I was a part of their clique and would get invited to all their soirées. I know I sound pathetic, hardly a role model for strong single mothers. If Arun had not left me so unceremoniously, I would not be sitting here, questioning my self-worth and feeling like discarded flip-flops. Abhi and I would be in California with Arun, going for long walks on quiet, sandy beaches, or for scenic drives where the zigzagging roads jut out above breathtaking views of the Pacific Coast. The familiar rush of low self-esteem and self-doubt washes over me. And the nauseating trauma of broken dreams threatens to envelope me. But for Abhi, I would be a complete basket case by now. I bite my lips to stop them from trembling. I remind myself again that I have come here for some fun, girly chit-chat.

'By the way, where is Avantika?' asks Hutoxi.

'She is terribly busy. Her sister is visiting from Toronto,' says Riya. I do a silent whoo-hoo. My attempts at striking polite conversation with Avantika have so far yielded only frosty smiles. She loves sizing me up through the dark shutters of her Aviators as if she were a wildlife photographer observing a rare animal. I wonder what she has against me.

I try to join in the laughter as Carol, looking pretty in her peach sleeveless tunic, describes Anna's escapades. Carol is my favourite. But isn't she everyone else's too? In the pecking order of moms from Abhi's class, she is the most popular and well-liked. All she has to do is show up at the Bumblebees gate looking fresh as a lily and, within nanoseconds, other moms swarm around her like ants around sugar. Some people are blessed with the innate ability to command attention without even trying. Even Shelly smiles a wee bit extra when she sees Carol and lavishes more attention on Anna than over all the other kids. I guess Carol receives at least five compliments a day; I can't remember the last time anyone complimented me on anything. I think it was when my mother said how beautiful I looked during my pregnancy. It is funny how, when women are pregnant, fat is beautiful.

I glance at the fat-free, low-cal, multigrain vegetarian sandwich that the waiter places before me. If I had come alone, I might have ordered two greasy samosas at one-third the price.

'When is your husband getting back, Ira?' Riya's sing-song voice cuts into my thoughts like shrapnel. I feel like laughing. The word husband makes me either laugh or cry. I take a bite of the sandwich to bide my time. I haven't come prepared to answer questions about my absentee 'husband'.

I carefully chew the cucumber, wedged between two

lettuce leaves, before looking up at Riya. 'Pretty soon,' I reply vaguely.

'Being away from him must be so hard on you,' adds Carol in a kindly tone. 'How do you manage?'

Hutoxi, Tina. and Jasmine look wide-eyed with curiosity. I can count on Riya to give them the low-down later. I give a practised shrug. 'Oh, I manage quite all right, thanks. Abhi and I have got used to being by ourselves.' There is an awkward silence and I hasten to clarify, 'I mean, until my husband joins us in India.'

'Are you on Facebook?' asks Carol, slicing her quiche.

I am grateful for the change of subject. Yes I am on Facebook, the boon and bane of twenty-first-century friendship. I have 217 'friends' of whom only five are 'real' friends. On my list, I have almost everyone who has entered my life (besides my ex, of course): from kindergarten bumchums to World Ink's office boy. Who isn't on FB these days? Jennifer, my former colleague from Hepworth Allen, has created a profile for her Beagle. Barton's latest Facebook status reads: 'Relaxing by the poolside; it's a dog's life. Woof!'

We all exchange our Facebook IDs and flit from topic to topic—kids, parenting methods, Bumblebees, Bollywood, clothes, TV reality shows and the Bon Jovi concert that's coming to Delhi in December. This is what I love about women—we have way too many things to talk about in our rushed existence. By the end of a good two hours, I feel a little more relaxed in the company of these moms. It's remarkable how motherhood can bring the unlikeliest of women together.

There are the younger moms, like Tina and Jasmine, who are twenty-three-years old. Then there is Riya, twenty-seven, and planning her second child. Carol and I are thirty-five and thirty-four respectively. Hutoxi is the oldest at thirty-nine. 'We had Jhanvi after eight years of marriage,' she reveals, biting into a juicy chicken fillet. I am amazed at how confidently she carries off her scalloped spandex T-shirt and track pants despite her ungainly flab. How are you so confident in your skin? I want to ask her.

I tell myself to be less judgemental about the women around me and not view them as mere frivolous affluent wives. We all have our stories and, maybe, one day, I'll get to know some of theirs. I take a sip of water and look around the table. I wonder if any of these women has the potential to become my genuine friend or would she remain yet another conquest for my Facebook list? I am shrewd enough to understand that, while they may invite me for coffee and pedicures, they don't necessarily consider me as a part of their inner circle. The best I can get is probably a ringside view into their lives. And they, into mine. These are the moms who huddle under the shade of the jacaranda tree and animatedly discuss their in-laws, husbands, servants, vacations and everything else that makes their lives go round. I know, for I have often overheard snippets of their conversation. Yet, regardless of the disparities amongst us, a thread of camaraderie binds us together. We are on a level playing field because of our children. In some ways, we mothers are painted in the same hues.

Carol opens the leather folder and studies the bill. I am

about to give her my share of Rs 89 when she reaches out and stops me. She does some quick calculations on a napkin. 'The total amount is Rs 1,255,' she announces. 'So it's Rs 179 per person.' But my sandwich is only Rs 89, I want to explain. Then it strikes me. She has arrived at this figure by dividing the total bill by the number of people.

My middle-class sensibilities want to protest at this unfair method of calculating each person's share of the pie.

Instead, I ask timidly, 'Is this what you guys always do?'

'Sorry, I don't get you.' Carol looks quizzically at me while the others watch with interest.

'This…um…this calculation,' I say, turning a little red in the face.

Carol smiles sweetly. Seeing her, the others too relax and break into grins.

'Oh, this? Yes, always.' Carol shrugs. 'It's simpler than all of us paying for our titbit orders. Then it gets so confusing, na?' The women titter their approval. I gaze at the chunky left-over chicken fillets on Hutoxi's plate. *Yeah, right. Titbit orders.*

Ah well, yet another lesson learnt from the Bumblebees Mommy Diaries, I think, as I follow the women through Brew's door and step into City Market's rarefied air.

Ten

Abhi and I are sitting inside the cramped confines of a frayed multicoloured tent. The September sky has turned a heavy indigo and the last rays of the sun pour through the flimsy fabric. Abhi's face is tinged orange with the light reflected from the tent's red panel. He is sitting opposite me with his soft toys crowded around him: Fido, his beloved Dalmatian pup; Karl the kangaroo; Eeyore the donkey puppet; the one-eyed tiger cub; the chimp missing a tail; the soiled dachshund, Mr Jumbo the elephant; the green python with magenta stripes; the tiny teddy with large black eyes; and the furry white teddy with devilish red eyes.

'Give them lunch!' Abhi instructs me, pointing to his friends.

I make small laddoos out of the yellow Play-Doh and oblige. Abhi giggles.

'More!' he cries. I repeat the act. He giggles even harder.

'Brush chimp's teeth,' he orders like a drill sergeant. I do so with my index finger. Abhi collapses on the floor with laughter and the tent tilts to one side. Mr Jumbo loses his balance and falls on all the other animals. Abhi finds it so hilarious that he flings the animals one by one out of the tent's narrow opening. 'Go, go, go!' he shouts, making me laugh. Playing with Abhi is a great stress-buster for me. I reach across the darkening tent and hug him tight. He smells like the warm milk and butter cookies he's just had after what has been a very long day for us.

Post the Brew get-together, I picked up Abhi, fed him lunch at home and then rushed for the paediatrician's appointment at 4 o'clock. He was due for a shot that I had kept postponing till Bumblebees sent a health report card asking for information on annual inoculations. Abhi was so cranky after the shot that he cried all the way home. I carried him kicking and screaming upstairs to our second-floor apartment and, like so many mothers across the world, sought the refuge of the idiot box to bail me out. Thank heavens for *Mister Maker*, Abhi was back in his element in no time.

I fold away the tent and deposit Abhi's soft toys in a cane basket already overflowing with his paraphernalia. Single-parenting is a blessing as well as a challenge. While I get Abhi all to myself, I sometimes crave for that mythical, incredibly supportive, husband who could be my equal partner in so many small and big things that go into bringing up a child. Be it doctor's appointments, school drops and pick-ups, potty training, after-school activities, assembling hi-tech toys, bath time, story time, disciplining issues, or any of the million other things that a parent has to do. Parenting is a 24/7 task and, being Abhi's sole caregiver, I often wish there were forty-eight hours in a day. The chaos of parenting can be overwhelming on certain days and exhilarating on others. On the odd day when stress levels escalate, I feel like flopping on the bed and having a good cry, ranting to the gods for unfairly making me a single parent. But I can't squeeze in time for even that. My life is a constant work–life juggle, even though I am one of the fortunate mothers who can exercise flexibility in her work hours. A good day for me is when I get to take a twenty-minute shower and properly run a comb through my hair. If I get additional time for applying lipstick and changing my earrings, it's like a day spent at the spa. Okay, I am probably exaggerating a bit.

'Look!' Abhi comes running and points to his feet. He has worn a red sneaker on his right foot and a white sneaker on his left foot. Though it's comical, I am proud to see him achieve yet another milestone of independently wearing his shoes. His gross motor skills are still developing, so the laces are understandably undone. I subscribe to at least five toddler milestone e-zines and have an entire bookshelf dedicated to parenting books. This helps me record his milestones with the keen eye a scientist would reserve for studying bacteria under a microscope.

'Sweetie, that's fantastic,' I say, reaching out to remove the shoes.

'Nooo!' he cries, inching away from me. For a pint-sized man, he has quite a boom-box voice, my son.

'Baby, it is time for dinner, please take off your shoes,' I say. He races to the living room and I chase him.

'Abhi, when I say no, it's a NO!' I growl in my meanest evil-mom voice, *Five Calm Buddha-like Steps to Disciplining a Child*—a book I finished reading last night, forgotten.

Abhi giggles and jumps on the glass coffee table like it were a bouncy. I feel too pooped to be patient.

'Get down! Please. Take. Off. Your. Shoes.'

But Abhi continues to dodge me and runs all over the house. I wait for his hyperactive mood to subside and chide myself for choosing a weekday for administering the shot. I fret that he has to get up early for school. After hiding behind the curtains, doing a dog trot on the carpet and whizzing around the house in his scooty, he finally crashes on the sofa, his curls sticking to his sweaty forehead, and his cheeks flushed a tomato red. His eyes are already drooping, though the impish grin remains plastered on his face.

'Abhi, dinner!' I gently shake him. 'Wake up, baby!' For the next fifteen minutes I do my best to wake him up for dinner but he is already fast asleep. I try to put aside my motherly guilt for allowing my child to go to bed hungry and stare at his angelic face. I love the way his fingers curl up when he sleeps, and how his tummy rises and falls in small rhythmic motions. I remove his sneakers and carry him to our bedroom. I tuck him in and switch off the lights. I am ready to crash out myself, but crave for a cool shower. My cell phone trills. It's Priya.

'Hey, what's up?' I ask, my hand randomly picking a nightie from the wardrobe.

'Hey. Wanted to remind you about Jonathan's forty-third birthday party on Saturday. '

It suddenly strikes me that Bianca's party is on Friday! I need to RSVP her on FB. It's going to be a busy weekend.

'Yeah! Of course we'll be there,' I say distractedly, searching for a bath towel. 'You need help? I can come in early to help with—'

'No, that's fine, the caterers are coming. But…but I thought you should know…' she trails. Priya never trails. She spews words, but never stops mid-sentence. My in-built woman's antenna perks up to receive significant signals.

'What is it?' I ask suspiciously. 'You preggers, Pri?'

'Oh please, of course not!'

'What is it then?' I repeat impatiently. 'Make it fast, I have to go for my beauty bath.'

'Never mind,' she sighs dramatically after a pause. 'I'll see you Saturday then. Ciao!'

'Priya!' It's the same tone I use for Abhi when he does mischief.

I hear her inhale an expert yogic breath. 'Okay, it's about Vasu. I have invited him for the dinner party. I just thought you should know…you know…to give you a head's up…' she trails again.

I feel my body stiffen. I blink stupidly at the open wardrobe and swallow hard. Vasu. *Vasu*! I haven't heard his name in fourteen years. I close my eyes and a million memories of my college days get tossed around in my mind. I try to remember Vasu—the way his eyes would search for me in the packed college canteen; his sunny personality that could make even the grim canteenwallah smile; how he would throw back his head and laugh; his strong chin set in stubbornness; his teasing voice whenever he pulled my leg; his non-stop chatter; but mostly his profound silences…our words unspoken till it was too late to turn back the clock.

'Ira?' Priya's voice is gentle, probing. 'Vasu has broken up with Usha.'

I am a little too stunned to react. I feel no joy in hearing this. It doesn't matter to me today though I may have wished this upon them many moons ago.

'Is this information vital for my peace of mind?' I ask finally, only half in jest.

'Maybe,' says Priya, her voice heavy with meaning. I choose to ignore that.

'I did not know you were in touch with him.' My tone is accusatory.

'I haven't been. I ran into him at the Kamani auditorium yesterday.'

'He still watches hoity-toity Shakespearean plays, is it?' I say mockingly, though my lips are upturned in a smile.

'It was a Carnatic violin concert,' corrects Priya.

'Oh? When did our Shakespeare start liking classical ragas?'

'Maybe his tastes have changed. It's been fourteen years since we left college, remember?'

'Maybe his girlfriend dragged him to the concert.'

'He had come alone.'

'That doesn't mean anything.'

'What do you want it to mean, darling?' Priya asks coolly.

'Priya, are you on his side or mine?' I bristle, sounding juvenile even to my ears.

'Ira,' says Priya. 'Why are you getting so worked up? Shall I tell Vasu not to come?'

'No, that won't be necessary,' I speak too swiftly. 'You are free to invite whomever you wish.'

I can picture her amused look.

'Okay, whatever. Do you want me to come or not?' I ask.

'There won't be any party without my best friend,' says Priya indulgently.

I smile despite myself.

'Deep breath, Ira, deep breath,' she adds, in the calming way I've heard a famous Brahmakumari speak on television. 'Release your pent-up feelings. Re-discover your latent feelings. Empower yourself by freeing your mind from painful thoughts. A whole new happy life awaits you.'

It's no wonder my friend is such a success at what she does. Her clients eat out of her hands but I am in no mood for pranayam now.

'I gotta go, Pri,' I say.

'Don't forget to deep-breathe.'

'Bye,' I hang up. My hands are trembling and my heart is beating wildly. *Vasu has broken up with Usha.* The words keep spinning in my head till they become a din.

When I last saw them the summer we graduated, Usha and Vasu were walking cheek by jowl along our department's corridor, their voices bouncing off the walls of the deserted college building, their laughter pricking my skin. Our entire batch had come to collect our College Leaving Certificates on a muggy June afternoon when the leaves lay supine on tree branches, and the still, hot air swathed itself around us like a sticky plastic wrap. Unknown to Vasu and Usha, my gaze followed them as they crossed our college's century-old quadrangle where our tight-knit group had idled away many an afternoon, down the weathered stone steps that led to the main red brick building with the high turrets, and finally, along the front lawn's winding path to the grand wrought-iron gates that opened out to the waiting world outside. Then I lost trace of them forever.

Eleven

I am unable to sleep after my shower. My mind is a maze of memories revolving around Vasu, making me feel confused and perplexed. I had met him for the first time at the fee-paying counter in our college bank. I was standing right behind him in the serpentine queue of students on the first day of our term. I remember him as this tall, bespectacled, handsome guy who was fumbling for change in his jeans pocket. He turned back, adjusted his glasses, and smiled at me with hope. 'Would you have a fiver by any chance?' And that did it for me. There was something so wholesome and honest about his expression that endeared him to me instantly. We hit it off from there and went on to become dependent on each other for class notes, and for coming up with innovative excuses to miss the subsidiary Philosophy class that we both hated. Priya was the other close friend I made that year. She was my opposite. While I was more the quiet, submissive type, she was tomboyish, a fiery feminist and unafraid to speak her mind even before the most daunting of professors, Monster Manchanda, the head of our Economics department.

Soon Priya, Vasu and I became an inseparable trio. We were different in our own ways, yet, were able to forge a deep bond of friendship that made the first year of our college absolutely magical for me. And so it would have continued between Vasu and me had Usha not entered the picture...

I rise and go to the kitchen. I am suddenly miffed with Priya for bringing Vasu back into my life—rather, into my thoughts—after fourteen years. I am in no mood to work tonight. Feeling restless, I put tea to brew in a saucepan and potter around the kitchen. I am suddenly hit by a wave of nostalgia as recollections of my cheery New Jersey kitchen come to mind. I miss its wide French windows; its floral curtains reminiscent of an English garden; the little pots of petunias on its white countertop; the oak cabinets where my precious spices were neatly lined up in glass jars; and the bright knitted mittens, a Christmas gift from Jennifer, that hung alongside the wooden and copper ladles from hooks on the wall. I remember chilly winter evenings stirring spicy soups in the Crockpot, the steam rising to my face in gentle wispy curls. I remember slaving in the kitchen over a three-tier chocolate cake for Arun's birthday—two months before he left. I remember Abhi learning to crawl on the kitchen's white-and-black linoleum tiles, his wide toothless grin when he first experienced the freedom that comes from mobility. Then I remember the family pictures on my refrigerator... and Arun's note. I flinch, and slowly add milk to the swirling Darjeeling, turning it a rosy brown.

For the third time, I check whether the main door is

double-locked and whether the curtains are fully drawn. Five years ago, I would have balked at the thought of living alone in Delhi, let alone with a child. The capital has been grabbing headlines for all the wrong reasons: murder, rape, Eve teasing, burglaries and road rage. My parents had been concerned about my decision to relocate to Delhi but let me take the final call when I got the job offer. I strain the tea into my cup and take it to the living room. I curl up on the couch and stare at the sliver of the moon visible through the gap in the curtains. I thoughtfully take a sip of the tea laced with cardamom. It's not that I don't feel scared living by ourselves in this flat. But it was anyway a toss between living with Abhi in the US—where I don't have an extended-family support mechanism—and starting afresh in India. At least Priya and Jonathan are just a phone call away, I sigh gratefully.

But it's not all bad. I am a lot more confident and positive about life now than I was when I first landed at Arrivals with a cranky toddler strapped in his stroller. I search again for the reasons why I returned to India: to begin life on a clean slate after my divorce; to escape the gnawing loneliness of American suburbia; to be near my parents; to expose Abhi to his Indian roots; to make new friends and to build a social network around Abhi and me. Furthering my career opportunities was incidental to the plan. But the most overriding reason why I took this humongous decision was to prove to myself—and to the world—that life would take a turn for the better; that it would come up smelling of roses again. Arun can't ruin me.

So far, my friends' circle has not extended beyond Priya. My school and college friends are scattered across the globe, and now are mere mugshots on Facebook. And I can hardly call the stylish moms at Bumblebees 'friends'. Then, there are the endless drawbacks of being a single parent. I will no longer belong to the exclusive club of married couples and jocularly whine with other wives about husbands throwing wet towels on the bed. But what hurts the most is that Abhi will never grow up knowing what it is like to be a part of his parents' network of friends, and play with the children of family friends. When I was pregnant, I used to envision camping trips, RV vacations and play dates on the beach for Abhi. So maybe, my plans went awry. But I have come to love this arrangement. Abhi is now the only family I shall ever need. Just Mama Bear and Baby Bear. Okay, so Papa Bear chose not to be in the picture. That's his karma. I sit upright on the couch as if stung by a bee. Maybe my subconscious is trying to tell me something. That I am finally coming into my own after my divorce. I have lost count of the nights I would weep inconsolably into my pillow in New Jersey. I would wait for Abhi to fall asleep before having a good cry. I would tear up on hearing romantic songs, seeing couples holding hands, and parents bonding with their children in malls and parks. I would steel myself for visits to the paediatrician when the blue-eyed matronly receptionist would talk cutely to Abhi who was merely eight months then, 'Oh look at those gorgeous long lashes! Betcha Mommy and Daddy spoil you!'

I shakily place my empty teacup on the glass centre

table. Thankfully, those days when I felt utterly helpless and miserable are slowly ebbing away. Of course, there are moments, like during the orientation at Bumblebees, when I missed having a husband beside me. And then it strikes me—the reason why I lied to the mothers at Bumblebees is not because I was missing Arun the *person*, but Arun the *husband*. A husband who would lend me respectability in society; a husband who would partake in the troubles and joys of our married life; a husband who would coo to his child. And a husband who could transform into a generous lover for his wife: hold her, caress her and passionately kiss away her blues...

My lips curl when I think of my ex. He had never been such a man. My parents had received his horoscope from a marriage bureau and the alliance had been fixed over tumblers of steaming decoction coffee during a bride-viewing ceremony that is best forgotten. I had come to India on a brief vacation, and the US-based Arun too—the marriage broker had enthusiastically informed my parents—was visiting his family in India. I remember wearing a green silk sari for the occasion, my long hair braided and bedecked with jasmine strings. Anusha had been contemptuous of this bride-viewing business and had termed it archaic. Being the more sober and traditional of us sisters, I had shrugged off her criticism. I didn't mind doing this if only to please our parents, I explained. They had given me the freedom to study and work abroad, and going through the boy-meets-girl rut was the least I could do for them. Arun came unchaperoned and sat quietly opposite me in the dining room. He was a few inches taller than me, of medium build, had bushy eyebrows and an umbrella-shaped moustache that almost concealed his upper lip. But what I couldn't gauge properly were his eyes, hidden as they were behind thick-rimmed spectacles. He had tiny peppercorn eyes, the eyes of a penny-pinching moneylender, darting from here to there but never settling on me, the woman he had come to see.

I shake my head in disbelief. Talk about karma! Till date, I have been unable to fathom why I agreed to the match. We hardly spoke across the dining table, just exchanged basic information and discussed the American East Coast climate with the accuracy of a weather reporter. In hindsight, the only time he made eye contact with me was when he inquired in a high-pitched tone, 'I hope you will continue working after marriage.' I had foolishly mistaken this concern to stem from a mind enlightened enough to allow his wife to have a career and exercise financial freedom. I wish I had had the foresight to ask if he had a proclivity to hoard money like Uncle Scrooge, or to abandon his wife and infant some day. Arun had always been a bit of an enigma in the years we were married. Though he was a silent and stoic type, I psyched myself into believing that we were quite happily married. Isn't that what a successful arranged marriage is all about? Gradually, I came to accept the fact that perhaps he was just a quiet and tight-fisted person. You can't label anyone bad for these reasons, I would tell myself whenever a small voice in my head taunted: *Do you know the real Arun?*

I get up and press my face against the living room window. I see nothing but the dark blanket of night along the length of my veranda. Abhi was not the accidental product of some steamy romp in the bathtub of a mountain cabin. With Arun, everything had to be planned—from buying toothpaste to my getting pregnant. By the time I expressed the desire to become a mother—my fourth attempt at broaching the topic—I knew the drill by heart. He unhurriedly flipped through the pages of his little black diary (his lifeline), adjusted his spectacles that didn't need adjusting, and unnecessarily cleared his throat. He dramatically snapped the diary shut. It had all sorts of information: from stock market tips, the best deals on laptops, his shirt size in UK and US, to his Delta Skymiles. 'Hmmm…this month won't be possible, we have the Beta release of the new software coming up,' he drawled in his fake American accent, common to desi IT workerbees. 'How about beginning the process early next quarter?' I was momentarily gobsmacked, for shouldn't it be the woman checking her cycles and ovulation calendar? But I jumped at the offer. Heck, I needed a sperm to make my baby. So, becoming pregnant had been a well-thought-out decision akin to the production precision involved in making a classic Bugatti Veyron. I often wonder why Arun agreed to start a family when all he wanted was to flee from his own? But I have to give it to the man for being such a smooth operator...and for giving me my precious Abhi.

I flick off the living room and kitchen lights. I wonder where Arun is now and what he is doing. I have resisted all temptation to Google him. I have even instructed Anusha and Venkat never to tell me what they may unearth about him online. It has taken all my resolve to move on after the divorce. A day may come when Abhi will ask about his father. Until then, I want to push away all thoughts of Arun.

I snuggle up near Abhi and fall into a deep and disturbed sleep. I see so many disjointed events in my dream: Arun kissing a Michelle Pfeiffer lookalike; Avantika mocking *my* garish make-up; the party in full swing at Priya's house; the door opening and me almost colliding with...Vasu...

Twelve

The next morning goes by in a blur. Abhi chooses today, of all days, to wake up at 4.15 am, demanding a glass of 'cooold otter' for which I sleepwalk to the fridge. Then at 4.50 he shakes me to be taken to the loo. Five minutes later, he flings away his bedsheet and Eeyore and hops down from the bed. 'Good morning, Amma!' he chirps, planting a wet kiss on my cheek.

'Play with me, no?' he whines in a scratchy voice while I press my face against the pillow craving for ten more minutes of sleep. Ah, to sleep undisturbed for a hundred years like Sleeping Beauty.

'Why no Sun Uncle in sky yet?'

'It is morning, no? Not night?'

'Have go to school quickly and play in mitti.'

'Where is my blue ball?'

'I want to wear Spiderman T-shirt.'

'Read me Noddy, no? I luurve Noddy and Bumpy Dog.'

'Why you sleeping, Amma? Get up! Quickly!'

'Ammaa!'

'AMMMAAAAA!!'

Right. My son who, I once used to worry, was not talking enough for his age, has now got a case of verbal diarrhoea. Having no choice, I rise and shine and turn into a Supermom Turborator: bathing, feeding Abhi his breakfast, whipping up pasta for his lunch, spring-cleaning his school bag, unearthing my blue clip that I thought had gone with the garbage, pinning a hanky on his Spiderman T-shirt, combing his hair, grabbing my keys and wallet, and pushing us out the door. I come back to check if I have turned off the gas. I dash to the car and then run home again to kick off my flip-flops and slip into my moccasins. Phew! How do these Bumblebees moms get time to look like ramp models? At 8 o'clock in the morning?

I am home after dropping Abhi at school. I enter my study that is the smallest but also the airiest room in the house. My desk is near the window, framed by a large neem tree and home to a garrulous crow. The sky is a deep aquamarine and visible in patches between the silvery neem leaves. The weather is especially pleasant today, providing relief from the usual mugginess that marks September. I throw open the window and immediately, a small gust of wind sweeps inside, teasing my hair that I have left loose. I settle down at my desk and take a deep breath. I love this time of day when I am able to put in around three hours of solid work before going to pick up Abhi. This is my sacred office time and I try to accomplish as much as I can during this chunk of the day. Some evenings, if there is a work overload, I try and work between cooking dinner and playing with Abhi in the park. However, my next block of office hours is at night after tucking in Abhi. I love working late into the night with Bob Dylan, Aretha Franklin, Nat King Cole and Pat Boone for company. Yeah, I am an oldies girl.

I consider the neat pile of manuscripts stacked on one corner of the desk and feel a rush of gratitude for working in publishing. Multicoloured Post-its, with my comments scribbled on them, stick out like small tongues from these pages. I feel reassured seeing my aunt's bookcases stacked with books, worn and new, containing stories from worlds in which I have lived vicariously through their pages.

Jagan, the office boy, will be coming tomorrow to drop off some manuscripts. He comes every week to drop and collect manuscripts and other paperwork. He is a fresh graduate from Jabalpur University and aspires to write a book some day. Even though he struggles with English, I admire his spunk and ambition. A friendly enough chap, he is my lifeline to office gossip and news. It is through him I learn about Vinnie hitting the ceiling last week when one of the junior editors overlooked glaring typos and sent a book to the printers. 'Vinnie Madam wants everything purr-fuct, even her black coffee,' he grinned ominously.

I look at the watermelon wall clock, a gift from Priya to Abhi, and panic at the melting minutes. I rub my hands together; I need to fine-tune some ideas before I next meet

Vinnie. I have so far met her only four times and each time feels like the first time with her. She can be very intimidating.

The last few months have gone in brainstorming over book ideas with Vinnie through phone calls and emails. However, after the October and November festival season, I may have to start frequenting World Ink's Noida office to become a more visible entity there. But this means I have to get serious about hiring a full-time maid. I let my shoulders slump. It kills me to think that a strange woman will be bonding with my son while I work twenty-five kilometres away. *Focus.* I train my eyes on the bound manuscript I'm working on, and for the next two hours concentrate on wrapping up *50 Smart Investments for Women*, which I can sense will be well-received. An SMS beeps.

It's from Nikki: Hi, please remember to join us to celebrate Bianca's third birthday tomorrow.

I slap my forehead. There is no time, but I have to buy Bianca a present this evening. I reply to Nikki, confirming Abhi's and my presence at the party.

Five Friend requests await me on Facebook: Carol, Riya, Nikki, Hutoxi, Avantika. I have also been invited to join 'The Avantika Sen Sexy Saris and Cholis Party Collection' and 'The Avantika Sen Sexy Saris and Cholis Wedding Collection' group pages. I accept all the Friend invites but dilly-dally over the group ones. However, Facebook etiquette demands that one accepts requests sent by 'Friends', including FarmVille gifts of cows and goats. So I grudgingly join Avantika's business pages.

I find Bianca's birthday page and click my confirmation. It has a whole album of professionally shot photos of the girl in various outfits: fairy, ballerina, ladybird, Hawaiian dancer and butterfly. I am guessing some princess pictures will be uploaded after the party.

Then I glance through the pages of the Bumblebees moms. There are tons of albums on each of their pages: wedding, father-in-law's birthday celebrations, children's photos from their birth onwards, sundry family outings, and miscellaneous photos with family and friends. Then there are the albums showcasing their family holidays in Switzerland, New York, Mauritius, Thailand, Amsterdam, London, Niagara Falls, Miami, Goa and other exotic locations. I gape in awe at a particularly stunning photograph of Carol and her husband with Interlaken's snow-capped peaks as a backdrop. They make such a good-looking couple, I think. They are laughing into each other's eyes, Carol's cheeks flushed a rosy apple tinge. Then I open an album on Nikki's profile titled, 'London Dreams'. These contain several sepia-tinted photos of Nikki and her husband taken in a dimly lit London hotel room. She is wearing scandalously brief denim shorts and a snug, white, knitted T-shirt. In one of the pictures she is perched on her husband's lap. And what exactly is her husband wearing? Are those boxers—can't see much except his hairy torso and legs. Eugh! This photo looks more slutty than cute. There are more such provocative shots in the album exuding the sinister setting for a Ram Gopal Varma underworld film.

I move on to Hutoxi's profile. My eyes pop open seeing her in a strapless one-piece lemon yellow swimsuit—cellulite and dimpled thunder thighs be damned. She is lazing by the pool of a luxury resort in Goa, her husband and daughter splashing in the water.

It tickles me that Riya's profile photo captures her speaking on her phone. There is an endearing picture of her husband, Rahul, embracing her on a star-spangled terrace while she coyly smiles into the distance in the album titled, 'Our First Anniversary'.

Avantika's albums are a full-throttle tribute to her. Her 'profile' album alone contains fifty-three shots of her: in a red sheath holding a goblet of red wine; in a sari during Diwali celebrations; in a strappy satin number; in a black lingerie-like lacy dress, and so on. Most of the photos have been laboriously doctored by Photoshop, making her blackish lipstick devilishly darker, her skin tone shades lighter, and her kohl-lined eyes spitting fire and ice. Her photos, including the one in which she is glaring into the lens like a serial killer, are bombarded with compliments. Told you she must have been one of *those girls* in high school. Her He-Man husband, Promod, has got to be in love with his yellow-tinted sunglasses if he can't part with them even while working out in shining Lycra on the treadmill.

A quick glance at Avantika's profile confirms that her two favourite words are sexy and darling (synonyms: pet, sweetie, doll), liberally sprinkled in the comments boxes, in lieu of 'thank you'. For example:

Friend: You look gorgeous in this photo!
Avantika: You are such a pet…lol!

Avantika's business pages have hundreds of photographs of her and an emaciated ebony mannequin draped in sheer saris and barely-there cholis. I am a little taken aback at the price tags—Rs 1,900 for a no-fuss cotton choli with not a hint of embroidery work? It's nothing more than an ordinary hanky-sized blouse, I snicker. Which person in her right mind would blow up so much money on this 'designer wear'? But apparently there are three women—including Carol—who have ordered this 'sensationally sexy, scooped-neck cotton choli', as the description reads.

I move on to my profile page. The only photo I have uploaded is of Abhi when he was a year old with long flowing locks that made other moms in New Jersey stop in their tracks and coo to him. These days I am happiest capturing 'Abhi moments' and recording his every milestone, though I shy away from bragging about his cuteness on Facebook that has become everybody's free publicist. People are so needy for conversation that even loo breaks make for interesting status updates. Or how about those globetrotters who love announcing their stopovers: São Paulo–Heathrow–La

Guardia. Regardless, Facebook is so addictive and integral to our existence that I can't imagine life without it. But it's also a complete waste of time, I groan, as I glance at the clock. I shut down my computer and bolt to the door to get to Abhi's school.

My mother calls me just as I pull into the car park at Bumblebees.

'Amma!' I say, thrilled to hear from her. 'I meant to call you tonight.'

'Ira, why don't you come to London for the Durga Puja break?' Amma asks without preamble.

The thought is tantalizing but I grimace thinking of the expense involved and my packed work schedule.

'Venkat and Anusha want to buy you and Abhi tickets,' Amma adds tentatively.

The corners of my mouth lift in a smile and then set in a grimace. I am an independent working woman and don't want to sponge off others, even if it is my sister. Anusha and Venkat know I would refuse, which is why they are using my mother as their mouthpiece.

'Nope. Sorry, Amma. Things are getting too demanding at work...and I can never do this,' I sigh, knowing my mother would be disappointed.

The twenty-something gang of mothers is making a slow procession across the sun-dappled lawn.

'But you can always return the money to them!' my mother sounds a little exasperated, like I do when Abhi refuses to obey me.

'But coming there for just a week when I have so much work piled on my desk—'

'Your father and I are so eager to see Abhi,' Amma's softly pleading voice makes my eyes sting. 'You know we can't leave Anusha's side even after the baby is born...'

I strain my eyes to see if the gate has opened.

'I think it will be difficult to make it for the Puja break,' I say finally, my free hand still clutching the gear. 'I am so sorry, Amma.'

There is a momentary pause before my mother speaks again.

'Okay, Ira,' Amma says brightly. 'Though I am sad the two of you won't be able to come, I am proud of my daughter.'

I take a deep breath. 'Thanks, Amma.'

A lone tear rolls down my cheek as I flip the phone shut. I bang my car door and hasten towards the gate. I don't want to lose whatever little self-esteem and self-respect I am hanging on to by making my sister and brother-in-law pay for our tickets. That goes against the principles laid down in my 'Independent Career Woman and Tough Single Mom Handbook'.

Thirteen

Abhi and I are at GK-1 M Block market, which is bustling as always. We are walking behind a group of fashionable young girls sashaying down the narrow corridor where shop windows gleam with merchandise from funky hairclips to Swarovski-studded handbags. I can visualize these girls becoming worthy successors to the Bumblebees moms some day. I try overtaking them, but Abhi pulls me back. He has screeched to a halt outside a toy shop and is looking longingly at a red train.

'Not now, baby,' I say, aware of the impatient traffic of shoppers behind us.

But he tugs at my hand again and lisps, 'Want tlaaain, Amma!' His big eyes are dancing with lust at the train that seems to beckon: 'Come on, kid, take me home!'

'Not today, Abhi,' I say with the right amount of cheer injected into my voice. Isn't that what Brenda Gaiman advises in her book, *Saying No to Your Child is Easy-Peasy Lemon Squeezy*? 'Decline cheerfully, instead of scolding, and the child will understand.'

'No, waaant train now, Amma! Pleease!' My son shrieks between tremulous lips, clasping my hand tighter.

Brenda's approach is clearly not for me.

'I said not now,' I hiss through clenched teeth.

Just then, a shop boy waves us inside. Even before I can react, Abhi sprints inside. He then turns and grins at me wickedly, making my heart flip. I take a deep breath and succumb to my toddler's mafia ways. There's a reason the terrible twos are called that.

We finally leave the shop—along with a singing clown and a monkey mask—after forty-five minutes of haggling with the kid. My fickle son remembers the red train on our way out and beseeches me with a puppy-dog expression. I lift him and skitter away to the bookshop at the end of the corridor.

As I browse through the children's section at Bookworm, I wonder what the 'Bumblebees-standard' budget for toddler birthday presents is. How much should I spend on Bianca's gift? I had already decided against giving her any of those disturbingly voluptuous Barbies that the market is flooded with. Something tells me that the kid is anyway going to be given every type of Barbie by the mothers who themselves bear an uncanny resemblance to the plastic original. I finally choose a beautifully illustrated fairytale book and have it gift-wrapped.

When we get home, we run into our German neighbour on the staircase. He is short and stocky, with wispy reddish-brown hair like that found in corncobs. I am startled by his eyes, the colour of monsoon clouds caught in a storm. When he makes childish prattle with Abhi, I am amazed at how well Abhi responds to the man's heavy Anglo-Saxon accent, thick enough to slice a knife through it. He introduces himself as Fritz Traugott and has a faraway look in his glazed eyes when he mentions his wife and two teenaged daughters who live in Stuttgart. He hasn't been home in two years, he says. I feel sad for him as I say goodbye and make our way to our apartment.

Fourteen

It's Friday morning and Abhi's school has declared a holiday on account of Founder's Day. Abhi is still asleep and I have the entire afternoon ahead of me before we have to leave for Bianca's birthday party in the evening. My son has reminded me about it only about a million times so far: 'Amma, let's go to Bianca's budday!' The thought of having to figure out my wardrobe for the occasion makes me wince. Argh! I curse myself for enrolling Abhi in Bumblebees.

I settle back comfortably in the cane garden chair and open *Delhi Times* only to come face-to-face with a luminous photo of Priya doing the Trikonasana, the triangle pose. It is a full-page interview on yoga's benefits for pregnant women. Priya is looking svelte in her ivory body-hugging outfit. I find it ironical that my friend, who wants to remain childless, is an expert on bolstering women's reproductive health. Then I cringe, thinking of how irrationally annoyed I was at her for inviting Vasu. Once again, my insides feel knotted up at the thought of meeting him tomorrow. Though it has been so many years, if I close my eyes long enough, Vasu's face drifts at the edges of my memory like jetsam. I still remember the red-checked shirt he wore once too often to college, his Beagle, Wolfgang, and the way his floppy hair would fall on his forehead while strumming *Hotel California*. I got goosebumps when I first heard him play it at an inter-collegiate fest; his technique was so raw and zealous that the notes washed over me like a tumultuous tide. Tumultuous was also how I felt when Vasu gravitated towards Usha in our second year. But the real cracks in our friendship had started developing on the first day the gorgeous Usha walked into our Macroeconomics class, her lissome frame and flickering mud-brown eyes making all the boys swivel their heads from the laws of supply and demand scribbled on the blackboard to the strikingly attractive, olive-skinned woman who stood at the door. When we found out later that her father was a diplomat, and that she had attended schools in Japan, Hong Kong and Paris, Usha's world travels made her even more alluring to my batchmates. Soon Vasu, to my utter envy, started mooning over her. I was astute enough to catch the extra boom in his voice when in Usha's company, the effort he invested to make her laugh, and the copious notes he wrote for her whenever she was absent. Gradually, my friendship with Vasu disintegrated almost completely as he increasingly started hanging out with Usha. I take a deep breath and try to analyse my past. If the beautiful and intelligent—unfortunately she had brains too—Usha had not entered the picture, would the trajectory of our friendship have metamorphosed into something more meaningful—like love, perhaps? Until I married Arun, I would fight memories of

Vasu who, I figured, occupied the grey area between a college crush and true love. But I now know that what I had felt for Vasu was just a deep crush; it was, obviously, an irrational schoolgirl infatuation.

I dial Priya's number.

'Ira! Have been meaning to call you,' she answers at the first ring.

'So glad to start the day by seeing your beautiful face, Pri.'

'I think my butt looks huge.'

'Cut it out, Jane Fonda. You're perfect.'

Priya laughs. 'I take it that you are coming tomorrow?' I love how our conversations have a seamless quality to them.

There is the slightest pause before I cheerfully reply, 'Of course.'

We chit-chat for some time, carefully avoiding the topic of Vasu, which is a hidden landmine waiting to explode. Just as I hang up, Abhi comes running to me, waving his denim dungarees, a gift from his indulgent aunt in London.

'Amma, dress me,' he says, kissing my hand. He kisses me a lot these days; soft wet kisses like a needy puppy. 'Let's go to Bianca's budday.'

'But her birthday is much later, baby. In the evening.'

'Why evening?'

'Because her mama says so.' I set down the newspapers and pull him close, revelling in his baby scent. I spot a parrot perched on the neighbour's balcony and point it out to Abhi. Sometimes, urban Delhi can surprise you with its beautiful sightings.

'Wooow!' Abhi gushes, his face lighting up. 'Why is parrot green, Amma?'

'Hmm…maybe God painted it green?'

'But why not red?' Now I know why the *Tell Me Why* series were conceived.

'Because green is God's favourite colour.' Abhi looks vaguely distrustful of my answer.

'Come on, lazybones,' I say, rising from my chair. 'It's time to brush your teeth and have breakfast.'

A few hours later, I fling one dress after another on my bed, rejecting each as I go along. I have nothing worthwhile to wear except baggy salwars and oversized kurtas. My Dockers and skirts remind me of the Size 8 I once was. It has been ages since I have gone shopping. I feel frumpy and unfit, and want to do something about it. But what? I spend a moment fantasizing about getting back in shape and wearing cute skirts and tops like I used to in my pre-baby days.

Abhi shoots me a quizzical look before going back to playing with his blocks. Our man is neatly scrubbed and looks dapper in his denim dungarees.

I finally decide on a black salwar kameez with some glass work at the neckline. I apply kajal, dab on some lipstick, and pick up Bianca's gift and my car keys.

'Okay, let's go baby!' I say, slipping into my wedges, the only high heels I own. They had served me well during my single days when I had wanted to walk shoulder to shoulder with tall American women with swishy golden hair. Abhi whoops in delight and sprints to the door. This is going to be fun, I think, feeling apprehensive all the same about meeting the yummy mummies.

Fifteen

Vadhera Villa's ornate gates are swung open by guards who motion me towards a canopy of trees under which vehicles are parked. A uniformed man appears out of nowhere and takes my car keys. Abhi and I slowly make our way along the cobbled path that I suspect would have cost a fortune to landscape. My eyes sweep over the enormous property, which seems to be bigger than the average Mehrauli farmhouse. A thicket of soaring trees cuts through the deep ochre September sky, matching the gulmohars in lush bloom. The air is heavy with humidity and I can feel my lipstick starting to smudge. The shouts and laughter of children float towards us from a distance. A sprawling white house with stucco walls, green windows and a large porch, looms in front of us. I suck in my breath. Nikki's house looks like one of those gorgeous Spanish villas seen in *The Lifestyles of the Rich and Famous*.

Abhi's grip tightens on my wrist. 'Amma, cowns!' he shrieks. Two men, in polka-dotted jumpsuits, come cartwheeling down the path, their blonde wigs and bulbous red noses, incredibly, in place. Abhi jumps up and down and claps in delight. The clowns shake hands with him and start juggling some balls. He is spellbound.

I drag my reluctant son to the expansive garden. That's when I see the large, white, billowing bedouin tents with lanterns and tea lights flickering in the darkening evening. Brass hookahs, white mattresses and colourful bolsters add to the Arabian Nights theme. And if my eyes are to be believed, I even see some sheikhs milling about in a crowd that looks nothing like a three-year-old's birthday party. Two sultry women in chiffon pantaloons and tight bustiers are swaying to seductive Arabic music. Abhi looks at them with a wide-eyed curiosity that I hope he will reserve for studying astrophysics some day. I promptly lead him away from the dancers and go in search of familiar faces. My gaze sweeps over the gathering. The party is packed with adults; where are the children? Where is the Bumblebees gang? Have I come to the right place?

Abhi suddenly makes a dash for the table where chocolates and candies—of the variety of Rs 100 a pop—are heaped in large cut-glass bowls. 'Abhi! ABHI!' I yell and chase after him awkwardly in my high heels that suddenly feel like stilts. But before I can say 'Toblerone', he has started scooping up the goodies.

'Not so many choc—' My leg gets ensnared in something sharp and I land on my back, Bianca's present flying out of my hands and crashing onto an unsuspecting waiter's tray.

The garden is spinning around me and my heart beats like Sivamani's drums. I feel the gaze of a hundred eyes upon me. My face burns. Boy, am I glad that none of my skirts fit me.

'Ira. Good to see you.' I look up; it's Avantika in a shimmery purple sheath dress. Her red lips part and purse in amusement.

I unravel the errant wire and haul myself up in as dignified a manner as possible.

'Hello, Avantika, good to see you too.' I smile tightly, smoothing my kurta and readjusting my dupatta. The waiter returns Bianca's gift, shoots me a withering glance and smiles effusively at Avantika. She picks up a wine goblet from the tray and waves out to a woman who has a poodle haircut.

Abhi comes running to me, his face flushed with triumph at the success of his plunder. He is sucking on a lollipop that's a third of the size of his face. He grins. I try not to glare and flash him my most soothing maternal smile.

'You okay, Ira?' Nikki sashays over and cheek kisses me.

'I'm glad to be in one piece,' I laugh nervously.

I can't help staring at Nikki's Cleopatra get-up: heavy silver-and-blue eye make-up, a sleek bob cut with bangs covering her forehead, and a long, flowing golden gown with deep slits that reveal smooth long legs. I do feel rather inadequate in my salwar kameez. Even the maids milling around—jeans, churidars, sleeveless tops and freshly painted toenails—are better turned out than I am.

'A very happy birthday to Bianca,' I smile brightly and hand Nikki the present. She snaps her fingers and a young girl springs into action and places my package on a table that's heaped with gifts the size of Australia.

'It's a great...umm... party,' I venture. 'You must have worked so hard on organizing it.'

'Oh, I never lift a finger for our parties, sweetie,' Nikki waves dismissively. 'We have a party planner who handles everything.' Sure, what was I thinking?

'Abhi darling, why don't you join your friends over there?' Nikki points her talons at the only blue tent on the lawns. She blows a kiss to someone in the crowd. 'A magic show is about to start.' The same child, who had nagged me stiff about Bianca's party, shyly disappears into my dupatta folds. Something sharp lodges itself in my thigh; one must not underestimate the power of milk teeth.

'Ouch!' I yelp. Nikki bats her turquoise eyelids at us.

Why, doesn't your daughter bite you? Like ever? I am tempted to ask.

'Come on, Abhi,' I cajole. 'The magic show will be fun.'

I give Nikki a small wave and walk with Abhi to the blue tent. It's warmly lit with tea lights and candles, and crammed with children laughing uproariously at the magician extracting eggs from a child's posterior. Abhi spots his classmates and plonks himself next to a chubby little boy whom I identify as Josh. The magician calls out to the birthday girl to volunteer for his next act.

Bianca is dressed in a flouncy full-length, satin, off-the-shoulder pink gown. Her hair is done up in a stylishly tousled bun, and a sparkling tiara sits atop her head. Her face is slathered with make-up and when she does a small twirl, admiration is palpable on everybody's face. Bianca smiles, lapping up all the attention. She *is* her mother's daughter, all right. She has two maids in attendance, each trying to outdo the other in keeping 'baby' happy. One adjusts the tiara, and the other checks Bianca's necklace. I am suddenly filled with sadness at the loss of innocence amongst today's children and step outside for some fresh air. I remember simple birthday parties at home for Anusha and me, our mother slogging in the kitchen, preparing delicacies and payasam. We would play with our friends in the garden and give pencils and erasers as return gifts. These days, the gifts from the birthday child begin to arrive even ahead of the party: Power Rangers, Barbie castles and what have you. Spending big bucks to say, 'I love you' to your kid seems to be the latest parenting trend in Indian metros. Delhi is the new Beverly Hills, with our very own millionaire parents blowing up money—more to satisfy their own egos than to give their children a good time.

The garden lights up from all directions, snapping me out of my reverie. The house, bathed in dusty gold and saffron, looks even more spectacular from where I stand. I grab a tomato juice from a passing waiter's tray. Everybody appears to be part of a clique and I find it rather awkward standing all by myself, feeling somewhat lost and foolish. Everyone seems to be having a good time, including the poodle-haired woman. She is swaying to the Arabic music, while a hefty sheikh breathes down her neck.

I walk around, admiring the blooming gardenias and the exquisite papier-mâché lamps hanging from the trees. I am trying to figure out what to do when I spot Riya and Hutoxi stepping inside a tent. I suddenly realize the purpose of this birthday party. I am supposed to be here to bond with the other mothers!

As I am about to follow the ladies, I catch the animated chatter spilling out of the tent.

'What *is* Ira wearing, yaar? Such an out-of-fashion salwar kameez! Even the tents here look nicer,' a raspy voice, that's clearly Avantika's, floats towards me. 'And her hair is all wrong.'

Some giggles.

'She was in America, right?' That's Nikki, her tone laced with mirth.

'Right!' Avantika giggles, as do the others. What does that mean? That I should be roaming around in Anne Taylor and Forever 21?

'I call her a cuckoo bird,' says a third voice that I don't recognize. It's thin and high-pitched as if the woman has something stuck in her windpipe.

I freeze and hold my breath. I want to see where this is going.

'Why cuckoo bird?' says someone lazily. It sounds like Riya.

'Oh, I don't know. Maybe because she always seems a bit lost and a...a bit cuckoo to me?' says the shrill voice. More giggles.

'Yes, you are right, Nivedita,' says Avantika. 'She doesn't seem to fit in at Bumblebees...you know, with us...'

'Told ya, she is cuckoo,' says Nivedita.

'It seems her hubs is in California,' Avantika continues. 'Don't see his pics on Facebook though.' Whoa! Snooping, are we? I flinch and gulp down the tomato juice in one go. I need something stronger to see me through the evening.

'Some people don't like uploading their personal pics on Facebook,' states someone matter-of-factly. Carol.

Soon the topic moves away from me. I strain my ears to pick up the gossip streaming out of the tent. Nikki says the sheikhs have flown down from Abu Dhabi; they are her husband's business partners. *Oil money*. Someone compliments Nikki on her glowing skin that she attributes to her daily morning massage—apparently a masseur has been on her payroll ever since Bianca was born. 'Prince insists I get a massage done daily,' she purrs, the word 'massage' coming off as 'message'. I don't know why but, despite her Italian shoes and designer clothes, there is something small-town and basic about Nikki. Her thick Punjabi accent is a dead giveaway about her roots.

'Okay, ladies, let's go,' announces Nikki. 'It's time for the birthday cake to be cut.'

I hastily slink away to fetch Abhi. The eavesdropping has done my ego enough good, I think wryly. I would so like to get the hell out of here.

The birthday cake is a giant-sized castle with a golden-haired princess perched on a throne. Prince, Nikki's husband, is wearing a purple satin shirt, white loafers and enough bling to make Bappi Lahiri feel insecure. Bianca is cranky and refuses to blow out the candles. Of course she would be. It's 8.30 pm. After some coaxing by her parents, Bianca blows out the candles and is carried away by her maids to the house. I look at the little girl's sleeping profile and wonder if she would ever remember today's over-the-top birthday extravaganza that was probably intended more for her parents than her.

The buffet table has everything and more: live pasta counters, chefs flipping pizzas, noodles getting stir-fried and tossed in woks, appams and stew, prawn curry, tandoori kebabs, delicate pastries and rich truffles ensconced in fine tissue.

I join the gang of Bumblebees moms at their table. Go on, bitch about me to my face, I silently challenge the women seated around me. Carol announces to no one in particular that her husband is in Johannesburg for three weeks. I catch a hint of frustration in her voice. I wonder if this Alpha Mom ever regrets her decision to quit working. She must have been used to fat pay packets and junkets to Langkawi. With her husband constantly travelling, I suppose the responsibility of raising her daughters, almost single-handedly, is taking an emotional toll on her. I take a deep breath. If I am grappling with single-parenting, so is Carol in her own way.

Hutoxi is as sad-eyed as ever but looks smug about the red briefcase-shaped handbag she has placed on the table like a centrepiece. Its steel exterior and chunky chains are so ugly that I have to look away.

'Come on. Eat, Vansh,' says a woman, sitting across from me, to her son. I freeze; it's the same voice. Nivedita. She is petite and has shrewd, narrow-slit eyes, like she is perpetually weighing her options.

'Hi, I am Iravati,' I say cheerily, determined to speak to this woman who views me as a daft bird. 'I don't believe we have met.'

'Hi,' she says, her lips tilting in a lopsided smile. She turns her face away and starts chatting with Hutoxi. It's as if I don't exist. I shrug and coax Abhi to finish the pasta.

As I am scanning the crowd to say goodbye to Nikki, someone taps my shoulder. It's Urvi, Josh's mom. I've met her a few times at the school gate and she is the only one I don't feel compelled to do the cheek-to-cheek kiss with.

'Hey, where were you? I was looking for you everywhere,' she says. I smile for the first time that evening, pleased to meet someone who is more on my wavelength. Urvi is wearing an elaborate gold anarkali kurta that has a flowing dupatta with tassels. Like me, her wardrobe is all wrong, except that the poor girl seems pretty much oblivious of her fashion faux pas.

'I saw Josh and somehow missed you in the crowd,' I say warmly.

'Some party, huh? Kitna spend kiya hoga?' Urvi's eyes widen as she takes in the surroundings.

'Ummm...Lakshmi Mittal ki beti ki shaadi se thoda kum,' I grin wickedly. We laugh.

We spot Nikki and she directs us to a table where a six-foot-tall bouncer-like man is handing out the return gifts. Abhi and Josh squeal delightedly and pester us to open the gifts. Urvi and I exchange looks, trying to guess what the huge gift-wrapped parcels might contain.

As my car makes its way out of the gates, I glance over my shoulder to take one last look at the house. Its imposing beauty against the velvety night sky unnerves me for some reason. Priya's comment about socialite women comes back to me and I wonder what sordid secrets the villa's walls are privy to. Beautiful people and their beautiful secrets, I sigh, and get on to the Ring Road.

The return gift is a massive spiderman robot, which comes with a complicated remote control that looks daunting to operate. Abhi insists on sleeping with the superhero, which leaves me almost at the edge of the bed. Soon I drift off into a deep sleep and I dream of castles, noodle-eating sheikhs dancing with poodles, and a thin high-pitched voice that sniggers: 'Cuckoo bird, cuckoo bird...'

Sixteen

Dawn is just breaking in the skies. I sigh happily and curl up next to Abhi who feels warm and toasty. He smells the way fresh rain, fluffy clouds and warm blueberry muffins would smell if made into a purée. I run my finger along the curve of his chubby cheeks and look at his long eyelashes, the perfect button nose and sweet lips. I smother him with kisses and hug him tight. He stirs lightly and nuzzles closer to me.

My cell phone rings. It's Priya. I suddenly remember what the day will bring and hop off the bed with a clumsy jerk, stubbing my big toe on the bedside table.

'Hellooo...aaah...oow,' I say.

'Hey, is something the matter?' Priya says. *Yes, Vasu. I can only think of Vasu.*

I sit on the bed and rub my toe with my free hand. 'Nothing, just stubbed my toe.'

'Uh-ohh. You do remember it's Jonathan's party tonight, right?'

Vasu. I can't shake him off from my thoughts.

'Of course I do. Is he around? Let me wish him.'

'Nope, Jo has gone for a jog. Hey, listen, I need to go to the salon today. Please come with me, pretty please?' she says in a little girl singsong voice.

I smile and bite my lower lip. 'Sure...but what will I do with Abhi? He will get bored stiff.'

'Oh, don't worry, I have it all sorted out. My salon has a very child-friendly environment and the women there are used to having kids around.'

'Hmm...sure, so what time do we leave?'

'Say I pick you guys up at 2 o'clock?'

'Perfect,' I say.

It's been ages since I have been to a posh salon. I am more than happy going to the neighbourhood parlour for my basic beauty needs. I just can't bring myself to check out the many spas that seem to have mushroomed suddenly all over Delhi. The beauty business is big now, especially in a place like Delhi where everybody, from Jorbagh to Janakpuri, wants to look nipped, tucked, and fit.

The only time I had been to an upmarket salon was before my wedding reception. Anusha had insisted on booking me for a bridal make-up special, despite my vehement protests. To this day, the thought of my ghastly elaborate hairdo makes me cringe. The salon had tried out a French twist, with hairpins and bobpins poking me every time I turned my head—which was a *lot* during the five-hour-long reception. But what was supposed to have been a chic hairstyle turned out to look like I had a three-tier cake on my head. Marge Simpson, anyone? With my severely pulled back hair and gaudy make-up—all wrong for my skin tone—I looked more like Dracula's bride than a blushing one. Argh! To think that my father blew up a few grand on this!

Priya pulls over in front of a two-storeyed cream structure in a leafy part of Gulmohar Park. 'The Blue Organza—all the pampering a woman needs,' reads its board. The spa-cum-salon, Priya says, is run by two sisters, both former beauty queens. Apparently, the place is so much in demand that Delhi's socialites have catfights over appointment slots on really busy days. Priya is a regular here for her magazine shoots and television appearances. I can't wait to see her getting all dolled up.

The moment we step inside, the matronly manager and her two assistants greet Priya as if she were royalty. The interiors are done up in pastels and there are elegant leather loveseats in the waiting area. Vivaldi is playing in the background and the room smells of pine and cinnamon. I am so not a *Blue Organza* girl and am grateful to bury my face behind a magazine while Abhi happily waddles around.

A young girl with a dazzling smile approaches me. 'May I take your son inside, ma'am?' she asks in dulcet tones. 'He can play there.'

I have never left Abhi in anyone's care and this girl looks too young and inexperienced. Priya touches my arm. 'It's okay, yaar. Abhi will be *fine*. I know Dolly, she is great with kids.' She smiles at the girl.

'What if he spills hot wax over himself or empties the L'Oréal tubes? You know he can be quite a handful,' I protest.

'Just relax, Ira, he will be fine. I had already instructed Dolly to keep a sharp watch over him while we both have a blast.'

I look wide-eyed at her, finally catching on to her game plan. Priya smiles sheepishly and links her arm around me. 'We're going to give you a small makeover,' she says. I feel the way Abhi feels when the paediatrician tells him that he is going to give him a 'small' injection.

'Look, I'm outta here,' I drop the magazine into the rack and get up. 'I don't need a makeover, thank you.'

'Ma'am, we have booked you and Priya ma'am for a seaweed and avocado facial, waxing, threading, and mani-pedi,' the manager interrupts with a polite smile. She assesses me through her gold-rimmed glasses. 'Ma'am, you will also be getting a new haircut from our expert hairstylist, Roxy.'

I raise my eyebrows at Priya who looks terribly excited at the proposition. I pull Priya aside and hiss, 'Why are you doing this?'

'Babe, do this for me, not you,' she says. 'Trust me, you will feel wonderful.'

'Listen, there is no husband to admire me. So why even bother with all this beauty hoo-haa?' I scowl, heat rushing up to my face.

Priya looks incredulously at me. 'So, is that why a woman should look groomed and pretty? To please a man? Really, Ira, are *you* saying this?'

Then I remember something and look pointedly at my friend. 'Priya, are you doing this because Vasu is coming tonight?' I glare at her.

'Of course not, silly,' she lies. I cock my eyebrows at her.

'Well, okay, it won't hurt if he sees you in a more, um, glamorous avatar,' Priya shrugs. 'But I am doing this for your overall cleansing process. You know, the divorce...starting over... everything...*everything* has been so hard on you.' I see sincerity in Priya's eyes. I am touched but still don't see her viewpoint.

'Do you know how the moms at Bumblebees view me? A cuckoo bird!' I say indignantly, flapping my hands.

Priya rolls her eyes. 'Bah! To hell with your Bumblebees moms. They are a weird lot.' She takes my hand and leads me inside the salon. 'We have a lot of work to do and there is not much time before the party, sweetie.'

Abhi's giggles reach me as Priya and I enter the main area of the salon. He seems to be getting on famously with the young salon girls. I hand Dolly Abhi's bag, which contains all the paraphernalia mothers with young children need: diapers, wipes, crayons, drawing pad, blocks, storybooks, plastic bowl, spoon, toffees, tissues and Band-Aids; only the Eiffel Tower and the Taj Mahal are missing.

'Come on, Mother Hen,' Priya pulls my hand and leads me to the spa room. 'Dolly will bring him to you if there is any issue.'

I follow her inside. The door closes behind us as we are ushered into a quiet zone with two beds. The walls are wallpapered in powder blue and the hum of the air-conditioner is the only sound that cuts through the silence. Priya and I are instructed to disrobe and we slip into the flimsy lavender gowns the salon assistants hand us. I awkwardly struggle to keep the buttons from popping open at all the wrong places and scowl at Priya who is the cause of this discomfort. But she seems to have drifted off to sleep already. I lie down on my back and try to relax my limbs as instructed by the salon girl. The room lights are dimmed and I feel some cold gelatinous paste being brushed on my face and two ice-cold cucumber slices placed on my eyes. I don't know what happens next since I, too, doze off. When I finally wake up, after what seems like aeons, Priya is looking at me appreciatively from her bed. Apparently, the good ladies at the salon have worked on me like labourers hammering stone for constructing a mansion. They have massaged, scrubbed, and weeded out every impudent blackhead and impurity. 'Boy, do I feel like a new person!' I say, running my fingers over my face, thrilled by its silken texture.

Priya grins smugly. 'Told ya. Wait till Roxy works on your hair. But first, waxing and then threading.'

Half-an-hour later, I gratefully slip into my own clothes and proceed to check on Abhi before surrendering my much-abused limbs to the mani-pedi experts. Priya and I settle down with magazines.

'Thanks for doing this for me,' I turn to her and say in a small voice.

Priya laughs and gives my hand a squeeze. 'The Universe will take care of you, babe,' she smiles enigmatically. There she goes again, on her Brahmakumari trip!

'What colour nail polish should I apply, ma'am?' a woman asks me. She shows me at least eighty colours and I want them all.

'What are you wearing for the party?' asks Priya.

'No clue,' I shake my head ruefully.

Finally, I play safe and choose coffee mocha, knowing it will go with most colours. Priya chooses grape purple.

'Ooo la la,' I say. 'What are *you* wearing?'

'Just wait and watch,' Priya winks at me.

'Have you thought of the decision you and Jonathan have to take?' I refrain from posing a direct question in front of the women attending on us.

Priya shakes her head sullenly. 'I'm still not sure, Ira. It's *such* a major decision for me, I need more time to think through it...let's see...'

'The Universe will take care of you too, babe,' I quietly repeat her words to her. Priya's eyes twinkle at me.

'All done. Wonderful!' grins the middle-aged lady who has been supervising our beauty treatment. 'Roxy will now attend to Ira ma'am's hair.'

Roxy turns out to be a short, bespectacled and balding Chinese man who gives me a friendly smile. I sit in the chair and inwardly wince, as if I were under the guillotine. 'Don't cut it too short and no blonde experiments, please,' are my last words before Roxy unleashes the scissors on me.

Abhi settles in a chair and watches us like we were a Disney movie. My hair is washed and combed down over my face. Roxy snips away like an eager beaver, while I pray hard that I don't end up looking like Lady Gaga on Ecstasy.

After what feels like hours, Roxy whisks off the towel draped around my shoulders, not unlike the way a matador would swing a red cloth before a bull. He runs his fingers through my damp hair, tousles it a bit, presses his thumbs on the pressure points on my forehead, swivels my chair till I come full circle, and announces with much drama in his voice, 'Look in the mirror, lady!'

I hesitantly open my eyes, too chicken to meet my reflection. 'Amma, see!' Abhi hops down from his chair and reaches for my hair like it were candy. I look in the mirror. A shiver of relief courses through me; I kind of like what I see. The freshly blow-dried haircut is shoulder-length, and quite flattering on me. My face looks leaner and my features sharper. A slow smile spreads on my face. I guess I could get used to this look.

'It's a layered step-cut with enough vo-ho-lume to make

your hair bounce when you ru-hun,' smiles Roxy, the gold caps flashing in his front teeth.

'Run?' I ask.

'Yes, yes. When models ru-hun in shampoo ads, huh? Like that. Your husband will love.'

I can't help joining him and the others in the laughter.

'Roxy, you rock,' says Priya, giving him a high-five.

I stare at my reflection for a long moment and shake Roxy's hands. 'Thanks. I guess you have knocked off…umm…two years from my face?'

'More like ten! How does your mom look?' Roxy asks Abhi.

Abhi stares at my reflection before yelling, 'Boootiful!'

Despite my protests, Priya insists on footing my bill. 'It's my treat to a whole wonderful beginning for you,' she says in her usual dreamy style.

Seventeen

I am panicking. It's 6.45 and I am still agonizing over what to wear for Jonathan's party. My Western clothes don't fit any more and my salwar kameezes belong to the *Alam Ara* era. Priya should have included a shopping spree in the makeover project. All I have are some saris. *Saris*. Now why didn't I think of them earlier? My mother always says, when in doubt, wear a sari.

I lay out the Kanjeevarams, the Bengal cottons, the Venkatagiris, and the printed silks on my bed. I am torn between the burnt rose Bengal cotton and the maroon-and-black Venkatagiri. But my jewellery matches the Venkatagiri better: gold bracelets and a black Rajasthani choker that I pinched from my mother's collection. So the Venkatagiri it is. Now that was easy—who says girls take forever to decide on their wardrobe?

Abhi comes charging into the bedroom on his tricycle, almost running over my foot. He is only in his underwear and in a dangerously playful mood. He has recently hit the milestone of learning how to undress. I tried putting him to sleep after the parlour visit but his energy levels seem to be on an overdrive.

'Where are your clothes?' I demand, putting away my saris and bringing out the jewellery.

'Pata nahin,' he shrugs and cycles back to the living room. He has started speaking in Hindi these days, mimicking his friends at Bumblebees.

'Abhi!' I call out. 'Come on, let's get ready. It's Jonathan Uncle's birthday party!' He abandons the cycle and comes running.

'Let's give you a good scrub, Mr Smelly,' I say.

'No!' he shouts.

'Yes!' I say, tickling him till he giggles uncontrollably.

Fifteen minutes later, Abhi is ready to hit the dance floor at Priya's in his Hawaiian floral shirt, white shorts and blue sneakers. I feed him khichdi and curd-rice, for he is bound to sleep early at Priya's.

I glance critically at myself in the mirror. Thank God for the sari; the garment knows how to conceal a thick waist and accentuate only those curves that are worth being smug about. The step-cut cascades over my shoulders in even layers and gives my face an angular shape. I feel good about myself—after a long time.

I apply kohl and lipstick, and spray on some perfume.

'Let's go, baby boy. I am ready!' I say. But I am so not

ready. With every passing minute I feel the anticipation of meeting Vasu rise in my chest.

'Okay, champ, let's go,' I repeat, slinging on Abhi's diaper bag. He insists on taking Spidey along and I place the two-foot superhero in the backseat.

I stop at the market to buy a large bouquet of white lilies for Jonathan, and drive through the slow evening traffic. My stomach is in a fist, clenching together odd remnants of my undergraduate years in my head. I begin to remember things that belong so far back in my past that even I am startled by my vivid memories.

At the traffic light, I steal a glance at Abhi in the mirror. He is looking admiringly at Spidey whose head is skewed a little towards him. It's like they were carrying on a private conversation. While the lights at the intersection take an agonizing five minutes to change, my mind meanders to the last year of my college. Vasu and I didn't part ways in the most amicable manner. After he became close to Usha, I studiously started avoiding him and was withdrawn and aloof whenever our paths crossed. I would look coolly through him even on those few occasions when he had the grace to wish me. I wasn't proud of my behaviour but didn't know how else to react to his growing friendship with Usha. His closeness to her made me feel sidelined, betrayed and ignored. I wanted to shake her shapely shoulders and say, 'Vasu was *my* friend before you came along—all fancy and French, from your la-la land.' I would constantly gripe to Priya about how shallow Vasu had become and what a bimbette Usha was. I would ridicule Usha, calling her a plastic doll with a wooden brain. Priya would nod understandingly though we both knew this was far from the truth. Usha was a complete knockout with a ridiculously high IQ. 'Are you in love with Vasu?' Priya had finally asked me one day, to which I had snapped, 'Of course not!' But many years later, when I was going through an indifferent marriage in America, I had often wondered if mine had been a case of acute infatuation or of one-sided love.

By the time we were to collect our College Leaving Certificates that summer, I had decided to mend my relationship with Vasu. You could say the distance from him after our final exams had given me a fresh perspective; I had done some growing up. I wanted to tell him how sorry I was for my childish behaviour and how keen I was on remaining good friends. Till date, I wonder if Vasu had even noticed the undercurrent of tension between us. I had come prepared with an emotionally charged speech that would have moved even the hardest of cynics. So I waited that June afternoon for Vasu to emerge through our department doors and walk down the corridor. My palms were clammy and my throat felt all itchy. I held my breath when I saw him walk down the corridor, in his usual swagger, clad in jeans and a white T-shirt that ironically said, GO AWAY. I rehearsed my speech in my head and scanned my surroundings. There was no one in sight and it was the perfect moment to talk to him. But just as I was about to run in his direction, I saw Usha trailing him. She said something and they laughed, their mirth bouncing off the college walls. My throat thickened and my chest tightened. I wanted to walk away but I stood frozen to the spot. I could still have gone and asked to speak with him privately. But something held me back, as if I knew Vasu and I couldn't turn back the clock. Still laughing, Vasu and Usha walked right past me, barely noticing my presence. For many years, I wondered if it had been deliberate on Vasu's part or if he had genuinely not seen me. And then I had buried those thoughts, laid them to rest—till now.

Jonathan opens the door, holding a Coors Light. 'Happy Big Four-three, Jo!' I say, handing him the bouquet. 'Not too many years to go before you become a senior citizen.' Jonathan mock-grimaces and shoots me a murderous look.

'Happy Budday, Uncle. Where is my return gift?' My son always comes to the point. Jonathan gives him a tight hug. 'But where's *my* gift, buddy?' he counters.

'Amma just gave you flowers,' replies Abhi. Oh, to think this child made me cry many nights when there were no signs of him talking. When I had thought of engaging a speech therapist, my mother simply remarked, 'He will jabber so much by the time he is three that you won't know where to look.' That's exactly how I feel now. I cock an eyebrow at Jonathan who hoots with laughter and leads us through the foyer to the living room.

'You look nice, Ira. Priya told me all about your new haircut,' he says.

I smile. 'Yeah, thanks to your wife, I have now had the privilege of a makeover.'

I peep into the living room and quickly assess the gathering; it's small and intimate, about a dozen odd people in the room. Knowing Priya as I do, she would not crowd the party with more people than necessary. It is very important on her hospitality checklist that her guests have enough room to mingle around and get to know each other in a relaxed fashion. Scented candles are placed everywhere. The house smells comfortingly of camphor and lavender.

'Where's Priya?' I ask casually, trying to remain hidden in the foyer's shadows. I have no desire to run immediately into Vasu.

'In the bedroom, I suppose,' says Jonathan and excuses himself to join the others in the living room.

'Hello, pretty lady!' Priya's voice booms from behind. She is in a sleeveless sunset-purple knee-length cotton dress held together at the nape. Her naturally curly hair is worn loose, making her look like a teenager. Her face glows, more from the person she is than from the aftermath of the spa treatment.

'Right back at you!' I say and we embrace like we had not seen each other for years.

'And who is this handsome young man?' she asks, pulling Abhi's cheeks.

'Owww…' Abhi grumbles but gives Priya a wide grin.

'You are one kid I really love very much,' Priya says. I know she means it.

We settle Abhi with a mango drink and popcorn in the

TV room and pop in a children's movie in the DVD player. Priya's eyes run over me appraisingly. 'Wow, you look really nice. You should wear saris more often.' Then she looks at me curiously. Her finely honed yogic powers probably sense my Vasu-jitters. 'Ira, relax. We are not eighteen-year-olds any more. Go on, talk to him!'

'Stop bossing me around,' I mutter under my breath and follow her to the living room.

Priya hands me a glass of red wine and introduces me to Joji, a nattily dressed woman who is a hugely popular personality in the English theatre circuit. She also plays the hip mother in Hindi movies and recently acted in a Holywood production. My mind starts ticking and I wonder if she would be interested in writing a book. I have wanted to commission something on the English theatre movement in India and Joji would be perfect for it. She is articulate, feisty, and a veteran in her industry. I lean back on the sofa and sip my wine, forming the book pitch in my head. Just then I spot him. Vasu. He is tall and bespectacled, just the way I remember him—only nattier. My body tenses and my mouth feels dry. I try to concentrate on what Joji is saying; I hear her but I am not listening. Before I can avert my face, Vasu looks in my direction. I have a strong urge to run out of the room. Joji rambles on about Naseeruddin Shah, her Lhasa Apso pup, and Delhi's atrocious road manners. I nod absently, my thoughts elsewhere. I drain my glass and take another Merlot from the passing tray. It's been a long day and I deserve one more drink.

Vasu walks towards me, a hint of the famous swagger still intact.

'Ira?' he says, swivelling the wine in his glass.

I try to look astonished. 'Yes…Vasu?'

'Yep, that's me,' he grins. 'So good to see you!' He leans down and gives me a hug. I feel buzzed with the wine and the woody fragrance of his aftershave. Vasu sits next to me on the sofa. I turn to introduce Joji to him but she has left to mingle with the others. Poor woman, she must have thought I was rude.

I surreptitiously study Vasu. Though he has piled on some kilos and has a slight paunch, he still looks very handsome. He has what I call the Park Avenue look: stylish silver-rimmed glasses, beige Dockers paired with a powder blue tucked-in shirt and tan loafers. But the highlight of his appearance is his salt-and-pepper hair that makes him look distinguished. Vasu fits in the category of men who manage to look attractive with grey hair. It just enhances his sex appeal.

'Your hair is not as floppy as it used to be,' I remark before I can stop myself. The colour rises to my cheeks. *So gauche for a conversation starter after so many years!*

'Thanks. I'm so glad I've not started balding like the men in my family. *Yet*.' Vasu's mellow laugh washes over me. I suddenly yearn to be back in college with him, relive those years without feelings of rancour or jealousy.

I sip more wine. 'I mean you have a very distinguished look now, Vasu.'

'Helps me in my line of work, I guess,' he smiles. His voice has a clipped accent, speaking of his many years in London.

His twinkling eyes hold mine for a moment longer than necessary. It's a perfectly friendly smile but my pulse races. Behind him, the stunning twilight sky is streaked in dusty rose and lavender.

'What happened to your long hair?' he adds after a pause. 'I don't remember it being so short, though this style suits you.'

I blink. The man remembers my hair?

'Thanks, it's something Priya suggested I try.' I self-consciously run my fingers through my hair. I would never have thought we'd discuss our hair so much!

I inquire about his work though I already know enough about him from Priya. I know that he attended the London School of Economics and works for the World Bank. I know that he has returned to India to head a new project for the South Asia region. And I know about his break-up with Usha…

Soon the initial awkwardness melts and I tell him about what I do, Abhi, and my years in the US. As the evening wears on, I realize that life has rounded our rough edges, blunting the ego and the arrogance that come with youth.

'All right, folks, it's time for the birthday boy to cut the cake!' announces Priya. Everybody starts gathering around the dining table that's laden with delicacies and a chocolate fudge cake Priya has baked.

'Why is there only one candle on the cake? Scared to reveal

our real age, are we?' someone teases Jonathan. The room fills with laughter and conversation.

I let out an audible gasp seeing the wall clock. It's 9.30.

'What is it?' asks Vasu.

'I'll just check on my son and be back,' I say, and hastily leave the room.

Abhi is splayed out on the couch fast asleep, the overturned bowl of popcorn on the carpet, and the movie credits rolling on the screen. I carry him to the guest room, switch off the lights and tuck him into bed. I crave for a five-minute snooze, feeling light and dizzy after the lethal combination of wine and Vasu. I keep patting Abhi till I myself doze off.

Eighteen

All the way home the next morning, I can't shake off the warm fuzzy feeling that one experiences after drinking one glass of wine too many. Or after meeting an old male friend who discomfitingly makes you question his place in your life. Priya had teased me that I missed last night's dinner because Vasu had been my guilty snack. More like a blast from the past, I think. I straighten my shoulders and stare at the traffic ahead. Meeting him had not been too awkward; it had been just like old times, yet, not quite. I guess Vasu and I will have to work on getting re-acquainted with each other. But who knows when our paths will cross again. I wonder what he must have made of my abrupt departure.

I smile tiredly at my sleeping son's reflection in the car mirror. It's amazing how children have an effortless capacity to snooze without a care in the world.

My cell phone trills just as I enter my apartment. Vinnie's high-pitched voice assails me even before I can deposit Abhi on the bed. I am dying to take off my sari and get under the shower. I dismally wonder what my boss wants at 8.45 on a Sunday morning.

'This Svetlana woman has been driving me crraazzy,' Vinnie launches without a preamble. 'Tell me, Ira, how can I offer her a crore plus for her next book? How will I make a profit for the company if we splurge like this? World Ink is, after all, not funded by a bloody firangi conglomerate with tentacles stretching from New York to Hong Kong. And if she leaves, our revenues will take a hit. I need to keep the company afloat and not shut up shop. It's not for nothing that I have slogged my butt off all these years.' Vinnie might be a bit of an oddball, but she has a point. A crore plus is a steep figure for us. I take a deep breath and try to cut Vinnie some slack.

Publishing is a brutal business behind the glamour of six-figure book deals, fancy book launches, and wine soirées. Profit and loss spreadsheets and revenue margins are crucial, more so in today's scenario where billion-dollar publishing joint ventures and digital books are threatening the existence of home-grown outfits like World Ink.

Vinnie sighs. 'I would like you to come to office tomorrow, Ira. We *have* to discuss a strategy to make Svetlana see reason.' It sounds less an order and more a plea. As of now, I am the only senior editor in World Ink and I can see Vinnie is trying to take me into her confidence to share her burden. I can intuitively sense that work pressures are only going to mount in the coming days, not least of all due to Svetlana.

'Sure, Vinnie, I'll be there at ten,' I say, popping my head inside the fridge to see if there is any leftover I can mishmash for lunch.

There is a momentary pause before she adds, 'Let's also take stock of your imprint. We have to lock the list soon.' Her tone is hardened, the earlier nakedness missing. 'This baby had better bring in the moolah.' The line goes dead after delivering this veiled threat. That's Vinnie for you.

My mind is in turmoil as the hot shower rains down on me. I have work targets to meet with, Vasu is back in my life—or not—and there is the added stress of matching steps with the Momzillas in their Steve Maddens.

Priya opens the door with a wide grin the next morning. As always, she looks spa-fresh in a lemon yellow salwar kameez. 'Go on, Ira. Abhi and I will have a great time today,' she says, hugging Abhi and playfully shooing me away. Abhi had to miss school today and I'm not sure if he is looking forlorn due to that or because Mommy will be away. I smother him with kisses and hand Priya Abhi's bag. 'Bye, Abhi bear. Be good. Remember to ask Aunty to take you to the bathroom.' I look doubtfully at my friend who suffers from babyphobia. 'Sure you can handle him, Pri?'

'Of course! I handle cranky rich housewives all the time. And Abhi is not a cranky child,' she pulls Abhi's cheeks. "It's just you and me today, kiddo. Let's go to the park and eat ice cream.'

'Yaay Priya Aunty!' Abhi's eyes light up and he runs indoors, clutching his battered truck.

'Sure it's no problem, Pri?' I repeat my question.

'Oof, just go, woman!' she gently pushes me to the door. I give her a quick hug and run to the car park. Vinnie dislikes tardiness and will do a dizzy number on me if I keep her waiting.

I can sense that Priya looks genuinely at ease babysitting Abhi. Even though she loves him to bits I know that watching over a two-and-a-half-year-old wouldn't be her idea of fun. But when I had called her last evening for this favour, Priya's pleasure was most palpable over the phone line. As I turn the road from Asiad Village's verdant surroundings and merge with the morning rush hour, I wonder what might have prompted this shift in my feisty, career-oriented friend's personality. Is she willing to give motherhood a chance, after all? Have she and Jonathan officially started trying for a child?

Noida's scale of development is astonishing. Glitzy glass-and-steel corporate offices and swanky residential high-rises are driving the satellite city's real estate explosion. For twenty-five years World Ink's office had been in a modest three-room rental space in a cramped part of Connaught Place, sandwiched between a bustling sari shop and a seedy galli that led to nondescript business establishments and paan shops. Vinnie had joined the company in the 1970s as a bright young editor with innovative ideas. Her story has been written enough times for me to know it like the back of my palm. She was a Delhi University gold medallist in Literature and had been hired by the septuagenarian Sindhi owner of World Ink. The company had been publishing mostly academic books, legal journals, and Hindi detective thrillers at the time. Before the issueless owner passed on, he had bequeathed a share of the business to Vinnie who had by then proved her mettle manifold and risen through the ranks. Gradually, over a period of a decade, Vinnie had wound up the main publishing business and pumped in outside capital to venture into mass-market English-language fiction and non-fiction that seemed to be a far more lucrative and exciting market. She was astute enough to recognize the potential of the new anglicized India that was fast emerging; the MTV generation of readers with newfangled literary tastes. Soon the company started publishing authors who represented the educated urban middle class, poised to usher in liberalization that would forever change the country's trajectory. Then, when the digital wave entered the country in the mid-1990s, Vinnie got her act together and outsourced the digital filing of contracts and other office paperwork to an IT company. She rid the office of the stacks of contracts and musty files. Thus, World Ink started coming of age and no longer resembled a godown. But the euphoria of this makeover was short-lived. When foreign publishing houses forayed into the Indian market, even the indomitable Vinnie felt powerless to compete with the kind of money the conglomerates were splashing around.

The tiny but successful list of authors she had built was at risk of being poached by the MNC publishing outfits that wasted no time in luring Vinnie's authors away with higher advances and better marketing deals. Then, five years ago, just when Vinnie had started despairing over her company's prospects, Svetlana Swaroop's manuscript, *Lips*, had found its way to the slush pile that Vinnie had taken home for a weekend read. Erotica at the time was a risky genre to publish in a country full of so-called prudes but Vinnie had decided to take the risk, spurning the advice of her colleagues who feared that Hindu radical elements would pelt their office with stones and burn down their warehouse. *Lips*'s first print run of three thousand copies was exhausted in a month's time, and the more they printed, the more it sold. *Lips* is in its eleventh edition now and has been translated into several Indian languages. Talks are on for North American rights to her titles. Svetlana's surprise success story had captured my interest even when I was in the US. She has this spunk that I have gradually come to admire. I have to give it to her for never using her husband's connections to get published and for boldly choosing to write such steamy books under her own name. I remember her candid remark from a *Savvy* issue where she was the cover story: 'Who knew my manuscript would get picked up from the slush pile? I was just a rich, bored housewife who wrote *Lips* for a lark.' Svetlana followed up her success with two more erotica novels, part of the *Lips* trilogy. The book sales went through the roof, infusing life into the financial health of World Ink. The company finally started breaking even two years ago—thanks in no small measure to Svetlana. Vinnie had once confided to me that the company makes an annual profit of a few crores from Svetlana's books while the author herself receives a hefty income from her royalties.

I pull into the car park in front of the tall glass-and-steel structure that houses World Ink's office. When Svetlana's second book, *Hips*, sold triple the number in expected sales, Vinnie had wasted no time in relocating World Ink to Noida. This was in keeping with the trend followed by other publishing houses and media companies who'd discovered the benefits of moving to Noida and Gurgaon, the other booming satellite city. Rents in South Delhi were touching the sky and, besides, Vinnie had anyway been looking for an excuse to move out of her old establishment at Connaught Place. So it was fitting to move to the new office when World Ink completed its forty-fifth anniversary two years ago. I remember reading Vinnie's media interviews in which she had pooh-poohed the notion that World Ink would now be at risk of being pigeonholed as the publisher of erotica. 'Erotica, campus-lit, chick-lit, pulp crime fiction, who cares?' she had famously retorted. 'Give the reader his money's worth and you'll be surprised to see what the market can take. When I decided to publish *Lips*, many feared it was the deathknell for World Ink, but look what happened instead. We opened new doors that were earlier considered taboo—and now every publisher is betting on erotica.'

That's true, I think, as I make my way in the elevator up to World Ink's eighth-floor office. Erotica is now a hot genre, which is why Svetlana is playing hard to get. And that is why I am here, standing in World Ink's elegant lobby on a Monday morning, desperately trying to think of ways to keep Svetlana from straying.

Each time I visit the office, I am spellbound by the breathtaking view from the large glass panels behind the receptionist's desk. A vast expanse of Noida's landscape stretches over the horizon, with the buildings, greenery and city dust blending into a golden light. I look around the room. Stylishly designed glass bookcases proudly display a range of World Ink's titles; Svetlana's books occupy a separate privileged corner, her smiling—or is it taunting?—face looking at me from a laminated poster. She must have been a striking woman in her younger days, her doe-shaped brown eyes and bee-stung lips being her best features. Wassup, Svetlana? I ask silently and give her a small nod. 'She's waiting for you, Ira,' says Fleur, the attractive Goanese receptionist, gesturing with her thumb in the direction of Vinnie's office. It's 9.55 by the wall clock. 'Thanks,' I mock-shudder and make my way inside while Fleur giggles softly behind me.

Rows of cubicles face me—editorial, production, design, marketing, sales, accounting. I fleetingly wonder what tantalizing stories and jokes are flitting from cubicle to cubicle. But on the flip side, I am thankfully safe from all nasty office politics that come with the territory of working full-time. I greet everyone and proceed towards Vinnie's room. I take a deep breath and knock on the glass door.

'Come in!' Vinnie's voice reaches me.

I open the door and step inside a large room done up in black and white. Morning light pours in through the bay windows bathing the room in incandescent colours. Awards and trophies from the Indian Publishers' Association gleam from wooden shelves.

'Good morning, Vinnie,' I say. The five-foot Vinnie looks even more petite behind the large glass-topped desk. 'Morning, Ira. Come, come, sit down,' Vinnie smiles, displaying her tobacco-stained teeth. She lights a cigarette and offers me the open packet.

'No thanks, I don't smoke,' I say, occupying a chair from across Vinnie. She laughs like I had just cracked a joke. 'You don't know what you're missing.' I smile and take in Vinnie's short frizzy hair that's a lustrous silver. It's in contrast to her ebony skin, further tanned, I suppose, after her Bali revelries. There are many stories about Vinnie that I've heard, though nobody I know can vouch for their veracity. Rumour goes that her first husband was an American writer who died in an air crash, and her second husband left her when he caught her doing it in bed with a much younger man. Apparently, Vinnie's son is from her first marriage.

'So tell me, what do we do with Svetlana?' Vinnie comes straight to the point, her raspy voice cutting into my reverie. 'How do we make Svetlana sweat?' Vinnie's laugh is low and hollow.

'Isn't there some way you can make her see reason?' I venture.

'Bah, what else do you think I've been doing, hon? Our

initial offer was twenty-five lakhs, then, I made it forty lakhs at double our royalty percentage. We are willing to put ourselves out there for marketing and promoting the book. But…' She takes a deep drag. 'But the lady is still not happy. She wants a crore plus at triple our royalty percentage. Come on, Ira. Throw me some ideas. Anything.' Smoke curls escape from the corner of her mouth.

I squirm in my chair, feeling like an errant schoolgirl. I do some mental calculations to determine how much more we could offer Svetlana. 'Um…Vinnie, is there any possibility of increasing the advance by at least another ten–fifteen lakhs?'

'Of course not!' Vinnie snaps. 'It would take a huge toll on our finances.'

She stubs out her cigarette in the ashtray and observes me through hooded eyes.

I am eager to help and fold my hands on my lap. 'Vinnie, I think I would like to take a shot at this and meet her.' Vinnie reclines in her plush leather chair and closes her eyes in thought. My mind races back to the day when I was offered this job by her. I remember feeling thrilled to work under a publishing stalwart like her. But for someone of such a petite build, she is rather intimidating.

Vinnie's eyes fly open and she heaves herself forward. 'Sure, go ahead and meet her when she is in Delhi next. Let's see if your persuasive skills will win the day for us.' I search for sarcasm in her tone, but there is none.

'I'll try to sweet-talk her,' I say with a newfound

assuredness. I guess I've happily thrown myself into the deep end of the pool.

Vinnie gives a small nod. 'Time is running short, Ira. It would be a calamity to lose her.' She wears a woebegone look. 'Ah well, to think we found her.' I like the 'we' in the sentence.

I nod silently. 'If Svetlana goes,' Vinnie gesticulates expansively, 'we lose precious revenues.' Her face hardens. 'World Ink's profile takes a hit.'

She pauses dramatically. I lick my lips and wait.

Vinnie adds with emphasis, 'Svetlana is our cash cow, the hen that lays the golden egg—call her what you will.'

I nod silently.

'And we must make her stay, Ira,' Vinnie's eyes bore into mine.

'Sure,' I mutter. 'I…I'll think of something.' I suppose this is how a lamb feels in a slaughterhouse.

Vinnie smiles brightly. 'Great, moving on! What about your new imprint? Let's get cracking on it.'

At 5 pm, when I finally make my way out of World Ink's office and drive through the UP–Delhi toll gates, the evening sky is a glazed sheet of copper. I feel completely drained after spending an entire day with Vinnie and feel a sense of dread of how it would be to work full-time under her nose. There are so many loose ends to be tied up before my imprint can be launched, which means I will have to work doubly hard. I think of Abhi and wonder how I am going to pull this off—manage the work–life balance as per *Reader's Digest* guidelines.

A radiant Priya greets me at the door when I pick up Abhi. She gushes about all that she and Abhi had done the whole day and declares she has never had so much fun in her life. Ohmygod! My friend has changed.

Abhi flings his arms around me and starts regaling me with his day's adventures. Park, ice cream, Play-Doh, yoga, *Madagascar*, chocolates and finger paint are the words I register.

When we reach home, I cook a simple dinner and coax Abhi to eat. He is so exhausted that he falls asleep as soon as I tuck him in. I slip in a Barbara Streisand CD and am about to step in for a shower when my cell phone rings. It's an unknown number.

'Is this Ira? Hi, Vasu here.'

'Hey,' I manage after a stunned pause. 'How are you?'

'It was great meeting you at Priya's the other day, though you mysteriously vanished,' he says in a tone laced with mirth.

I flush and explain the reason for my disappearing act. *The man noticed my absence. But how did he get my number? Priya, of course. Wait a minute, is she trying to play Cupid?*

'I was, um, thinking if we could meet for coffee somewhere?' he asks.

Did he just ask me out? For some reason, my heart is singing so loudly that I can barely hear myself saying 'Yes' in response to his question.

Nineteen

October heralds the onset of the festival season in Delhi. With Durga Puja around the corner, puja pandals are being erected everywhere—from Chittaranjan Park to Mayur Vihar to Noida. Tall cut-outs of Durga, her large expressive eyes surveying us and the city, loom over the cityscape. A sudden lushness fills the public parks and gardens, and flowers in bejewelled hues overflow from flower beds and hang like trinkets from tree branches. I take Abhi for drives around Lutyens' Delhi and point out the different flowers in the manicured roundabouts. We go to India Gate at twilight, munch on cheap popcorn, and greedily suck on ice lollies before winter descends upon us. It's also the beginning of the theatre season in the capital, and auditoriums vie with each other to draw in the crowds. Delhi comes alive in October and the city is transformed into an alluring lady from the insufferable brute it generally is.

This is also the time of the year when mothers of young children go into overdrive, planning outdoor play dates. I wake up today to an SMS from Carol:

Ladies! Play date picnic @ LG on Sat? 3.30? Say YES.
Luv
Carol

When Carol decides on something, she sees it through to its logical conclusion. Once she even marched to the principal's office—something other mothers only fantasize about—and complained about the absence of Dettol in the children's bathrooms, despite several reminders to the school. The following morning—voilà!—brand new Dettol dispensers and hand sanitizers gleamed from the bathroom shelves. Carol has this aura around her that makes her the leader of our pack. In the pecking order of mothers in Abhi's class, Carol is the queen bee. She is a true Alpha Mom, always on the go and on top of everything, like the indefatigable Energizer Bunny. She knows when the fees are due; which class worksheets to return and which to keep; the centres where Julia Gabriel operates; the student–teacher ratio in top Delhi schools; the best herbal remedies for children's cough; where to shop for the perfect school bags; which agency's maids to hire; what colour Lala is; and how many Tombliboos there are in total. She is an uber-mom who approaches every parenting challenge with the management skills she picked up in B-school. She is always focused and prepared—a Type A Mom. If that were not enough, she is also perfectly turned out: her skin *always* glows, her teeth are superwhite, and she is blessed with zero bad hair days. So when Carol decides on a play date, I'm sure she'll make it happen.

It's one of those crisp early autumn afternoons when the sky is a clear blue and the sun is mild enough for us to enjoy the outdoors. Abhi and I arrive in Lodi Gardens before the others and settle down on a nice patch of grass, diagonally opposite the old tombs. I spread a bedsheet and place my casseroles containing pudina sandwiches and cheese fingers. I spot Urvi and Josh, and wave to them to join us. Urvi places her picnic hamper on the ground and exclaims, 'Hey, you look nice...did you have your hair cut? It suits you a lot.'

'Just like that, for a change,' I smile, running my fingers through my hair that's still damp after my shower. I can't thank Priya enough for giving me this haircut; short hair is so much more manageable. I get up and call out to Abhi and Josh. 'I'll buy these kids some balloons. Be back in a bit, Urvi.'

As we walk back with the balloons, I see Carol, Riya, Nikki and Hutoxi sashay across the emerald lawns. The scene looks straight out of *Desperate Housewives*, the women swaying their hips; their humongous glares shielding half their faces; their hair all bouncy and shiny; their dazzling smiles; and their stylish handbags swinging from their arms—everything reminds me of the glamorous American women on TV. Then my face burns when I remember their barbed comments about me at Bianca's birthday party. I straighten my shoulders and utter my new mantra under my breath: *Whom am I afraid of? I won't allow these women to hurt me. I won't be intimidated by them.*

The maids place the food baskets on the ground and disperse to form their own group a little away from us. Riya,

Nikki, and Hutoxi measure me up. Carol smiles sweetly but doesn't comment on my new haircut. I must have paid Carol fifty thousand compliments till date, so would it really hurt her to return the favour? But most of us women are like that; petty and insecure, even if some of us look like movie stars.

I see Nivedita and Avantika walking down the path but they stand at a distance to chat in private. My eyes follow Abhi who is playing with Josh. They squeal each time the wind carries away the balloons. Anna, Jhanvi, Bianca and Rimli walk past us, engaged in girlie chatter. It's hard not to notice how well-groomed these girls are, little fashionistas like their moms. Riya's son, Kunal, is playing with Vansh, Nivedita's son. My eyes travel back to Abhi. He and Josh are busy trying to extricate their blue balloon from a bush.

'The picnic was a great idea, Carol,' Urvi gushes, pronouncing Carol as in Karol Bagh. 'Thank you very much for organizing this.'

Carol shrugs elegantly. 'I figured it would be nice for all of us to meet.'

Urvi adds, 'I love your top, Riya. Where did you buy this?' I smile at Urvi's sincere attempts to endear herself to the swish set.

Riya looks down at her skintight red satin top, as if for the first time. She narrows her eyes to slits. 'I think in Singapore... no, wait, Hong Kong.'

'It's been soo long since we went to Hong Kong,' sighs Hutoxi, twisting open a two-litre Coke bottle. 'Harbhajan only likes London and Paris. Oof...I am soooo bored of Europe.'

'I love, love, love shopping in Hong Kong,' says Carol, passing around disposable cups for the Coke. 'You get such good stuff for such amazing prices.'

Riya nods. 'But Rahul wants to go to New York this winter. Maine bola itni thand hogi, but he says, "Chalo, snow dekhenge."' The women laugh heartily. I am suddenly reminded of the white Christmas Abhi and I saw through our frosted windows in New Jersey. He was still a baby and cocooned in my arms as we watched the flurries dance outside and settle on rooftops. Christmas carols were playing on the radio and tomato soup was simmering on the stove. It had been the most memorable Christmas for me in the US.

Nikki pushes up her glares and stretches her long legs out on the grass. 'Prince toh has already booked our tickets to Abu Dhabi. Hamara toh holiday hamesha wahin pe hota hai.' She looks so glum that I am tempted to say, 'I'll be happy to go in your place, dear.'

Carol looks at me. 'Where do you like holidaying? You must have been all over America, na?'

'Umm...any place with a beach will do, I guess,' I reply vaguely. These ladies would flip if I told them I never saw Las Vegas, the Grand Canyon, Disneyland or California in all my years in the US. Arun and I had not been on a single vacation and, before marriage, my annual holiday had always been in India.

'I love beaches,' Urvi interrupts my thoughts. 'We keep

thinking of going to Goa but hota hi nahin.'

'We were in Maldives last summer,' says Carol. 'Aaahhh...I could live there and never come back.'

Hutoxi opens a bag of chips and offers it to Nikki. She balks at its sight and touches her flat stomach. I notice she does that a lot, as if to assure herself that no cellulite and fat deposits have stealthily lodged themselves on her midriff.

'No thanks, I don't eat junk food. Did I tell you, I'm now on an all-organic diet,' she shakes her head. Her bleached blond hair makes her look older than her years. Getting copper, bronze and blond highlights is the signature style among Delhi women. These shades look so ridiculous on Indian skin tones that not even someone as pale as Nikki can pull it off.

'What do you mean by organic diet?' asks Riya, flipping open her phone.

'We buy our fruits and vegetables from an organic farm in Mehrauli. But I eat only steamed vegetables through the day—no rice, no carbohydrates, no starch, no sweets, and no non-veg. I am now a complete vegetarian.' She cocks her head at an angle and adds shyly, 'Like Kareena Kapoor.'

'That's absurd. I mean, how...how do you survive?' I ask before I can stop myself.

Nikki raises her pencil-thin eyebrows. 'Sorry?' she says.

'I mean, aren't you tempted to binge once in a while? At least on rice and roti?'

Nikki smiles beatifically, as if she were an enlightened soul. 'No dear, not at all. I have eating discipline,' she says, her gaze pointedly lingering on my midriff.

'I have been considering liposuction,' says Hutoxi, happily munching on the chips. She pats her backside and thighs. 'For these areas.' Urvi flashes a horrified look in my direction. Lipo and tummy tucks are the rage among moneyed women in India. I have read that they could pose immense long-term health risks. I wonder if World Ink should bring out a series of self-image titles for women. There seems to be a ready-made market for this.

I feel exhausted just listening to these women. It's sad that our gender is so image-conscious and harsh on themselves. Pick up any magazine and you'll find only super-thin women on its fashion spreads. Most of the clothing brands don't have the right size for women who are generously proportioned. And I don't believe fashion designers have heard of post-partum weight. Our society, like the West, is obsessed with size zero and women are setting bad examples for their daughters. Nikki looks so gaunt and frail in the afternoon light; her blonde highlights, her pink jumpsuit and her Burberry handbag remind me of someone. *Paris Hilton*!

I gasp audibly, making everybody look in my direction.

Just then I hear Abhi wailing. I scramble to my feet and walk across to where he is playing. 'What happened, baby?' I ask.

'Aunty, Vansh ne…Abhi ka balloon chheen liya!' Josh comes running to me and offers a breathless explanation.

'No, yeh mera balloon hai,' says Vansh defiantly.

'Nooo…mera!' Abhi cries even louder.

I've come to believe that mothers must tread carefully around children's fights. That's the first rule in the play date etiquette handbook. They are children, after all, and there is no point in openly taking sides with your own child at the risk of alienating other parents and ruining the very purpose behind the play date.

'It's okay, baby,' I soothe Abhi. 'Let Vansh keep your balloon, we'll buy you another one. So tell me, what colour do you want? Orange?'

'Yellow!' shrieks Abhi.

As I start leading Abhi away, Nivedita appears, wearing a hassled look. 'Kya hua, baba?' she asks her son, her hands clenched by her side. I wonder if she is going to punch me.

'Abhi ne balloon chheena,' the little brat says.

Nivedita throws a scornful glance at Abhi, and then at me. So not worth our time, her look says. She pulls the string from Vansh's grip and lets the balloon drop on the grass. She grabs his hand and walks away in a huff. She goes back to Avantika and whispers something conspiratorially, her feline features coming alive in the midday sun. Avantika's snakeskin belt shines ominously and I feel the women's combined glare on me. I am frozen to the spot and seething with rage. Abhi tugs at my sleeves and whispers, 'Amma, balloon uncle is theeere. I want a yellow balloon.' His eyes are puffy but a bright smile plays on his lips. I kiss his nose and lead him away.

For the rest of the picnic I diligently avoid Nivedita's gaze, afraid that I might pounce on her and wipe the smug smile off her face. I am still shocked that she could stoop so low as to be vicious towards little children.

Soon we get busy laying out the food. The next hour is spent in making the children eat and clearing up the place. As I walk to the restroom with Abhi, Urvi joins me, Josh trailing behind her.

'What happened, Ira?' Urvi asks in a low tone, sensing my mood. 'Did Nivedita say something?' I tell her what had happened.

'She was rude to me too,' says Urvi. 'I wished her today and she didn't wish back. I didn't knew she was so utpata.' I laugh despite myself. Urvi's earthy sense of humour and quirky grammar make her even more endearing to me. I take in the long floral skirt and the buttoned-down ill-fitting blue shirt she is wearing. Her hair is tied in a sloppy bun and she has slapped on too much foundation and mascara. The orange lipstick doesn't help matters. She looks so wannabe that I feel like hugging her and saying, 'Don't bother, dear. You will never fit in.' But I know that behind this gaudy façade is a perceptive woman who is aware of her place in the Bumblebees mothers' hierarchy. She knows that she can *try* to be like them but can never really enter the system. It is a gated community that is password-protected. The sooner she—and I—realize it, the better the rest of the journey in Bumblebees would be for us.

Moments later, I see Abhi sharing his toffees with all the children, including Vansh. I am proud of his clean heart and straightforward dealings. I wish things were as straightforward as climbing monkey bars in Mommydom politics, too. Come to think of it, we mothers are adept climbers of monkey bars. While some of us know when to get off, others climb too high and need help getting off. And still others refuse to come down till it's too late. My eyes wander to the picnic spot; the women's chatter and refined giggles rent the air. I feel Nivedita and Avantika might be climbing the monkey bar a bit too high. And if they don't get off fast enough, they are in danger of toppling and having a bad fall.

Twenty

It's been two weeks since I met Vasu at a coffee shop, a cosy little Sri Lankan joint that has opened in the tranquil Malcha Marg market. Being the sort of person to overanalyse everything in my life, I had wondered why Vasu had asked me out to coffee. Though I had stupidly, albeit fleetingly, imagined it to be a date of some sort, within minutes of meeting him I realized he was just genuinely interested in catching up with me on the lost years. He had simply wanted to meet an old friend, as did I. There was nothing else to it. I surmised he would have done the same with any of our batchmates. Vasu had always been popular and easy-going, and had had tons of friends hanging around him. But most of all, he had an irresistible warmth that had drawn me to him in the first place.

As at Jonathan's party, we lapsed into an easy enough banter, recalling old friends, teachers, and our shared college days. He told me about his UK years and I, about my years in America. Abhi, who was in school, also figured heavily in our conversation, without any mention of my ex, of course. I couldn't bring myself to inquire about Usha after what Priya had told me. But without any probing, I gathered he was now single and living in a rented apartment in Chanakyapuri. And there were no children in the picture as far as I could see.

But I was dying to know why he had broken up with Usha. Could anyone break up with that gorgeous woman? I didn't even know whether she and Vasu had been married or simply living together all these years. Surprisingly, neither of them is on Facebook, and other Internet searches revealed only their professional details. Even though I am bursting with curiosity, I dare not ask Priya for the inside scoop. As it is, she would be only too happy to get me hitched up with Vasu. And I am not ready to give up my Independent Woman status for any man right now.

In the three hours Vasu and I spent at the café, we expertly skittered around the subject of our exes and heartbreaks. Though my mind kept skipping back to the scene of Usha and Vasu in the corridor—a moment I can't seem to erase from my memory—my practical side told me to move on and get acquainted with Vasu as if we had never known each other before. It was pointless and silly even, to carry the irrational baggage of our past with me. Moreover, seeing it from Vasu's perspective after all these years, I'm not even sure he realized the heartache he had caused me when he got close to Usha. It's not as if he and I had been dating at that time. We had only been good friends—and, hopefully, we still have it in us to rekindle some of that old friendship.

I stole quick glances at him while he sipped his fancy black coffee. He was in crisp formals: white shirt, brown corduroys, and brogues. I ribbed him about turning out all preppy and sophisticated, a far cry from his rugged-jeans look in college. The hint of a Brit accent went well with his overall hotshot policy wonk profile. He grinned. 'Looks like I have grown up, Ira.' I wondered—or rather worried—how he viewed me. Did he notice my flaws or view me with gentle eyes? I hoped it was the latter and then berated myself for being a sell-out. Why do we women try so hard to impress men? Why can't we all be a bit more accepting of our imperfections? Why do we crave perfection? Isn't this what I find appalling about women like Nikki who want flat stomachs and flawless lives? At that moment, there seemed to be no difference between her and me.

Looking at myself in the bathroom mirror, I part my hair and check the roots. More grey strands; do I start colouring my hair? However much I criticize women who are obsessed with their appearance, I absolutely dread the vision of me with a head full of grey hair. I brush my hair till it shines and flatteringly frames my face. I add eyeliner, a touch of lip gloss, and look this way and that. *Enough preening, Queen Mother.* Abhi and I are having dinner with Vasu, Priya, and Jonathan tonight. It was Jonathan's idea that we try out the new Italian restaurant that has opened in Vasant Vihar. I am wearing a black skirt that sweeps gracefully down to the ankles and a white top with a V-neck—spoils of my recent shopping with Priya! Maybe due to being constantly on the go and immense work-related stress, I seem to have lost a couple of kilos. I haven't felt as high on life as this for months. The retail therapy and the miraculous weight loss seem to have revitalized me. But deep down I know the real reason for my effervescent mood. Just the thought of hanging out with Vasu makes me feel buoyant.

My phone rings. 'Are you ready, Ira? I am here,' Vasu says.

'Hi! Be down in a sec,' I give myself a final glance in the mirror, grab my handbag, and go down with Abhi who has been particularly cranky today. He refused to drink his evening milk, was adamant about changing his clothes, and kicked up a big fuss when I hid his crayons after he had doodled on the walls. He seems more settled now and content to carry his precious Eeyore for our outing.

Vasu leans across from the driver's seat and opens the rear car door for me.

'Hey, champ!' he grins at Abhi. 'I'm Vasu. What's your name?'

'Abhi,' my son says, looking cautiously at Vasu. 'And my school's name is Bumblebees.'

Vasu and I laugh. Vasu is looking dapper in jeans and a blue-checked shirt, a whiff of his now-familiar aftershave lingering in the car. He engages Abhi in easy banter as we drive to the restaurant. I experience a sudden rush of happiness. It's nice to have Vasu around in Delhi. *In my life. In Abhi's life.* Then I shake my head and push the unruly romantic thoughts away. *Vasu is a friend. And that is that. Besides, he can get anyone he wants. Why would he want to be with a divorcee with a kid?*

Spiaggia is filled with Saturday diners, a happy buzz swarming the air. As the waitress leads us to a table, I pull out my vibrating phone from my handbag. It's Priya and I get a premonition of what she is going to say.

'Ira, so sorry, but Jo and I won't be able to make it tonight. Some last-minute work-related stuff has come up.'

'For both of you?' My eyebrows lift automatically.

'Yes.'

'On a Saturday?' I persist. You can't fool me, Priya.

'Yes,' sighs Priya. I can visualize her winking at Jonathan.

I glance at Vasu suspiciously. Was he involved in this set-up? He shoots me an innocent enough quizzical look. I shake my head uncertainly.

'Couldn't you have told me sooner? We are already at the restaurant,' I try not to hiss out the words.

'Last-minute work shows up only at the last minute, sweetie,' Priya responds. I hear her giggle. *Giggle*. Okay, now I know for sure. She and Jonathan *are* trying to play Cupid. 'Have fun,' she says and hangs up.

While Vasu is fine company, Priya and Jonathan's presence wouldn't have put all the pressure on me to carry the evening forward. I vow to strangle her tomorrow.

'Was it Priya?' Vasu asks.

'Yep, they're not coming, some last-minute work, it seems,' I try to sound casual.

Vasu is about to respond when Abhi yells, 'Look, Amma! Rimli and Vansh!'

I swivel my neck and sure enough, Avantika and Nivedita are two tables away with their husbands and kids. I go cold at the sight of them. Avantika—snakeskin dress, loud make-up and thrice-ironed hair—is having a giggle fest with Nivedita—sleeveless black tunic, high ponytail—her spectacular yellow topaz eardrops glinting like snake's eyes. Nivedita's husband is two heads shorter than the burly Promod who, I still find hard to believe, is a fitness expert.

The familiar bile rises to my throat when Avantika spots me and shimmies over to our table. My mind is racing. The woman must have an agenda for coming and wishing me. Dengue-infected mosquitoes matter more to her than chatting me up. I look at Vasu through hooded eyes—his broad shoulders, kindly eyes and smooth clean-shaven face. He looks way more handsome now than he did in college. Will Avantika assume Vasu is my husband? Will she ask him something that will make me want to bolt out the door? Will my fake husband game be up tonight in this plush restaurant—like the dramatic final act of an Italian opera, with the soprano's lyrical climax and all?

'Hi, Ira,' Avantika leans forward and does her customary cheek kiss. Her overpowering perfume almost makes me pass out. She looks appreciatively at Vasu, her gaze lingering longer than is politely permissible. I don't blame her. Vasu is a dishy-looking guy.

'I don't believe we have met,' she extends her hand to him.

'Avantika, I am a fashion designer.'

'Saris and cholis are her specialty,' I pipe up automatically. Avantika's patronizing smile freezes on me.

Vasu smiles politely. 'I'm Vasu—'

'Oh, Ira has told us so much about you,' Avantika cuts in, resting her hand on Vasu's chair.

Okay, this would be the perfect moment for me to die. I don't dare meet Vasu's perplexed gaze.

'So how is dreary Delhi after sunny California?' says Avantika in the huskiest voice she can command. 'When did you get back from Cali?'

Vasu darts me a confused look. 'Um...actually, I lived in London and—'

'That's a great dress you're wearing, Avantika,' I interrupt, wildly thinking of ways to make the woman vanish. Going by the rate at which my mind is ticking, I think it will explode. 'Is it from Zara?'

She raises a condescending eyebrow at me. 'Mango.' She leans closer to Vasu, her ten-foot-deep cleavage a perfect V. 'Oh? I thought you were in California,' she adds.

I clutch my goblet of water so tight that I'm afraid the glass will crack. I tip it slightly, on the ready to drench Avantika's nude pumps.

Vasu shakes his head. 'I was never in the US. I was always in the UK.' Avantika's eyes widen. I sense her registering something, stashing away information to be data-processed later.

I start coughing loudly. Vasu looks at me with concern while Avantika frowns in consternation.

'You okay?' Vasu asks.

'I'm fine, thanks,' I gulp down some water and clear my throat. 'Just a seasonal allergy. So irritating, really.'

Avantika opens her mouth to say something, but Rimli comes skipping to our table, pulling her mother's hand with demands for garlic toast and cheese ravioli.

Avantika flashes a flirtatious smile at Vasu and wiggles her silver-tipped fingers. 'Ciao, nice meeting you, Vasu.' Her eyes sweep over me. A disturbed feeling settles in my stomach. Has she caught on to my Big Lie? Does she now know what I don't want her to know? I have never been able to fathom why she is hell-bent on knowing more about me. What does she have against me? As soon as she is out of earshot, Vasu asks, 'Is she always like this?'

'Yes, only much worse,' I mutter, and we both start laughing.

'Have you been talking to your friends about me?' he asks, his eyes dancing mischievously. I see a bit of the old Vasu when his eyes crinkle in a smile. I tell myself there is nothing attractive about this man and that he is just a friend. But my body is sending me contrary signals. I flush and dip a slice of garlic bread in olive oil. 'I...I must have just mentioned something about meeting up with an old friend—you—from the UK that...that Avantika obviously mistook for the US.' I let out a low whistle. 'Phew, she is weird and says all sorts of things.' My response sounds lame even to my ears but this is the best explanation I can come up with. I must remember to think through the geography before I lie next time.

All attempts at playing with Rimli and Vansh prove futile for Abhi and he comes running to me, lips quivering, eyes glinting with tears. Vasu brilliantly catches on to Abhi's mood and engages him with jokes. Soon, we three are having an enjoyable dinner and for the second time that evening, I feel my chest squeeze tightly. I suddenly want to feel Vasu's strong arms around me, telling me all is well with my world. But I banish the thought immediately. I am afraid of feeling attracted to him just when our old friendship has got revived. But what I am most afraid of is falling in love and rocking the cosy life I have built with Abhi. I am a single mom who must focus on raising her child. I have no time for romance in my life. And I certainly don't want a man to complicate my life again.

Abhi falls asleep on the ride back home and, despite my protests, Vasu insists on carrying him up to our apartment. He lays Abhi on the living room couch and gives me the briefest of hugs. 'Take care, Ira,' he says gruffly, looking at me like he might want to say something. There is a light in his eyes that makes me feel weak in the knees. I don't offer him coffee though I wish he would stay. But he is too much of a gentleman to linger on.

As I see him off, once again apprehension washes over me about what and how much Avantika might have caught on to tonight. Is my Big Lie soon going to unravel at Bumblebees?

Twenty-one

As on most days, Abhi and I reach Bumblebees early and spend time on the lawns facing the school. Abhi is on the swings, jabbering something to himself, while I lazily leaf through a manuscript. I love coming to Churchill Lane at this time of the morning, even if it means waking up half an hour earlier than required. The sun is always mellow at this hour and there is hardly anyone on the lawns. It feels like Abhi and I are in our private garden with the dazzling jacaranda trees fanning out in a cheery welcome.

I am trying hard to concentrate on the manuscript but my mind keeps wandering to last week's dinner with Vasu at Spiaggia. Thankfully, I haven't run into Avantika all week and haven't yet heard headlines screaming, 'Ira's Fake Husband Act Busted!'

I see the frail Hiroo Zardari make her way to the lawns, Bonny walking slowly alongside her. The old Lab seems to have aged suddenly. He is twelve years old, which makes him a grand old man in human years. Abhi jumps off the swing and runs to pat him. 'Bonniiieee, Bonniiieee!' he shouts, but

Bonny doesn't turn in Abhi's direction. Mrs Zardari had once mentioned that his hearing has weakened and that he is not as sharp in his reflexes as he was even last year. Abhi and Bonny have developed a strong bond in the four months since Abhi started school and there are some great moments of theirs that I have captured on camera. I suddenly notice Abhi's pants are two inches above his ankles and his toes are jutting out of his sandals. My little boy seems to be undergoing a growth spurt that I hadn't noticed before.

'How are you, my dear?' Mrs Zardari comes up to me and pats my shoulder. Her face is like an ancient map, weathered and full of criss-cross lines. Her tiny eyes wear a remote look that I now recognize as sadness. I am consumed with guilt for not keeping my promise of helping her bond with her grandson in Dublin. Acting on my advice, she had booked a trunk call to her son and got his email ID, and passed it on to me earlier this month. It had completely slipped my mind to visit her and have an email dictated for her son.

'I am so sorry, Aunty, for never making it to your place. It has been incredibly hectic for me,' I say sheepishly. 'I shall come during Abhi's Dusshera holidays that start next week.'

Mrs Zardari smiles and grips my hand. 'Don't worry, dear. You are young and lead a busy life.' She points to her apartment with her shaky index finger and gives me her door number. 'I look forward to having you and Abhi visit me.'

I smile and stand up. I sling Abhi's schoolbag on to my shoulder and call out, 'Come on, let's go, baby.'

There is a festive air at the Bumblebees gate today. The

mothers seem to have discarded, en masse, their tank tops and skinny jeans for flowing organzas, chiffons, and silks. They are draped in bright jewel-toned saris, and have sindoor smeared on their foreheads like a gash of blood. They look straight out of TV soaps with their maang tikkas and bedecked avatar. Their gold bangles and diamond rings glitter against the delicate henna designs on their hands. If Ekta Kapoor were to conduct auditions for her next serial at the Bumblebees gate, she would probably select them all. The women are busy chattering about Karvachauth and the fast they have to observe through the day. I hear good-humoured cribs about fasting for their husbands and muffled titters about what they would demand in return. Some boast that they are already aware of the iPhones, designer jewellery and perfumes their husbands are planning to gift them. Avantika, in a shimmery yellow chiffon sari paired with a backless red choli, is holding court before a captive audience. Riya, in a red silk sari, is paying Avantika compliments. 'You should be a supermodel, babe,' she says. I must have heard her plea to Avantika at least fifty times since I have known these women. Avantika beams at Riya and cocks her head to one side. That's when her gaze lands on me. Her expression immediately changes to unmasked scorn as she looks me up and down. I hold her gaze and silently challenge her, though my heart beats like a train chugging along in the dead of night.

'Aren't you Bengali? Do you too observe Karvachauth?' Nikki asks Avantika. I am so grateful for the interruption that I want to hug Nikki who looks like a stick draped in a sari. Her blue organza sari sits stiffly on her flat figure. Does she really need to fast any more? I wonder.

'I am half-Bengali and half-Punjabi, darling,' Avantika winks at Nikki. 'That's why I am so exotic-looking.' I stare at her blankly, wondering how this woman could be so vain.

'I can't wait to see the moon,' sighs Riya. 'Rahul is such a sweetie; he always fasts along with me every Karvachauth.'

A dark shadow flits across Nikki's face. 'Lucky you! Prince hogs all day, a typical Punju who can't survive without his paneer and dal makhani.' There is an edge to her voice that makes everyone look at her quietly. Nikki hastily covers up with a mirthless giggle. 'Oh, how Prince spoils me on every Karvachauth! I wonder what he is giving me this year.' When the school term had begun in July, Nikki had been fuller, livelier. But she has been looking different of late—brittle-boned, withdrawn and extremely gaunt, in a sickly sense. She looks frightfully anorexic. I wonder what is going on with her. Is she on one of those dubious fast-track weight-loss programmes?

'I know what Rahul will get me,' chirps Riya in a sing-song voice. 'The latest iPad.'

Before Avantika can throw any uncomfortable questions about husbands and romantic gestures at me, I slink away quietly. I see Shelly from a distance as she shepherds our children to a large banyan tree under which mats are spread out for them to sit on. A huge cardboard cut-out of Raavan is erected nearby, ready to be set on fire on the last day of school before the Dusshera break. All the teachers have been in a tizzy planning Dusshera celebrations and Abhi comes home daily with drawings and craft activities centred around the festival. Yesterday, he had coloured Rama and stuck glitter on terracotta diyas. Abhi has been terribly excited about school these days and I can see his personality gradually blossoming, in no small measure due to the good folks at Bumblebees. I weave my way between the women who are drifting in animated groups. While Bumblebees has done Abhi's confidence levels a whole lot of good, I'm not so sure about me. The women here have inadvertently made me feel insecure about my divorced status. I cast a sidelong glance at Avantika who is hi-fiving Riya about something. I swallow hard. I am not sure how much longer I can keep up with this act of having a husband. The lie is eating at my insides and I am unable to bring myself to confess to these women without worrying about the consequences. What if the news spreads and the principal, Mrs Sippy, hears of it? What if I am given a dressing-down by her for concealing my single-parent status from the school? It would be too embarrassing for me. Good Lord, what have I got myself into? I draw a deep breath, my mind made up. I will continue with the Big Lie as long as Abhi is in Bumblebees, which is only for another five months. And I make a silent promise to myself and God never ever to lie about my divorced status to anyone after this. It's much too stressful to lie about such an important aspect of one's life. It's better to admit to being a divorcee and a single mom, and deal with people's prejudiced notions than to fabricate this gem of a husband with an ambiguous geographical status.

The Karvachauth ladies are leaving one by one—their precious coffee hour at City Market forsaken for wifely duties. They are in a rush to join the women of their families in the day's fasting, and to supervise the cooks for the feasting that will follow upon moonrise. I feel a grudging admiration for these women. They lead the good life; they know how to balance Marks & Spencer's with the maang tikka, the parties with the pujas, and the Chardonnay with the sindoor.

I go back to the lawns and sit on a bench directly under a leafy tree. The park is empty and the surroundings deserted. I am in no mood to drive back home, and decide, instead, to hang around and work on my laptop for the three hours that Abhi is in school. World Ink's impasse with Svetlana continues. Vinnie has learnt through her intelligence network that the bidding war for Svetlana's book is heating up. Apparently, some publishers may offer her up to one and a half crores. I am meeting Svetlana next week when she comes to Delhi for a series of talks with the other publishers. Besides matching the monies, I don't know what else will make Svetlana stay with World Ink. I rub my forehead. What *is* going to swing the deal in our favour?

I'm not sure what I'm going to tell Svetlana at the meeting, though. It's not like we have much choice here—our cash cow seems all set to leave the building. I try to ignore the anxiety creeping over me and open my laptop. About ten minutes into my work, I hear a familiar voice float towards me from the car park that is directly behind my bench. I recognize that voice. It's Carol.

'No! You can't do this to me again, George,' she says in a shrill voice. I suspect she doesn't realize there could be people overhearing her conversation. A light wind rustles the trees and a few leaves fall at my feet.

'But how can I manage for three weeks by myself?' snaps Carol. 'You've just come back from Texas—' There is a long pause during which, I assume, she is listening to her husband have his say. I shift slightly on the bench, just enough to glance quickly behind me through the cluster of bushes separating Carol and me. Her back is turned towards me, her head tilted to one side, cradling the phone on her shoulder. Today, Carol, who always looks and sounds so pulled together, sounds stricken.

'This…I…can't go on like this,' her voice cracks. 'You are never with the girls…with me these days. I...' Carol's soft sobs reach me. She snaps the phone shut, maybe too distraught to continue. I want to go and put my arms around her but that would be so improper. She would be embarrassed that I had overheard her and caught her at a very vulnerable private moment. I had always believed that women like Carol were tough nuts to crack, that their world was always shiny, clean, and in order.

I carefully keep myself hidden and see her walk dejectedly to her Innova. For the first time since I have known her do I see her look underdressed—at least by Bumblebees standards. Her hair is bedraggled, and she is in jeans and a short kurti. The home flip-flops are a dead giveaway about her state of mind. I hear her car door bang shut and the engine rev up.

Within seconds, I catch a glimpse of her profile in the driver's seat as she whizzes past me on the road beyond the lawns. I would never have guessed that trouble was brewing in this supermom's paradise. First, Nikki—if my instincts are right—sounded vexed about something in her marriage. And now, Carol. These are women whom I have envied for having everything. I bite down on my lower lip. Was I too harsh in judging them? Are they also real women with real problems? Should I cut them some slack? I slowly shake my head and resume my work. With some women, you can never tell.

Twenty-two

I reach The Imperial hotel lobby at exactly 3.30 pm. My palms feel clammy, though it's pleasantly cool inside. I have come to meet Svetlana, the desi E.L. James, as the media calls her. I am wearing a powder blue chikan-work salwar kameez and have tied my hair in a ponytail. There was only one mantra I kept on reciting before I got here: *Act cool and confident*.

But when Svetlana glides across the lobby in her gorgeous, sleeveless, red, flowing dress and stilettos, my confidence crumples. She looks stunning, her step-cut hair bouncing around her smooth, exposed shoulders, her perfectly even teeth breaking into a warm smile at nobody in particular. The whole room lights up with her presence. There is admiration and awe on the faces of the other guests milling about. The hotel staff collectively train their eyes on her, in anticipation of fulfilling her commands. I gather myself and tentatively approach her. 'Svetlana? Hi, I am Ira, from World Ink.' I fish out my visiting card from my handbag and give it to her.

Svetlana beams down at me from her five-foot-ten frame. *Goodness, the woman is tall.* She envelops me in a hug. Her perfume smells rich and lush. 'So pleased to meet you. Come, let's go to the coffee shop.'

Twenty minutes later, we are looking at each other with polite expressions as we wait for our orders to arrive. The small talk is over and I need to launch my attack now.

I lean forward slightly and rest my hands on the table. 'Svetlana, let me cut to the chase and be honest: Vinnie and I would really appreciate it if you didn't move to another publishing house.' I pause and try to read her mind from her face that has suddenly turned expressionless. She is a smart cookie, this one. 'It has been a privilege having you as our prized author all these years and we have huge plans to leverage your—'

'Where is the money, Ira?' Svetlana cuts me off smoothly. Her doe-shaped brown eyes flicker in the afternoon light. 'Please tell Vinnie to increase the offer. Forty lakhs doesn't quite cut it. Others are offering me that much only for the marketing spend.'

I want to tell her that we are not a foreign publishing house, flush with funds. But, of course, it's like stating the obvious and Svetlana must be aware of this. Besides, I have always believed that World Ink is far superior to any of the other publishers in India. One has just to glance through our enviable fiction backlist and frontlist that Vinnie has painstakingly built over the years. She has also started putting into motion her plans to expand her editorial team.

World Ink has everything going for it, but desperately needs the revenues from its star author, Svetlana Swaroop.

'Please try to look at the bigger vision we have for you, Svetlana,' I urge. 'I daresay we understand the Indian mass market better than our competitors and have a wider distribution network at our disposal. Vinnie has already included double the royalty percentage and a refresher advance to make up for any shortfall in the total advance amount.' I look at her with hope. 'You will earn the royalties and square up eventually.'

Svetlana sighs exasperatedly as if I were a child harassing her. 'Considering my Twitter following that's now over a lakh, my own efforts to market my books, and the mentions I have received in the international press, I don't believe forty lakhs does justice to my brand.'

I stare at the brilliant ruby drops in her ears. A double row of intricately cut diamonds sparkles on her ring finger. I know she has married into wealth, and I would now like to read up on her husband's business some day. I tear my eyes away from her jewellery and look her in the eye. 'Vinnie is widely acknowledged as the best editor in the publishing business and can drum up the sales, as you well know.' This is a fact: Vinnie is a maverick when it comes to pushing books into the market.

'Ira, I adore Vinnie but I want a better offer,' says Svetlana crisply. 'Let's talk after you've discussed this with her. I would like to close this in the next few weeks.'

I open my mouth to reply but no words come out. I understand from her closed expression that the meeting is over.

Twenty-three

'Ladies, come on! Get your act together. You are women of the world. Women of substance. Superwomen. Give yourselves a hug. We all need a li'l bit of lovin' to keep the mojo going.' Priya beams at the group of women gathered in her newly opened yoga studio in upmarket Sunder Nagar. They are standing in a V-formation, hands on hips and hanging on to her every word. The women are the pick of Delhi's high society with impeccable grooming oozing from their every pore. They may look casually attired, but their sharp tracksuits and hair accessories are sourced from high street shops in Europe and America. These are women who find City Market boring and take off on a whim to Gstaad and Fiji whenever India's manic energy wears them out. These are women whose husbands are industrialists, banking gurus, and entrepreneurial wiz-kids. Some of these women were air hostesses, PR girls, beauty queens, and Bollywood starlets in their previous lives—before the Mrs So-and-So tag became their all-consuming identity. I recognize a former Bollywood item girl who shot to fame with a pole-dancing number in a Hindi movie and her much-publicized break-up with a Pakistani cricketer. And then there is a former Miss India with the elevated eyebrows and abnormally taut forhead.

One would think the dozen-odd privileged women in this room—all set to defeat the onslaught of age—wouldn't need lessons in self-esteem, women's empowerment, self-worth, body image, and all that jazz. And yet, as I scan the room from the corner where I am seated—as inconspicuously as possible—their tired eyes and anorexic frames tell me another story. To the world, these women have storybook marriages. But in reality, they are caught in abusive relationships and are slowly coming apart. Notwithstanding the M·A·C and the Lancóme make-up, their complexions look pallid in the afternoon light. Priya had earlier introduced me to them as a partner in her self-esteem coaching enterprise—a new offshoot of her yoga consultancy outfit—making me almost sputter on the tomato juice her office boy had served. My dear friend Priya, as I am learning every day, is capable of all kinds of guile beneath her innocent girl-woman façade. But, to cut her some slack, I know why she introduced me so. These women, who come to Priya's thrice-weekly Delhi Power Girls sessions, lead schizophrenic lives. They live under the glare of Page 3 flashbulbs and are scrutinized like biology specimens by the media. While they are fiercely competitive about acquiring the latest IT bag, they also lead a darker life, cloaked in insecurities, shame, and secret fears. Given their place in society, it makes sense that they would be worried if a stranger like me were to sit through their session. What if I were to record everything and leak it on YouTube! My being introduced as Priya's business partner allows them to let down their guard, relax and immerse themselves completely in what they have come for. The first hour was spent in group workshops and play-acting, aided by two personable young girls who are fresh psychology graduates. It taught them how to deftly handle situations of abuse—verbal or physical. I was terribly impressed with Priya's personable and calm exterior as she went around the room and talked to the women. She told them that the best way to handle an abusive spouse was with kid gloves, instead of resorting to aggressive tactics. I am not surprised to see Priya become a self-esteem coach. Even back in college, she had been a supporter of various women's causes and would volunteer for women's helplines, sometimes bunking classes if there was an emergency call from an NGO.

'Don't feel ashamed of your situation,' Priya advised the women. 'And please don't blame yourself. You have to recognize an abusive situation and remove yourself from it.' She paused and scanned the room with her soft brown eyes. 'Remember, abuse can happen to anyone and sometimes it happens to smart, beautiful women like you. You cannot allow someone else to destroy your inner confidence and drive you to become suicidal.' Priya went on for another half an hour, explaining the different kinds of abuse against women—the obvious, violent ones and the more subtle ones where the victim is made to feel guilty. A deathly pin-drop silence hung in the air after Priya had finished addressing the women. Even in the dimly lit room, I could sense the women's palpable fear and anxiety. And something happened to me too that left me feeling a little breathless. *Arun*. He had been clever enough to make me feel worthless and unloved in our marriage without resorting to physical abuse. I too, like these women around me, had been in an abusive relationship where I had always felt isolated and demeaned—but, I hadn't known this back then.

'Gorgeous ladies, let's wrap up the class with our mantra,' Priya's dulcet tone rings in the silent room. She inhales deeply and punches her right hand in front, 'Heil Hitler'-style.

The women follow suit, the collective punching and their audible exhalation creating a whoosh sound. Their voices rise in unison, as if they were army recruits in the National Defence Academy: 'We are Women. We are daughters, sisters, wives, daughters-in-law and mothers. But first, we are US! I am ME! And I LOVE myself the way I AM. Be GENTLE with me. I have EARNED the stretch marks, the C-section scars, the grey hair, the love handles, the crow's feet, and the fine lines on my face. So SHOVE it if you want me to change. I am BEAUTIFUL and I LOVE ME...even if you don't!'

I get goosebumps on my arms as I hear this. There is so much anger, resentment and frustration laced into their collective chant. I instinctively know Priya wants them to let off some steam by using strong language. The words roll off their tongues without any awkwardness. Are these women really so scarred in life? One would never guess it, going strictly by their appearance and lifestyle. I lean back on the sofa and quell the beating of my heart. I feel something shift within me—a cold realization. A rush of unsavoury memories assails me.

Arun, too, had tried to make me something I was not—he tried to *change* me into a different personality. Like the numerous times he made me feel guilty for enjoying life's small pleasures, be it going for a movie or shopping for dresses. He wanted me to be a working woman for his sake though I might have liked to exercise other options had the marriage continued. In small ways and big, he had always wanted me to adjust to his way of thinking, and not vice versa. It was not a relationship of equals. It was he who held the remote control. But he had a knack for conveying his point across so subtly that it is only now that I can fully comprehend the mental power game he had been playing all those years. I set my mouth in a firm line. *Shove it, Arun, wherever you are. I AM beautiful. And I am worth every bit of heartache I have gone through because of you.* I rise to my feet, my skin tingling with newfound determination to bury the dead.

The two-hour session with Priya seems to have done me some good too! I am glad I took up on her invitation to be present here today. I think she had wanted me to realize that there are so many other women—more privileged and blessed than me—who also go through life's grind in various demeaning ways. I admire Priya for starting Delhi Power Girls, even though it caters to a very niche clientele. Despite its low-key, unpublicized existence, the client base has been steadily growing due to word of mouth and endorsements.

Priya receives calls from unhappy wealthy women every day, swearing her to secrecy before they reveal their true identity. That makes me wonder about the blackhole that Delhi's high society is in. It must be the same in other metros too—rich, beautiful, sad people caught in indifferent, poisonous relationships.

Priya's face shines with happiness as she sees the women off at the door. While this is certainly a lucrative market for her to extend her lifestyle/yoga guru brand to, I know that the self-esteem coaching is not just about the money for her. She finds a deeper meaning in her chosen profession. 'It's an inner calling, Ira,' she often tells me and I know that it's not a Miss India statement in Priya's case. She ventured into the self-esteem coaching consultancy three months ago when she realized that her upmarket yoga clients had far graver issues to contend with than just weight loss and aching joints. Thus began her coaching academy of sorts for the well-heeled ladies of Delhi. She came up with the name Delhi Power Girls because she wanted to empower these women with the right tools for being happy in life—not just the Bobbi Brown cosmetics and platinum credit cards that serve as an instant pick-me-up for them.

Overhead, the clouds are gathering in full force. Rains in October are a rarity in Delhi. But this October, Delhiites have experienced an unusually wet spell. Abhi is playing on the small patch of grass near the driveway with Priya's office boy. As I am about to join Abhi outside, I do a double take on seeing a familiar skinny figure in a pink Juicy Couture outfit framed in the door. It is Nikki. Her brown eyes flicker and then settle on me with a blank look. I must have missed seeing her earlier in the class since Priya had dimmed the lights for the most part. And besides, most of these women look alike because of their attire, streaked hair, and fatigue-worn expressions. A low rumble reverberates in the vapour-laden skies. With a curt nod at me, Nikki hastens out the door with her mini entourage of two maids who are carrying her handbag, sports duffel bag and umbrella. Nikki puts on her humongous glares even though the last of the sun's rays are ebbing, slips into the backseat of her silver Mercedes and takes off in a cloud of dust before I can even gather my thoughts.

'Amma!' Abhi comes running and grabs my knees. I thank Priya's office boy and lift my son, and kiss him. Abhi and I join Priya inside for a cup of tea. When I tell her that Nikki is a Bumblebees mom, Priya sighs and shrugs in a 'What can I say?' manner.

'What?' I remark. 'What is the dope on her? She leads a perfect life as far as I know.'

Priya gives me a closed smile and remains silent. I know client confidentiality matters a lot to her but I am in no mood to follow protocol.

'What? Come on, Pri. You know I won't tell anyone,' I say exasperatedly.

Priya sips her green tea and presses her face against the window. A thin drizzle has started outside. 'You think it's a perfect life when your husband only knows how to demean you every day? You think it's a good life when all he does is call you fat when you're actually only forty-five kilos? Tell me, if it's a perfect life when he pressurizes you into losing weight soon after your body has gone through a C-section. When he calls you imperfect although all your time goes in cellulite massages, acid peels, lasers, dermabrasions, and countless other treatments to reverse the signs of ageing? You think it's a perfect life when he doesn't allow you to have another child because you will gain weight?' Priya pauses and looks at me. I am too speechless to react. It has started pouring outside, the shards of rain drumming against the window in a harsh rhythm. 'Ira, do you know Nikki was almost killing herself by being on random, dangerous, and impossible diet plans? She would eat and puke the entire day, absolutely neurotic about getting fat. She was so depressed when she came to me a month ago—I suspect even suicidal. I am trying to get her on track and give her a shitload of self-esteem.'

'But what about her husband, Prince?' I ask in a thin voice. 'Does he know?'

'Are you crazy? The woman comes here stealthily. If he knew about the self-esteem that's being pumped into her instead of collagen on her lips, the marriage would go bust. That man is maniacally insecure and needs to be handled with care.'

I place my teacup on the table with an unsteady hand. A lump forms in my throat. What Priya has just disclosed makes me take another look at my own life with renewed respect and gratitude. I realize I have lucked out by getting out of a toxic relationship in the nick of time.

Twenty-four

It's a packed Saturday morning. Abhi and I are going to Mrs Hiroo Zardari's house today. But before that I have a mountain of dirty laundry to put in the washing machine, another to send to the neighbourhood istriwallah, channas to soak for dinner, bills to pay online, my TV satellite service to renew, Abhi's photos to email to Anusha, Abhi's toe and fingernails to clip, plants to water, and so many other pending tasks screaming for my attention. And most of all, I want to take a nice long, luxurious shower. But when I see the work piled up on my study desk, I balk and throw away thoughts of beauty baths, face masks, hot-oil hair massages, and other such fancy indulgences. They will have to wait till tomorrow…or till Abhi goes to college. Such is a mother's life. I don't know how women with a brood of children managed it back in the old days. Did they catch even five winks of sleep? Or get three minutes to themselves? My great-grandmother had eleven children and still managed to have a creamy, glowing complexion, well into her eighties. Maybe the stress of urban living, junk food, hours on the computer, and other modern-day lifestyle hazards contribute to how women of my generation look and feel.

Abhi's giggles reach me from the living room. I feel guilty about putting him in front of the TV when I am busy. But it's something I need to wrap my New Age parenting head around. I'm not sure if there are kids Abhi's age on the street where we live. The houses around us, though spick and span, always wear a deserted look. I see the gardeners, drivers, servants, and watchmen—but never the residents. I see a line of gleaming cars parked in the driveways, but never their owners.

I shut the washing machine lid and turn it on. Raising a child single-handedly is tough in today's Delhi, where people view each other with suspicion and distrust. Back when Anusha and I were growing up, we and our friends would happily skitter in and out of each other's houses, freely help ourselves to snacks in our mothers' kitchens and whisper adolescent secrets to each other from our adjoining balconies. More importantly, our mothers never had to bother with that thing which I have come to dread, called a 'play date'. Organizing a play date for Abhi is proving to be an insurmountable task. I think it would be far easier to take off on a rocket. None of the Bumblebees mothers is someone whom I can just call and ask to come over with her kid. We don't as yet share that kind of comfort level. Okay, maybe Urvi is an exception, but even she is busy running a joint-family household. In the busy times we live in, women find it tough to plan play dates at the drop of a hat due to work and home pressures, commuting time, and so many other day-to-day responsibilities that pile up over the week.

Half an hour later, when I am working on my computer, Abhi comes crashing through the door in a superman cape. I was bullied into buying it last week when we had gone shopping to Sarojini Nagar for Abhi's clothes. The cape flows two feet long and he almost trips on it while running to me, and gives me a tight hug.

I hold my little boy close and smell the delicate scent of Johnson's Baby Powder on his skin. 'Come, Amma. Pillow fight!' he says. We hop on to the bed and throw the pillows at each other—it's Abhi's favourite game this week. Last week, it was 'Find the handkerchief'. I tickle him till he squeals, wriggles out of my grasp, and dashes to the door. I run and grab him and swing him around like I used to when he was a much lighter child. We play hide and seek and then leave for Mrs Hiroo Zardari's house.

I pull into the parking lot in front of Bumblebees. Abhi's Dusshera break has started and it feels odd to come here without carrying his school bag and water bottle. It's a balmy evening after three days of continuous rain. The trees have started shedding their leaves for autumn, their gnarled branches spread out to the skies.

'Amma, when will school open?' asks Abhi, kneeling down to pick up some soggy leaves from the ground. They look like tiny, limp fish in his clammy little hands.

'After a week, sweetheart.'

'Tomorrow?' he looks at me with bright eyes.

'After seven days,' I say, tweaking his nose. 'Seven days make a week.'

'Seven days make a week. Seven days make a week,' Abhi sing-songs and goes skipping in front of me.

We enter Mrs Zardari's apartment block and climb the wide steps to the second floor. At the entrance to her house hangs a charming Tibetan brass bell with intricate workmanship. Abhi clangs it a couple of times despite my stern admonishments. The door opens and Mrs Zardari's profile peeps through the crack. I hear Bonny's heavy breathing behind her. The old lady peers with her weak eyes at us standing in the dimly lit foyer and then breaks into a smile of recognition.

'Come in, darlings,' she says warmly and lets Abhi and me inside.

As imagined by me on many an occasion, the living room is humongous and the floor is a dark wood covered with Persian rugs. Vintage lace curtains are neatly pulled back from the tall French windows, revealing a brilliant view of the lawns facing Bumblebees. Bonny wags his tail soporifically and licks Abhi's feet. Abhi giggles and pats the shiny coat sprinkled with grey hair. Heavy chestnut glass cases display lovely knick-knacks from another era: a pair of Victorian porcelain jugs with fish-head spouts; an engraved candleholder reminiscent of children's fairy tale books; a dainty antique doll with golden hair; and enamelled pottery pieces in various sizes and colours. Weathered spines of Tolstoy, Fitzgerald, Hardy, Dickens, and other classics line the book cases. Even the furniture is quaint: two chaises longues with carved walnut frames and a mahogany three-seater, upholstered sofa. The dank smell of untreated wood and old books, and of dog breath hangs in the air.

Mrs Zardari seats us and goes inside. She returns a few minutes later with a young boy who serves us cake and cookies on a tray.

'Come on, eat, Abhi,' she says. 'I made these for you.' The cake is spongy, lemony, rich and moist. Abhi, to my surprise, licks the plate clean in two minutes. He is usually such a fussy eater.

'Mmm…it's heavenly, Aunty,' I say, as my teeth sink into the cake's gooey core.

'I learnt this from my grandmother sixty years ago,' Mrs Zardari says with a weak laugh. 'Oh, people went wild eating her cakes and pies.'

We get to talking about her life and I learn that her husband was in the Indian Civil Service and had passed away twenty years ago. As she had told me earlier, she has only one child, Siddy's father.The mantelpiece above the fireplace is crammed with photos. There are photos of her and her husband in oval silver frames as handsome newly-weds; on the deck of a ship ('We were sailing to China'); with foreigners at dinner parties; with their son at various stages of his life;

and sundry family photos with relatives and friends. My eyes travel to a sideboard where more photos are on display. I immediately know the toddler and little boy photos are of Siddy. She catches my glance, gets up and brings me a beautiful collage of Siddy's photos, capturing him from newborn to pre-school days.

'I'm afraid I don't have any of Siddy's from the recent years, though I can well imagine him having turned out to be a good-looker like his father and grandfather,' she says, in the hazy evening light.

Her helper boy brings us tea and Abhi a glass of hot chocolate. Abhi crinkles his nose and declares, 'No milk.'

'You have to drink it, my dear, or else the big bear from inside my room will come to your house and take away your toys.'

Abhi gapes at Mrs Zardari, registering her words. 'Okay,' he says meekly and sips the hot chocolate from a blue Noddy plastic cup that I suppose must have been Siddy's.

Mrs Zardari winks at me. 'Worked like a charm every time I tried it on Siddy.'

I suppress my giggles. I pull out a notebook and pen from my handbag. 'Aunty, please dictate a letter to your son. I'll create an email ID tonight and send it to him.'

The next half-hour melts in taking down a heartfelt intimate letter from a mother to her son, bottled-up emotions breaking free and drenching the page. Bonny is sleeping contentedly at Abhi's feet, happy to be stroked by soft little hands.

By the time we leave Mrs Zardari's house, evening is falling outside, some early stars popping out in the inky blue sky. Abhi is wearing an oversized hat that Mrs Zardari has gifted him. It is made of suede and trimmed at the rim with genuine leather. 'My husband loved collecting hats and this was bought in England all those years ago,' she had explained. I am touched that she thought of giving away a part of her precious memories to Abhi.

Something catches in my throat on the drive back home. Do little boys who snuggle with their mothers grow up into callous sons one day? Abhi is humming a tune to himself. I turn around and smile at him. He looks at me with questioning eyes. 'Amma, do doggies have Mamas? Who is Bonny's Mama?'

Twenty-five

The Dusshera holidays stretch ahead of Abhi and me in a vacuous haze. I wish we could have flown to London to be with my parents. But I am careful not to say this when I chat with them on Skype. I try to sound as if their daughter is doing it all—managing a child, home and work responsibilities with aplomb and enviable organizational skills that would once have landed me on Oprah's show as a role model for working mothers. But only I know the manic work–life jugglery that goes into everything I am doing. These days, it feels as if my cell phone is a body part—I'm constantly on the phone talking to authors, office colleagues and Vinnie. My book titles have started going to press and the pre-production stages of each book—editing, typesetting, proofing, book jackets—leave precious little time for anything else in life. Abhi has missed going to the park for three days in a row but I try not to beat myself up about it. Work emails and SMSs have tripled and the number of hours spent on the computer has exponentially increased, making me a potential candidate for Cubital Tunnel Syndrome. This hi-tech term for elbow pain has the potential to be a great conversation starter at parties. 'You know, Tara, I have a case of CTS.' Not to be outdone, Tara may reply: 'Honey, I have a case of WMASFL (Working Mothers Are Screwed for Life).' I let out a deep sigh as I fold the laundry piled up from last week and try to recall the number of whistles from the pressure cooker—was it three or five? There are blurbs to be written; catalogues to be prepared for the trade; book jacket briefs to be discussed—or argued over—with designers; manuscripts to be edited; and marketing strategies to be chalked out in consultation with World Ink's marketing team.

Vinnie is a little down in the dumps since I couldn't convince Svetlana to stay when I met her the other day. I have been to World Ink's office twice to discuss the Svetlana Crisis (as I have come to call it) in more detail. 'We can do sixty lakhs tops,' Vinnie had finally conceded after speaking to our financial adviser. But Svetlana had declined our revised figure with an unmasked snicker.

When Vinnie had called me last night—she has a knack for calling at only odd hours—she was sounding despondent. The publishing grapevine has it that Svetlana is signing up with our biggest competitor. 'They are giving her one crore fifty lakhs and 30 percent royalty,' Vinnie had almost wept into the receiver.

How grossly I had underestimated the workload of mothers who work from home! I wish Vinnie would allow me to continue to work from home after the year-long contract expires. Why hasn't telecommuting caught on in India? Why make it so tough for working mothers who are in professions where a fair degree of flexibility can be exercised?

I finish my shower and go to my study, still lost in my thoughts. Should I opt for freelance work on a retainer basis and be a stay-at-home mommy who doesn't have crazy work deadlines to meet? I immediately regret my choice of words. Stay-at-home moms *are* working mothers. In fact, they work much harder than moms with regular jobs and without getting any validation, promotion, perks or pats on the back for a great job done. Anusha and I were raised by a stay-at-home mother who was—and is—the strength and pillar of our family. She would welcome us returning from school with a hug and warm food; kiss away our bruises; play referee when we fought; nurse us to health when ill; cheer our every achievement; wipe away our tears; and contribute to our growing years in big ways and small. Seeing our mother as a formidable example of a fully invested stay-at-home mother has made a huge impact on us sisters, which is why I, too, want to be there for Abhi in his childhood years. Even Anusha has been talking about taking a sabbatical or quitting her job when the baby comes along. She often talks about taking up salsa dancing! What happens to the most hard-core career woman among us when we become mothers? It's like we metamorphose into a different personality at the flick of a switch. One day we are in masculine boardrooms delivering powerful presentations and the next day we are in sloppy tracksuits, chasing our kids in the park. I sigh with happiness. Motherhood is the best thing that has happened to me.

Twenty-six

'What are you doing this evening?' asks Vasu in that deep sexy voice that makes my breath catch in my throat.

I am suddenly, unreasonably, annoyed with him. My life—with my compact family of two, happily ensconced at its new moorings—had been sailing smoothly, till this impossibly handsome man from my past waltzed back into my life after fourteen years. And complicated it again. I can hear Vasu smiling broadly at me through the phone. I know I am being unfair to him. He has been nothing but a gentleman, a genuine friend, since the time I've reconnected with him. Even so, I am miffed with him. He has stirred within me a longing for a man, a happy married life and all the picture-perfect, cheerful family scenes that glossy magazines capture so beautifully and that little girls grow up believing to be true.

I take my cup of tea and go to the study. I can visualize Vasu seated in his plush office, dressed in crisp formals and looking out the window at the manicured lawns outside.

'Don't you have work to do, Vasu? Pressing policy work

for a developing nation?' I ask playfully, I daresay, even flirtatiously. There is something liberating and reckless in being a single woman, albeit divorced. It makes me want to believe in love again, even though my ex has shattered my faith in men. Why, oh why, has Vasu returned to Delhi? Couldn't he have got posted to Africa instead?

'Well, now that you mention it, I do have work,' Vasu chuckles. 'But funding water irrigation projects in rural Maharashtra doesn't compare with talking to you, Ira.'

My cheeks burn. Is he trying to flirt with me?

'How is Abhi?' he asks.

I launch off into the minutiae of his Dusshera break. I've enrolled him in a neighbourhood painting class that keeps him busy for two hours in the morning. In fact, that's where he is right now. 'I need to pick him up in an hour,' I say.

Vasu adds softly after more chit-chat, 'You have still not answered my question. What are you doing this evening?'

'Nothing much, really. Why don't you come home for dinner?' I ask impulsively.

'Great, I'll see you guys at 8 o'clock,' says Vasu and the line goes dead.

Apparently, the man doesn't believe in polite demurs. It is as if he has been waiting for me to invite him! I drain my tea and dump the cup in the kitchen sink. Now I'll be left wondering why *he* had asked me about what my plans were for the evening. Damn you, Vasu!

Abhi is splayed out on the floor with his crayons, drawing a house. Shelly has given the class activity sheets for the Dusshera break and this one requires the child to use his imagination to draw his family. Abhi's house is round with a tall door and crooked windows. There are flowers and bees outside. Then there is a stick figure with long hair and a shorter stick figure with giant red shoes. 'Abhi and Amma,' he looks up and tells me.

Sure, that's us. Mama Bear and Baby Bear. I look at Abhi's rounded chin and cheeks, still plump with baby fat. I feel a tightness in my throat. He is too innocent now even to realize that a regular family unit also has a Papa Bear, though I think the world is breaking away from this norm. I mentally brace myself for the day when people may ask him uncomfortable questions about his father. Abhi vigorously colours the sky a light purple and adds a yellow blob of sun with a smiley face.

'Great job, baby!' I remark. I am so glad the activity sheets don't have to be returned to Shelly for she may wonder why our family has one member missing. And that might result in further inquiries with my Big Lie unravelling in the presence of the tittering Bumblebees moms.

Avantika's smug smile clouds my vision. I shake my head to drive away these thoughts. *Stop overanalysing*. Abhi scrambles to his feet. 'Piggyback, Amma.' I carry him on my back and drop him on the living room couch. I slip *Toy Story* into the DVD player and sing along with Abhi to *You've Got a Friend in Me*. We must have watched the movie at least twenty times together. I stretch my legs out in exhaustion and cuddle up with Abhi. I have slogged for the better part of the afternoon, whipping up a baked cheese dish, pulao, korma, raita and custard for tonight's dinner. It's been a while since I've cooked for guests and I feel a little nervous about the outcome. After a shower, I stood in front of my wardrobe for a long time, agonizing over what I should wear. I finally chose a white churidar kurta with a thin gold border at the neck and the sleeves, accessorizing it with gold ear drops and a thin gold chain. My hair is loose and brushed to a shine.

The tantalizing smell of spices and anticipation hangs thick in the air when the doorbell rings. I quickly smooth my dress, take a deep breath, and open the door.

'Hi!' says Vasu, his warm smile reaching up to his eyes. At almost six feet, Vasu has a certain presence about him that makes my knees a little wobbly. His coffee-coloured skin is offset by the white Polo T-shirt that is stretched taut against his torso. I summon every muscle in my body not to hurl myself into his arms. He hands me a bouquet of white and yellow roses.

I feel the same fluttery feeling I had experienced when I had first set eyes on him in college. It suddenly strikes me that I am not over him—I may never be. I am so not the staid divorcee who is immune to this man's charms.

'They're lovely, thanks,' I say, stepping aside to let him in. This is the first time a man has given me flowers and I am secretly thrilled and a bit embarrassed about my adolescent reaction. I remember the way he had looked at me the night he had dropped me home after the dinner at Spiaggia. It was as if he had wanted to say something but didn't know how. *Shut up. There you go again on your fantasy trip.*

'Nice place you've got here, Ira.' Vasu's voice cuts into my reverie.

'Yes, I really lucked out with accommodation.' I explain to him whose place this is.

Abhi comes running to us, shouts a 'Hello, Uncle' to Vasu and runs back to the couch. Vasu follows him and gives him a large box of assorted chocolates. The photos on the box show dark and white chocolates shaped like shells, conches, and seahorses.

'Please open, Uncle,' Abhi says distractedly, his eyes glued to the television screen.

'Abhi, what is the magic word when someone gifts you something?' I ask.

'Thank you, Uncle,' says Abhi in a low voice and flashes me a sly smile.

'You're welcome, champ.' Vasu ruffles Abhi's hair and opens the chocolate box. 'Having fun in your holidays?'

'Yes, so so much fun,' Abhi says, stretching his hands and bringing them together in a small clap.

'Waiting for school to start again?' asks Vasu.

'Um-hmm…' Abhi nods. 'You know, there is a doggie in my school.'

'Really? What's his name?'

'Bonnie. He is black in colour and very very old. Hundred years old.'

'Wow, I too am hundred years old,' says Vasu.

'No!' says Abhi and giggles.

Vasu asks Abhi a few more questions about his school and sundry things. I flit in and out of the living room, bringing Vasu bowls of nibbles and a soft drink. There is absolutely no pretence in his interaction with Abhi and it's nice to see them warm up to each other. I return from the kitchen with a ceramic vase filled with water. I carefully arrange the roses in it and place it on the glass-topped coffee table.

'So, how is work?' I ask Vasu.

'Crazy!' he laughs, running his fingers through his hair. 'I've been travelling all week and I'm gone for a fortnight again at the end of the month.'

'Where to?'

'Manila.'

'Sounds like a dream job to me,' I smile. 'Want to trade places?'

'Sure,' says Vasu holding my gaze with a smile that makes me take a quick breath. There is nothing flirtatious about his smile, yet, it's powerful enough to set my insides a-fluttering. Yes, the man *is* gorgeous. His dark liquid eyes and sensual mouth are enough to melt any woman worth her hormones. I excuse myself and go to heat the dinner.

The rest of the evening goes so smoothly that I don't want the night to end. Abhi joins us at the dinner table and wolfs down his food for a change. He brings out his file of crayon drawings and shows them to a very appreciative Vasu.

'Did you cook all the yummy food, Abhi?' asks Vasu in all seriousness.

Abhi stares at him, a perplexed expression on his face. He shrieks with laughter, 'No! Amma cooks. I am a child and fire is dangerous.'

'You have a very precocious boy, Ira,' Vasu laughs.

After dessert, while Vasu watches TV, I change Abhi into his pyjamas and help him brush his teeth. I tuck him in and kiss his cheeks. 'Love you, baby,' I whisper against his face.

'Lurrve you, Amma.' Abhi shifts to the other side and almost immediately falls asleep.

Once again, a warm fuzzy feeling creeps up on me without warning and makes me wonder what it would be like for Abhi to have a real, caring father in his life. And me, a husband. Are my parents, Anusha, Venkat and Priya right, after all, about wanting to see me re-married? I know that what I feel for Vasu now is different from the first rush of love—or infatuation—I had felt for him in college. I am a different Ira now—not the immature woman who had shown flashes of possessiveness about Vasu. I wonder what it would be like to be Vasu's wife. Though we go back a long way, we are strangers in one sense—there is so much we don't know about each other. I don't even know something as basic as what his favourite colour is. We have a lot of catching up to do, before—if at all—things can progress between us. As always, I am quick to chide myself for entertaining such thoughts. Why should I be married to feel complete? I can't risk marriage again. I am a single mother who can take care of herself and her kid, thank you very much.

When I return to the living room, my mind fuzzy with

confusion, Vasu is getting ready to leave. He switches off the TV and gets up from the sofa.

'It's quite late, I should be getting back now,' he says, sending a pang into my heart. 'Thanks so much, Ira. I had a great time.'

I am a bit startled to realize how much one part of me wants Vasu. But I can't bring myself to offer him a glass of wine or coffee to make him linger a while longer. Going by whatever I have gleaned from movies, nightcaps have a way of sending wrong signals. What if he misinterprets it and I lose him again?

As we walk across the room to the front door, I remember something and open my mouth to speak. But all I can do is take a big gulp of air.

Vasu looks sideways at me. 'What?' His eyebrows come together in a question.

I shake my head emphatically. 'Nothing.'

'What? Come on, tell me. I know you were about to say something.' Vasu gazes deeply into my eyes, startling me with the intensity of his look.

I sigh. 'Okay, since you insist. Why did you ask me on the phone what I was doing this evening?' I look at him expectantly, feeling foolish. 'Why did you want to know?'

Vasu reaches for my hand and pulls me gently towards him. His touch sends a current under my skin. I can smell his aftershave, a clean masculine fragrance that reminds me of sea-surfing and wind-swept hair.

'I wanted to take you out for dinner,' he says. 'That's what I had wanted to ask you.'

'Why?' I half-whisper, my eyes closed, scared that the magical moment would vanish if I opened them.

'We were once such good friends, Ira...' He gently strokes my cheeks with his fingertips. His eyes light up. 'Remember how we used to bunk those boring Philosophy classes? And I'll never forget the detailed class notes you'd prepare for me when I was absent.'

I hug him tightly, not believing I am actually doing so. 'Oh, Vasu,' I say, my voice choked with emotion. 'You remember after all...'

The house is quiet and the pale moonlight filters in through the windows. Vasu leads me back to the living room.

'Can I ask you something?' Vasu says, putting his arm around me after we sit next to each other on the sofa.

'Sure.'

'Why did you get divorced?' I tense. My skin prickles with shame.

'Don't bother answering that. Sorry, that was rude.' he says.

I shake my head. 'No, no, that's fine. There was no choice, really; he just upped and left.' Swallowing hard, I add, 'Guess he didn't love us enough to want to stay. I'll tell you everything some other day.' We sit in companionable silence for a while. The last time I had sat so close to Vasu was when we were in the college auditorium, watching a play. But that was when I was too naïve to realize the depth of my feelings for him.

'How did you know I am divorced? Did Priya tell you?' I ask eventually, my curiosity killing me.

'Yes, but that's only because I asked about your husband,' Vasu smiles sheepishly.

I roll my eyes at him. 'I think she has been desperately trying to set us up.'

Vasu laughs. We both know our friend Priya well enough.

He assumes a serious expression. 'Is he...your ex...is he in touch with you? Does he visit Abhi?'

'Nope.'

Vasu squeezes my hand. 'I'm sorry I brought it up.'

'That's fine; I think I've moved on.' I turn and face him. 'What happened between you and Usha?'

'We were really happy for the first couple of years,' he responds after a moment.

'How long were you guys married?'

'We were living together, not married.' Vasu's eyes turn narrow and thoughtful. 'Which is good in a way—no messy divorce and no kids to have custody fights over.'

I flinch. He looks at me apologetically. 'Sorry, didn't mean to phrase it like that. As you can see, I am not the most tactful guy.'

My lips stretch in a sardonic smile. 'You have just stated a fact.'

Vasu adds, 'After we graduated from Delhi University, Usha and I got accepted at the London School of Economics. We started living together during our college years in London.

Then we got busy chasing our careers and moving from one professional goal to the other.' He pauses and stares into the distance. 'We often talked about getting married but never got around to doing it.'

'Was there no family pressure?' I interject.

'Of course, incredible pressure—from both our families,' says Vasu. 'And I did propose to Usha a couple of times.'

I try to ignore the sting of envy coursing through me. 'Did she accept?' I ask in a quiet voice.

Vasu sighs. 'That's the thing. She could never bring herself to say, "Yes". She figured she wasn't the marrying type.'

'Did that bother you?'

Vasu nods. 'We started having arguments when, somewhere down the road, I realized that I wanted something more meaningful from our relationship. I wanted to get married and feel "settled" like most guys my age.' He waves his free hand in the air. 'I guess I was ready for a wife, kids, a backyard barbecue and the works...but Usha was not ready.' He leans back against the sofa and closes his eyes. 'She may never be ready.'

I nod understandingly. 'Where is she now?' I ask, although my Internet search has revealed that she is teaching at Cambridge.

'She is a professor at Cambridge.'

'Are you guys in touch?' I try to quell the beating of my heart.

'No, she and I split up almost two years ago. We decided

to go our separate ways amicably and set each other free from our shared past.'

'That sounds poetic,' I say.

Vasu laughs weakly. 'What can I say? I am a man of many talents.'

'Are you over her?' The words tumble out before I can stop myself.

Vasu meets my gaze with gentle eyes. 'Yes, absolutely.'

I rest my head on his shoulder and feel the rhythmic rise and fall of his chest. Before I know what is happening, he buries his face in the hollow of my shoulder and kisses me, his breath hot against my skin. I find myself responding, returning his kiss with equal fervour, feeling his mild stubble under my fingertips, caressing his hair, losing myself in him.

When we finally pull apart, my whole body feels tingly and warm. What had just transpired was surreal, but so perfect. Is the Universe really looking out for me? Vasu is great for me; we could probably have the best life together. But I am a bundle of nerves, scared to make the wrong move when it comes to men. Destiny has thrown us together again, though I am really not sure in which direction Vasu and I are headed.

Twenty-seven

The following morning I wake up feeling like a new woman. I still can't believe what had happened last night. It was magical, as if it was all a chimera. Vasu had left shortly after our kiss, holding me for a long time in his arms before he went out the door. We didn't converse much but connected eloquently through our silence. We fit so well against each other, I muse, like two logs that have come together again after years of drifting in different streams of the ocean.

I go to the living room and bury my face in the roses arranged in the vase. I carry the vase to the dining table and place it in the middle, the sun-dappled flowers instantly spreading cheer in the room. I sit down to have my morning coffee, trying to clear the buzzing sounds in my mind. I am still trying to figure out my life and am uncertain how a man will figure in the larger scheme of things. I moved to India to re-evaluate my life and to reclaim the self-respect and confidence that Arun had robbed me of. Am I ready to allow another man into my life, even someone who is an old friend, for whom I have always had a soft spot?

I bite into a biscuit. I know that Vasu is a good man but am uncertain of what he is to me after the kiss—a lover, or something more? Do I see a future with him? What is my sub-conscious mind telling me? Am I done coping as a single parent? And what does he feel? Is he serious about wanting to settle down or did he act out of unbridled desire last night? I let out an exasperated sigh. I haven't the faintest answer to any of these questions crowding my head. But what I do know is that Vasu has given me hope, a fire in my heart that's going to be difficult to extinguish. Then a dark thought clouds over me like mist. I can't risk getting hurt again. It will kill me to get rejected by someone as wonderful as Vasu.

Twenty-eight

'I can't believe you guys didn't go all the way,' says Priya above the din of the voices in the mall.

We are at a coffee shop in the new mall that has opened in Vasant Vihar. I have dropped off Abhi in the play area that's just across from where we are sitting. At Rs 175 an hour, modern-day parenting doesn't come cheap in India. But it's also a convenient way for parents to catch up with their adult world while their kids play in these fancy, enclosed recreation areas.

'I should never have confided in you in the first place,' I grimace at Priya. I had called her last night when I could no longer control my confused state of mind.

'Is Vasu a good kisser?' asks Priya in a matter-of-fact tone, sipping her green tea.

'Focus, Priya, focus,' I scowl. 'I got a—'

'Is he or is he not?' she cuts me off impatiently.

'He is the world's greatest kisser, all right? Happy? Now can I move on?'

'You guys should have gone the whole nine yards,' she cribs.

Priya is so sensitively disposed towards her clients but can be absolutely frivolous and infuriating with me. But this is what makes our friendship so special. 'Okay, are you done with dispensing your advice?' I flash her a mock glare.

'Not the *Kamasutra* ones,' she retorts. 'There is a client of mine who is an expert in that sort of thing. Boy, does she know some moves to "please" her husband!'

My eyebrows lift. 'How do you know?'

'She showed me the stuff she can do with her Size Zero body during my power yoga class. I think *I* should become her student. It will be such a treat for Jo.' Priya winks at me. We erupt into a fit of giggles, attracting stares from the sophisticated elderly couple sitting at the next table.

'Vasu called me this morning, asking me out for a movie,' I say in a low voice.

Priya reaches across the table and squeezes my hand. 'So he *is* serious about you! That's great.'

I remain silent and take small sips from my teacup. Abhi is on the bouncy playing with two other boys who look a couple of years older than him. Young girls in yellow T-shirts and navy-blue trousers are guiding the smallest children onto the plastic horses and into something that looks like a lion's cave. The whole play area has been designed to look like a jungle.

Priya frowns. 'What is it? Why so glum?'

I shake my head. 'Nothing. Don't you think things are moving too fast?'

'Oh, Ira. At least you know the man is interested. Take all the time you want but don't close your mind to new possibilities.'

I rub my forehead. 'See, that's the thing. I am not ready to get hurt and dumped again. You know how wary I have become around men these days...I...I have trust issues...'

'But it's our Vasu we are talking about, not some random bloke who has landed at your door,' says Priya, a tad exasperatedly. 'Like that oaf Arun.'

I shake my head. 'Yes, Vasu is a dear friend and we have come to know each other better in these few weeks than we ever could while in college. But—'

'But what?' interrupts Priya.

I hold up my hand. 'Let me finish. I am done with living under the thumb of a man. The sole purpose of my life is not to dance and sing to a husband's every whim.' My voice rises and I jab my finger in the air. 'I need financial freedom, love, trust, respect, compatibility, and friendship in a marriage. And the man needs to accept and love Abhi as his own son. Don't you think that is a tall order?' I look defiantly at Priya.

She sits up with a jerk. 'Why do you jump to conclusions, Ira? Doesn't Vasu know enough about you by now?'

My face feels hot. 'It's easy for you to say this because you weren't married to someone like Arun.' I blink at her and mutter, 'Sorry, but you know what I mean.'

'Darling, if Arun had been my husband, he would have had

the pleasure of receiving several strategically placed karate chops from my toned legs. I would never have let him forget that I am a Black Belt.' We laugh. From the corner of one eye, I can see Abhi tenaciously trying to climb the bouncy's netted wall, clinging onto the net like a baby monkey. Ordinarily, I would have gone inside the play area and brought him down, but I am too caught up in our conversation to register the precarious nature of his moves.

'Marriage terrifies me, Priya,' I say. 'What if it doesn't work out again? Remember, I also need to keep in mind Abhi's welfare.'

Priya places her cup on the table. 'Just because Arun hurt you and dumped you and Abhi like factory rejects, doesn't mean all men are like that. You need to move on and place your faith in the *right* man.' She pauses and leans back in her chair. 'I know Vasu is very fond of Abhi because he told me the other day about a conversation he'd had with him. I interact a lot with people and can gauge such things. I am quite convinced Vasu is the right man for you. Trust me, it's karma that has reunited you both.'

My throat feels scratchy and my eyes mist over. 'My standards are too high now, Priya. If at all I remarry, the man has to love me and my child. Is that asking for too much?' I search her beautiful brown eyes as if the answer to my doubts lies there.

'Of course not, you goose!' Priya squeezes my hands again. 'Talk things over with Vasu. You absolutely must come clean with him about your past, your fears—be it money-related or just that crazy thing called love that you were denied in your marriage.' She points an admonishing finger at me. 'And you shall not be prejudiced and judgemental about him. Take your time and get to know him better. There is no pressure riding on either you or him.'

'And you know I am a marrying kind,' I add as an afterthought. 'I don't have the time or the inclination for one-night stands and frivolous dating.'

Priya smiles at me kindly. 'I know, sweetie. You will make a great wife to someone. Just go with the flow, don't follow a script for finding love.'

I consider Priya's words; they make sense. 'Okay, how about I give in this time and see where it goes? I will keep my mind open and talk things over with him—if it comes to that.'

Priya beams. 'Atta girl! Yes, that's the spirit.'

I grin at her. Just then I see Abhi topple from the net and fall on the bouncy. Priya and I run in a daze towards him. *It's my fault, it's my fault.* I scoop him up and hold him to my chest, uttering soothing words. Luckily, he is not hurt since he landed on the bouncy and not on any hard surface. But he is in a state of shock, as I am. Priya admonishes the young girls for not being alert enough to the potential danger the play area poses for small kids. 'Poor baby,' she coos to Abhi. She makes funny faces and tickles him under his chin. Abhi feebly giggles and responds to Priya's jokes. I sigh with relief and kiss my son.

As Priya drives us home, I mull over the conversation I've had with her. I feel lighter and more relaxed and I tell myself that all will be well. I cast a sidelong glance at her and notice the tenderness with which she is looking at Abhi who is sleeping in his car seat. She has always been fond of Abhi, but of late she has been displaying a side to her personality that borders on the maternal. I am about to ask her if she has made up her mind about having a child. But I stop myself short thinking that even amongst the best of friends, some confessions and secrets should come out spontaneously, not through being nosy and inquisitive. I am unable to bring myself to ask her directly, though I should be able to. I shall wait for Priya to talk to me about this... maybe she needs more time to think through such a life-changing decision.

Twenty-nine

Bumblebees re-opens after the Dusshera break on a crisp November morning that promises an early winter. There is an autumnal nip in the air as Abhi and I make our way across the dew-kissed lawns to the school gate. I love this time of the year when one can look forward to snuggling under Jaipuri razais, drinking unlimited cups of chai and treating oneself to hot jalebis at Haldirams. The pleasures of Delhi's winter are endless. In another fortnight, everyone's woollens will be out for the four-month season ahead of us.

Parents and children are crowding outside the gate and the teachers on duty are instructing the drivers to keep moving and not clog the narrow road. Mrs Sippy is all over the place, welcoming the children with hugs and exchanging polite hellos with the parents. Abhi runs ahead of me to his class, caught up in the excitement of his first day back at school. I hustle through the crowd and make my way to his classroom. Shelly opens her arms out to Abhi and gives him a bear hug.

She looks even younger in a smart new haircut with bangs accentuating her heart-shaped face.

'How are you, Ira?' she greets me warmly. I quickly get updated by her about Abhi's progress in school and wave her goodbye. There is no quarterly report card system here and the school gives one only at the time the child graduates to go to a 'Big School'. Shelly tells me to focus on Abhi's gross motor skills and encourage his musical abilities. 'He has a great ear for music,' she says.

The school music teacher is setting up his synthesizer under the banyan tree and I see Abhi and some of his friends dragging their small modhas over there. I hurry along, anxious to go home and get started with my office work. Someone touches my arm and I stiffen on seeing Avantika smiling at me through her headlamp-sized glares. My eyes move to her lips that are painted a vixen-red. She is wearing jeans and a red T-shirt so tight that her underwire-supported breasts are screaming for attention. I wonder what she wants from me.

Avantika lifts her glares and perches them on top of her forehead. 'Hi, Ira,' she says. 'We are celebrating Dad's Day at school next Saturday and would love to have all the dads participate in the event.'

My heart starts pounding and I can feel a thin film of sweat settling on my upper lip. Avantika's steely gaze is fixed on me, as if waiting to catch any slip-up on my part. Her clunky eyelashes look like they have got multiple coats of mascara. Her cheeks are brushed a dusty rose that starts from her temples and ends at her jawline. I keep staring at her make-up for, at some level, the overkill fascinates me. I think she has utilized the Dusshera break to pluck out almost all the hair on her eyebrows, for there are only two thin lines that look like they have been drawn with a pencil.

'So, please tell your husband about this. Vasu, right?' Avantika's voice interrupts my thoughts. I could swear that she almost giggled at the word 'husband'. *Bitch*. 'It's going to be a fun day for fathers and children.' She looks at me pointedly, her pout swelling by the second like some invisible bee is at work on her mouth.

I take a deep breath and force a smile out of me. 'This sounds great, Avantika. Whose idea was this?'

'Mine, sweetie,' she replies tartly and slides the glares down over her eyes. 'I suggested this to Mrs Sippy and she absolutely loved the idea. You know, we all need to acknowledge a dad's presence in a child's life. We should be more appreciative of what our husbands do for our kids.'

'Of course,' I say, in an even tone.

'So, anyway, I am in charge of the event and will be texting everyone a reminder closer to the date,' she says. 'Tell your hubs to participate, sweetie. Hope he is not going back to California...er...London?'

I squint my eyes in the morning light and for the umpteenth time try to fathom why she is doggedly interested in peeling off the layers of my personal life. Her eyes are obscured by the glares, though her smirking mouth is a dead giveaway about the private joke she is having at my expense. Something snaps within me and I return her simpering smile. 'My hubs wouldn't miss this for the world, Avantika.'

I leave her open-mouthed and a bit stunned, and walk out of the Bumblebees gate to my car.

Thirty

Oh, God, what have I done? Have I just smugly told Avantika that Abhi's 'dad'—my 'husband'—would be there for Dad's Day? *You moron.* Why do I so like taking her on? How difficult would it have been to tell her that my 'husband' was travelling? When did I start getting a kick out of such idiotic challenges? When did I start sacrificing my dignity at the feet of Bumblebees mothers? I pace up and down my balcony, thinking how I could wriggle out of the situation. Two things can happen if my 'husband' doesn't show up at the event due to 'some pressing work commitments':

1. Nothing. Life goes on as usual.

2. Avantika digs deeper and finds out that I am a single mom. Mrs Sippy learns about this and questions me about why I didn't disclose this vital information at the outset. The rest of the mommy brigade gets wind of it and ostracizes me from their group...forever. Liar, they smirk and turn their powdered noses up. Not that I am an 'insider' anyway, but whatever little access I have to these women will get cut off

and, more importantly, Abhi will suffer the brunt of the boycott. No more birthday parties or play dates for him. Even Josh, his best friend, may be advised by his mother to ignore Abhi.

I grip the balcony railing. No, I can't risk Abhi getting caught in this complicated mess I have created. I have to resolve this situation somehow without losing face before Avantika. Her mocking voice rings in my ears: 'Hope he is not going back to California...er...London?' I take a deep breath and close my eyes.There is only one person who can bail me out of this. *Vasu*. I go inside, sit at the dining table, and count to ten. Then I dial Vasu's number and wait for him to pick up.

Thirty-one

India Gate radiates a majestic ivory glow at this twilight hour. Vasu, Abhi and I walk on the crowded footpath, behind a newly-wed couple who amble along sharing an ice cream. Abhi is playing with a yo-yo that dangles from a flimsy elastic thread. He whirls it around a couple of times, its fluorescent yellow light blinks rapidly, the thread snaps and one half of the ball drops on the ground. Vasu picks it up and joins the two halves together. 'Here you go,' he grins at Abhi and hands it back to him.

'Thanks, Uncle,' says Abhi, promptly twirling the ball again, even though I tell him not to.

'If he doesn't twirl it, what fun is a yo-yo?' counters Vasu, turning to face me.

'I repeat, the fellow overcharged you,' I complain. 'Rs 20 for this flimsy thing?'

'Even these guys have to make their living, Ira,' replies Vasu with a small shrug.

I cluck my tongue in exasperation. There is no point in arguing with a developmental economist. A man approaches us, his arms weighed down by large plastic bags stuffed with yo-yos, trumpets, dolls, and other cheap toys. Like so many vendors whom I see at traffic lights, he is wearing a pair of devil's horns that glint red in the enveloping darkness. For some reason, these tacky horns give me the creeps. Abhi is so not asking for this!

'Amma, I want honns,' says Abhi, tugging at my hand.

'Nope, not today, chellum.'

'Yo-yo?' he looks at me hopefully.

'Hello? Isn't that what Uncle has just bought you, baby?' I say.

'One more yo-yo,' he pleads with his limpid eyes. 'Pleaaase?'

'I'm sorry, but it's a no,' I say firmly. 'Let's buy you a balloon instead.'

'Oh, come on, Ira, let the kid have another yo-yo if that's what he wants,' interjects Vasu, reaching into his trouser pocket for his wallet. 'What colour do you want, Abhi?'

'Umm…yellow. No, green!' Abhi smiles sweetly at Vasu. Bravo, my kid knows which side of the bread to butter, after all!

Vasu ends up buying Abhi a yo-yo, a trumpet and a balloon.

'What's up with you?' Vasu grins, seeing the sulk plastered on my face.

'You really spoil him, Vasu. I would not have bought him everything in one go. How will he learn to appreciate the value of things?'

Vasu puts an arm around me. 'You take life too seriously, lady. Chill, let Abhi enjoy his childhood. These days won't come back.'

'You make me sound like Tiger Mom,' I mumble good-naturedly. 'You have no idea; I am constantly playing the good cop and the bad cop.'

'Let me play the good cop today,' Vasu's eyes twinkle behind his glasses. I can't help but return his smile.

Abhi trumpets loudly. I put the yo-yos inside my handbag and Vasu carries the balloon. We make our way towards one of the lawns surrounding India Gate. We find a patch of relatively clean grass and sit down. Abhi drops the trumpet on my lap and takes the balloon from Vasu. To any passer-by, we could well be the average family out for a nice evening. But my insides are churning in anticipation of the 'small' favour I am going to ask Vasu. When I called him in the morning, I had suggested that we meet at India Gate. I wanted a neutral outdoor location where there would be ample exit routes to make a dash for my car in the event that Vasu erupted at the audacity of my request. If Vasu and I had a spat in a mall, it would attract too many stares. And after what had happened between us the other night, I can't trust myself to invite him over to my apartment. My eyes sweep over our surroundings. *This is perfect. There are many exits you could take, Ira. Take a few moments to locate your nearest exit. In the event of a scene, make a dash for your car. Inhale. Exhale. Inhale. Exhale. Inhale. Exh—'*

'Hey, what's up?' asks Vasu, snapping his fingers in front of me. 'You look pale.'

I remain silent and give him a dim smile.

'Would you like some popcorn?' Vasu gets up. I nod enthusiastically. He goes and returns with three packets of masala-sprinkled popcorn and a bottle of mango drink.

Barring the subtle accent and natty dress sense, I am surprised that nothing much has changed in him. He is as easy-going, grounded and charming as he used to be. Even his glasses are just an upgraded version of what he used to wear. I relive in my head moments of our shared past, with hazy images of our college classrooms, gang of friends and canteen scenes flashing like a film strip in front of my mind's eye.

'You haven't changed much,' I tell him, watching Abhi toss the balloon around in front of us.

'Is that a good or a bad thing?' he asks with a crooked smile.

'Good, all good,' I say, munching my popcorn.

'Hmm...but *you* have changed.' He says the words slowly and stretches out his legs on the grass.

My head jerks in his direction. 'Yeah? In what sense?'

'For one, you look much more attractive now than when we were in college.'

I throw popcorn at him. 'Cut it out, Vasu. You're not getting another kiss from me.'

'We'll see about that,' he states matter-of-factly, sending a shiver through me.

'All right, what else has changed about me?' I ask cautiously.

He takes a moment to think and shrugs. 'I don't know, there is a sense of calm in you, a quiet confidence, I think.' He looks serious when he says this, so I know he is not pulling my leg.

'I think Priya's Buddhist chants and yoga-shoga have rubbed off on me,' I reply. We laugh. Poor Priya, she always ends up being the butt of our jokes, and she knows it. But that is the great thing about true friendship, the liberty to laugh at one another and trade inside jokes.

'Isn't it nice that we have re-connected, Vasu?' I ask softly. I don't feel awkward even about the passionate moment we shared at my place. It is as if it was all pre-ordained. Destiny wanted us to be together but we had lost our way in the middle. There was a reason why I had to go through my bad marriage and Vasu his break-up with Usha. It has made us—at least me—realize the worth of our friendship.

Vasu smiles weakly. 'Trust me, I did think about you when I was in London. I would often wonder where you were. We were, after all, a great gang, especially in the first year...' he trails. I instinctively know that he is thinking about Usha. I can never forget the moment she walked into our classroom and changed the course of the friendship I shared with Vasu. My prejudice against Usha is difficult to shake off. I know it's immature but that is how the human heart and mind work. I decide to be brutal. 'If you did think about me, why didn't you reach out on Facebook or through one of our friends?'

Vasu gives me an inscrutable look and shrugs. 'You have got me there. I guess I am not a Facebook person. I can't imagine spending hours reading about what people are eating for lunch and their travel itinerary. That's just not me.'

I laugh. 'That's so true.'

'Usha and I had sort of cut ourselves off from our batchmates...we...we were blissful in our own bubble I suppose...' he elaborates. 'But after our break-up, I felt the need to come out of my shell and, luckily for me, I ran into Priya, and then you...' Our eyes meet momentarily. It's hard not to feel the unmistakable chemistry happening between us, making me feel a little breathless. To use Marc Anthony's words, I think I am 'crashing into love'. The feeling is at once exhilarating and scary. I want to ask Vasu if he ever sensed the breach in our friendship after Usha entered the picture. I want to confront him about that June afternoon when he and Usha had walked past me in the college corridor. I want to ask him the question that has tormented me for so many years: 'Did you really not see me standing there, Vasu?'

'Do you still play the guitar?' I ask instead.

Vasu's eyes light up. 'Oh, yeah. I was part of an amateur guitar club and have done some gigs with them.'

'Wow.'

'You know, Ira, that's what I miss most about London,' he stares into the distance in the twilight. 'This group was really good and helped me hone my skills.'

'Will you play *Hotel California* some day?' I ask quietly. 'I want Abhi to hear you play it. He loves music.'

'Of course,' he responds, 'though it would be nice to dedicate a number to us...our friendship.'

I hold his gaze, a thrill running down my spine. 'Which one?'

Vasu smiles mischievously, 'Keep guessing, I'll tell you at the right time.'

I jokingly roll my eyes at him. The very act of doing so reminds me of Avantika for some reason and I sit up with a jolt. The words that have flowed so freely and flirtatiously this evening now get choked in my throat. A panic rises inside me. I don't think I can talk to Vasu about this madcap quick-fix solution to my problem; it would just ruin the evening and, quite possibly, even our friendship. It is one thing to start dating Vasu, but quite another to take advantage of our relationship by putting this ridiculous proposition to him.

'Ira, can you please tell me what is suddenly bothering you?' Vasu's voice drifts towards me, as if from afar.

'Nothing,' I reply, refusing to look him in the eye. Abhi yawns and rests his head tiredly on my lap. 'I think we should leave now, Vasu. It's close to 8 o'clock and it's getting late for Abhi's dinnertime.'

I move to get up but Vasu gently clasps my hand. 'There is something that you wanted to discuss tonight, you'd said on the phone. Hope all is well with your family? Or is this about work?'

I shake my head. I mentally rehearse the lines I had wanted to speak but am unable to gather the courage to do so.

'Ira,' Vasu prods.

I draw in a deep breath. 'Wi…will you be my husband for a day? I…I mean, only for Bumblebees Dad's Day?' I squeak.

'Excuse me?' says Vasu, looking at once amused and confused. I repeat my question.

His eyebrows rise. 'Is this a proposal?' he asks.

'Yes, and a very indecent one at that,' I flush. 'Okay, here's the thing. Abhi's school is having a Dad's Day next Saturday and Abhi needs a dad—and I, a husband—to take along. All the dads will be there…'

Vasu takes a moment to digest this information. 'Doesn't the school know you are single?'

I sheepishly shake my head and drop my gaze to the ground. The heat rises to my cheeks. I would now have to disclose the bane of my existence—my Big Lie. Vasu will surely stop talking to me after this. God knows why our relationship always seems to be on the path to getting jinxed.

'If I have got it right, you want to, ahem, "rent" a husband, like they do in the movies?' asks Vasu, his mouth twitching in an incipient laugh.

I nod silently.

He gives me a pointed look. 'Is there a back story to this?' Oh, how the man can read me.

I smooth Abhi's hair and study his sweet sleeping face, blissfully unaware of his mother's embarrassing lie uttered in a moment of weakness.

I look up at Vasu. 'When I was new to Bumblebees, I did one of those things that I am not particularly proud of.' I relate what had happened at Java Lava at the beginning of Abhi's school year. I add in a small voice, 'I lied because I was ashamed to call myself a divorcee.'

A flash of understanding registers on Vasu's face. 'Ah, that explains it,' he remarks, rubbing his forehead. 'Your friend that night mistook me for your "*husband*".'

I make a wry face. 'Avantika is not my *friend*.'

Vasu and I catch each other's eyes and start laughing. The situation is quite comical, really, and I try to see the humour in it as Vasu does. I tell him about Avantika's inexplicable and unsatiated appetite for trying to unearth the truth about my 'husband'. I tell him about the smug manner in which she told me about Dad's Day and the unspoken challenge she has thrown my way to bring my 'husband' and Abhi's 'dad' along.

'So you took up her challenge and made me the guinea pig of your experiments?' Vasu surmises.

'You don't *have* to oblige if you don't want to,' I reply grumpily. 'But there is a chance that she probably still believes you are my husband—since she saw us together at Spiagga—which will make it easier for us to pull it off. Just for that one day...'

Vasu chuckles. 'She is no Miss Marple, Ira. I think you are overanalysing the situation—don't you think so?'

'No, Vasu. I don't want to underestimate Avantika's potential for mischief. It's important to carry on the lie as long as Abhi is in Bumblebees.'

Vasu hears me out patiently as I explain my reasons to him. We see the dwindling evening crowd of families and lovers making their exit towards the roads. A long line of ice cream vans is parked parallel to the road, their fluorescent lights streaking the horizon.

'I accept your proposal, Ira Krishna,' Vasu finally says with a theatrical flourish. 'It's ridiculous but let's do it! It's been a while since I have acted in plays—or dabbled in something as adventurous as this. I'll be honoured to be your husband and Abhi's father for Dad's Day.'

I am relieved to see the grin on his face. I squeeze his arm in gratitude, touched by his gesture.

'Oh, thank you, Vasu. Thank you,' I gush. 'I'm so sorry, I never thought I would get into such a mess.'

'Or get *me* into such a mess,' he responds with such a victimized expression that I have to laugh.

I wring my hands in my lap. 'You may wonder if acting as Abhi's dad for a day will scar his psyche or confuse him. But I have thought this through. It's only for a day and the event will be over in a few hours. I doubt if Abhi will even register all this at his age.'

'Don't worry too much about it,' Vasu says. 'You have made a decision, so stick to it without worrying too much about the repercussions.'

I nod. 'You are right, Vasu. I guess I must just go with the flow and see what happens. Worse things happen to kids these days than getting a hot dad on loan for a day.'

Vasu's eyes twinkle. 'Okay, wifey, let's get moving. I'd better start calling you that to get into character as actors do these days.'

I quite like the sound of 'wifey' but tell myself not to get carried away.

Vasu carries Abhi to my car and buckles him into his seat. Just as he is heading to his own car, the strangest thing happens which, in hindsight, makes me believe that God is really watching over me.

Thirty-two

'Vasu? Ira?' a voice calls out in the semi-lit road. We turn to see a heavyset man in jeans and a designer shirt. He looks a bit like Cyrus Broacha, only shorter. He grins and slaps Vasu on the back. 'You bugger, you don't remember me, do you?'

'Chinmay?' I ask tentatively, recognizing our college batchmate from his Facebook photos. As Chinmay clasps my hand in a powerful handshake, I notice he has a ring on almost each finger. Then I remember his Facebook posts that are all about numerology, gemmology, and astrology. Chinmay was the class joker and we would all take potshots at him for his weight, Govinda-like sartorial sense and obsession with astrology. But he was a sport and would always make us crack up with his self-deprecating humour.

'Chinmay Mittal? Wow, how great to see you, man!' says Vasu, enveloping him in an embrace. Vasu and Chinmay were particularly close since they used to take the same Delhi University-Special to college.

'Where are you these days?' he asks Vasu.

'World Bank,' says Vasu.

Chinmay stares at him, mouth agape. 'Sala! You are too much, yaar. Such high-achieving friends give me a complex.'

'How about you?' Vasu smiles.

Chinmay leans back against my car door and crosses his arms. 'Arré yaar, you know I was cut out for one thing only—business. After graduation I joined Papa's auto parts business in Pune. I have come to Delhi on some work.' He looks at me. 'You are in the publishing field, na? I saw your Facebook profile.'

'Yes, I am with World Ink,' I reply.

'Arré, then you will know my good friend, Svetlana Swaroop.' He pauses and adds in an awestruck voice. 'She is super-successful—I hear her books sell in lakhs.'

'Chinmay, if you don't mind my saying so, she is super-successful but she is also super-greedy,' I say tiredly. I can see I have grabbed Chinmay and Vasu's attention with my tactless statement.

'Arré yaar, why should Svetlana be greedy?' pooh-poohs Chinmay. 'Do you know who she is married to?'

'Yes, apparently to some industrialist in Pune,' I reply with a shrug.

The gemstones on Chinmay's fingers flash as he animatedly waves his hands. 'Not to *any* industrialist! The Swaroops are so wealthy that they can buy half of India. They own race courses, islands, and private jets. They are filthy rich, Ira! Filthy rich.'

Vinnie's constant badgering has set my nerves on edge over

Svetlana. 'If that is the case, then why is she quibbling over the money we are offering her for her next book?'

Vasu shoots a quizzical glance in my direction. 'What is this about?' he asks. I have not bothered to tell him about the Svetlana Crisis. I debate whether I should discuss this in Chinmay's presence, especially since he says Svetlana is his friend.

Seeing me hesitate, Chinmay ventures, 'It's okay, Ira. Let me know if there is any problem with Svetlana, she is like family to me. I could help.' I remain silent mulling over his words. I eventually decide to place my trust in him and rattle off the details of the Svetlana Crisis.

Chinmay chuckles softly. 'Do you know, Svetlana owns saris studded with diamonds? Why is she being so rigid about what you pay her? She should show her loyalty and solidarity with the publisher who has made her the star she is today.'

I nod gratefully at Chinmay, wishing Svetlana shared his sentiments.

'Is she signing up with another publisher?' asks Vasu.

'Yes, when the news is announced, it's going to be a publishing coup,' I say quietly. I take a deep breath, 'And D-Day for World Ink.'

Chinmay looks at me thoughtfully. 'Does Svetlana mean that much for World Ink's revenues?'

'Absolutely, she has really resurrected our company's growth.'

Chinmay gives me a blank look. 'Don't worry, I will see what I can do to help.'

I give him a small smile. Why would Svetlana listen to him even if he were her friend? It is impossible that he will be able to salvage the situation for me but I am touched by the initiative he has shown to step in.

'I will kill you if you mention my name, Chinmay,' I say. 'My name has to be kept absolutely confidential when you speak to her.'

'Of course, no worries on that score.' Chinmay wears a determined expression. 'I'll see what I can do. Svetlana owes me big time for something that happened many years ago.'

'What is that?' Vasu and I ask simultaneously.

Chinmay smiles mysteriously. 'I'll tell you if I am able to successfully convince the lady.'

Vasu and I exchange a bewildered look when, after a few minutes, Chinmay bids us goodbye and drives away into the city.

Thirty-three

Three days later, I am on the computer at night. I have just logged out of Skype after chatting with my parents and Anusha, and I am idly surfing Facebook. There are thirty-seven promotional emails from Avantika that I delete without reading. I think this woman is hell-bent on avenging some past-life bad karma of mine. Since she has created two separate Facebook pages for her business, my Inbox is unsparingly bombarded with urgent announcements of last-minute sales and deals that mean zilch to me. To make matters worse, she models for most of her collections and so there is no escaping Avantika whenever I am online—as if seeing her at school were not enough! Then there are the million photos of Rimli or of herself captured on her web camera that she keeps posting. She is a chronic show-off and I am itching to 'unlike' her pages and drop her from my Facebook list. But I am too chicken to do so, though I keep telling myself that this is the first thing I will do after Abhi graduates from Bumblebees. 'Unfriending' Avantika will get top billing even over buying Abhi's new school uniform.

All said and done, Facebook has served as a great timepass for me ever since Abhi joined Bumblebees. Compared to the Bumblebees mothers, all my other friends lead mind-numbingly boring lives. It's especially fun checking out the profiles of a particular group of Bumblebees mothers whom I call the 'Party Girls'. They plan weekend get-togethers at Hard Rock Café and other cool places, and pose collectively in their cocktail dresses and party frocks, even in children's birthday parties. They pout and preen before the camera, and never ever forget to wear their ornamental glares, even if they are indoors. These women are queens of a practised pose which, when I imitate it in front of the mirror, comes off like a shoulder dislocation. Riya's posts are always about what she and her gal pals do on a week-to-week basis. Her latest batch of photos shows the blast she, Hutoxi, Nikki and some other mothers from the twenty-something gang had at a trendy nightclub in Gurgaon. A lot of bonding seems to be happening amongst the hubbies as well and, of late, I have also been seeing photos of combined family vacations spent at beach resorts and hill stations.

Though Carol is the queen bee in the Bumblebees mothers' gang, she doesn't seem to figure in all the photos. I now understand why; she must be bogged down with managing the home front while her hubby globetrots. Ever since the day I overheard her phone conversation, Carol has been looking a little withdrawn and cheerless, though this has in no way hampered her sharp dressing style. I continue to see her mingling with her admirers at Bumblebees, though only I can discern that she is putting on a charade behind her bright smiles and confident gait. Earlier, her posts would be like a Reuter's wire for parents with young children. They would be full of links and advice on breastfeeding, disciplining issues, DIY projects, reading lists, nutrition charts and such. She would also post romantic quotes about happy couples, Bible psalms about love, and spontaneous gratitude notes for her husband. But these days, her posts read more like angry rants about the unfair balancing act women have to do to keep the family machinery running. She posts links to news websites and academic findings that conclude that it's women—the wives and the mothers—who have to sacrifice their interests to make their marriages work. She often shares links that throw figures to prove this:

- Sixty-six percent of women are sleep-deprived. They don't get any help from their husbands in household chores.
- Forty-three percent of women have had to give up their jobs after the children came along.
- Seventy-eight percent of women feel they need more sex and stimulation to keep their marriage alive.
- Fifty-seven percent of women feel their husbands cook up excuses to dodge parenting duties, like helping with homework and carpooling.
- Eighty-three percent of women feel they would be happier individuals if their husbands shared in the parenting and household responsibilities.

A new post just comes in from Carol: 'Life is one roller-coaster ride after another. How much coping can one woman do?'

Two minutes later, she posts another: 'In my opinion, being a mom counts as a full-time job. I demand that husbands pay salaries to their wives.'

Five minutes later, she posts this: 'How about sending the wife on an all-expenses paid trip to a spa while the husband manages the kids and home? Yeah, right. And pigs will fly.'

My insides squirm reading the posts that are like arrows being aimed at her husband. Carol has always come across as a proud mother and a doting wife. She must be under intense pressure that's making her express her angst on Facebook. I want to tell her that it's okay if she feels this way, but it's not advisable to let it all out on a public forum. Though I am not best friends with her, I feel a sense of camaraderie, perhaps due to her 'single-parent-like' situation. I know what it's like to do everything yourself and feel the life energy sapped from you. Motherhood is a communal journey and we women should not hesitate to compliment one another for a job well done—or to call out a word of caution before bloopers are committed. It's 9.25 pm and I wonder if it would be inappropriate to call her at this hour. But my fingers are already dialling her number.

'Hey Carol, this is Ira,' I say.

'Hi!' she sounds a little stunned to hear from me. We have never spoken on the phone before, though I have received plenty of SMSs from her whenever she mass-texts quotes on friendship, motherhood, greetings on festivals and even on occasions like World Contraception Day!

'Hope it's not too late?' I ask, my mind suddenly drawing a blank. God, I can never understand how I routinely get myself into sticky situations.

'Not at all...hope you are well? How is Abhi?' she asks.

I feel my mouth go dry. But at the same time I feel this maddening urge to reach out to her woman-to-woman, mother-to-mother.

'I hope you won't get me wrong when I say this, but you seem to be under a lot of stress lately. Just wanted to check if you are doing all right.'

She giggles nervously. 'What makes you say this?' I can sense the shutters coming down. Of course she won't confide in me. 'Everything is great; Anna and Saira have gone to bed. I was just whiling away my time on Facebook.'

I clear my throat. 'Look, I know it's inappropriate to poke my nose into other people's lives but I thought of calling you for a reason. I would like to believe that we mothers are battling with the same things and should look out for one another.' There, I have prepared the ground.

Carol draws in a quick breath. 'Sure.' She must be thinking I am talking in my sleep at this hour.

'Carol, of late I have noticed your posts on Facebook. It's like you are overburdened with home and parenting responsibilities...' I trail off, waiting for her to grasp my point. I drop my voice to a decibel. 'I just wanted to tell you that you are doing great with the kids. Please don't beat yourself up about the parenting stuff.' I am careful not to take her husband's name. There is no need to; Carol is astute enough to get my point.

There is a long silence at the other end. 'Hello?' I say. I am about to hang up, thinking Carol has disconnected when she speaks, 'Thanks for your concern, Ira.' Her tone is not patronizing or brusque.

Her voice quivers, 'I hate sounding like a woman who has lost her marbles, but...but things have been so hard on me in the last few months that I suppose I have stooped to washing dirty linen in public.' Her laughter is small and brittle. 'I never knew I was being so obvious when I started posting stuff on Facebook.'

'No, no, don't worry,' I hastily assure her. 'Probably because I am always used to seeing your cheery posts, the recent ones got me thinking. I'm sorry, this was really none of my business but I just *had* to call you tonight.'

Carol lets out her trademark, full-throated laugh. 'It's fine, Ira. That's what real friends do—look out for one another.'

A shiver of relief runs through me. It would have been embarrassing if Carol had snubbed me. But she seems mature enough to hear me out.

'Is there some way I could help you?' I ask.

'Yes, please don't tell anyone this,' she says in a small voice laced with desperation.

I shake my head. 'Of course not and besides, you have done no wrong, Carol. I wonder if anyone would have caught on.'

'You did!'

I am certainly not going to confess that I had overheard her conversation that day. 'You have just been completely stressed,' I say in a reassuring tone.

'Don't get me wrong, I absolutely adore George,' she adds urgently. 'But...but he has been so caught up in his career and travels that he has had no time for the family for months now. I end up being both parents to the kids, and the never-ending chores and responsibilities are killing me.'

I pace the bedroom. 'Of course you love him, Carol. There was never any doubt about that!' I add as an afterthought, 'Why don't you guys take a break and go on a vacation somewhere? It will help you bond.'

Carols clucks her tongue exasperatedly. 'George has been assigned additional responsibilities in his bank and it's such a task for him to spend even a weekend with us without his stupid Blackberry.'

'Hmm...'

'But we'll see, a trip somewhere would be great, provided he gets leave,' adds Carol.

'But why should you wait till then?' I ask. My intern days of assisting the Agony Aunt columnist have proved to be beneficial after all! 'Tag along with George on his next trip.'

'But the girls will miss school...'

'I think it's quite all right if they miss a week or two of school—they are still in the lower classes. It's more important for you all to be together as a family.'

Carol giggles. 'Oh Ira, now you've got me all excited about planning a vacation that might never happen. Damn you!'

We laugh.

She adds softly, 'Thanks for your call, Ira.' It's a short sentence but I know it is infused with gratitude and warmth.

When we finally hang up after a good one hour, I am convinced that a simple phone call is probably all it takes to bring disparate women together.

Thirty-four

I lean against a tree and follow Avantika's gaze as she devours Vasu. I see her looking at him with an acute longing in her eyes that I have never seen her reserve for even her own husband. I catch my breath as this odd little thought whizzes through my mind like a bullet.

Dad's Day is in full swing at Bumblebees and all the fathers are prepping up to participate in the 200-metre running race. Vasu is in conversation with Nikki's husband, Prince, whose gold chains and diamond studs glint in the morning light. Vasu radiates an electrifying masculine sex appeal in a sky-blue T-shirt, fitting jeans and sneakers. He is wearing sunglasses and kneels down to tighten his shoelaces. I feel lovesick just looking at him. Avantika, too, can't seem to take her eyes off him. My chest swells with pride. I am kicked about bringing my swashbuckling husband…er…fake husband to Bumblebees today.

My gaze wanders to Abhi who is playing with his friends near the swings. We are all gathered on the lawns opposite Bumblebees since the school grounds don't have enough space for holding races. The referee blows his whistle and the fathers make a dash to the finishing line where Mrs Sippy and all the teachers are gathered. As Vasu takes long athletic strides, I can't help noticing how fit he is. Except for his slight paunch, he is the perfect weight for his height. Cheers emanate from the finishing line. I have been so engrossed in my Mills & Boon thoughts that I missed the last few seconds of the race. I walk over to Vasu. 'Who won?' I ask.

'Yours truly came second,' he grins.

'Good job,' I hi-five. 'Who came first?'

'That guy.' Vasu points to a tall, wiry father whom I recognize as a father from the class adjoining Abhi's.

From the corner of one eye I see Avantika hovering nearby, and I am quick to fling my arms around Vasu's neck and coo loud enough for her to hear me, 'That was so wonderful, darling.' Vasu pulls me closer and wraps his arms around my waist. We stand like that for a few seconds, neither willing to release the other. I am no longer sure whether we are play-acting or acting naturally. Our lips almost touch but we reluctantly pull away remembering why we are here. Abhi comes running to us, his arms outstretched. I just hope he won't ruin the moment for me by calling Vasu, 'Uncle!' Vasu scoops up Abhi in one clean motion and places him on his shoulders. I turn to look at Avantika to ensure she is noticing all the father–son bonding that is happening. I catch her whispering something into Nivedita's ear. They run contemptuous eyes over me. I stand tall and smoothen my blue skirt that I have paired with a white top. Oh, grow up, ladies, I smile disdainfully and walk away.

After a lemon-and-spoon race, a tug-of-war between two teams of fathers, and a relay race, Mrs Sippy invites everyone inside the school for refreshments. I am surprised at the ease with which Vasu mingles with the other parents. It is as if we were really married to each other. I find myself wishing how nice it would be if we really ended up doing so. Despite the brave, independent woman front I present to the world, I have missed being a wife and would love to slip into that role again with the right man. I drain the lemon juice from my styrofoam cup and trash it in the bin. Yes, it will be nice to feel settled again. I gaze at the sweep of greyish-blue skies above for a message. I really wish I knew what the future holds for Vasu and me.

'We absolutely loved having you over, Vasu,' gushes Avantika, handing him a miniature gold cup for his performance in the 200-metre race. She looks at him coquettishly, like one would at a handsome man at a singles bar.

'My pleasure,' says Vasu, his sensual mouth lifting in a smile. To my utter delight, he grabs me and links his arm in mine. 'Shall we go home, baby?' he asks, looking deep into my eyes. It's with great difficulty that I resist giggling till we are safely at the school gate. I look over my shoulder and feel Avantika's heat on me.

'Ira: one; Avantika: zero,' I mutter under my breath and leave with Abhi and Vasu with a spring in my step.

Thirty-five

It's been a week since Dad's Day. Something magical and indefinable was sparked off between Vasu and me on that day that keeps us for long hours on the phone at night like two besotted teenagers. I guess it's that phase in a relationship where you simply want to—or *have* to—hear the other person's voice and feel reassured of their presence in your life. Vasu has been in the throes of a project that is taking him to Manila the day after and I have been caught up with my own work. But this doesn't deter us from our nightly phone call routine after Abhi has been tucked in.

I lightly touch my face with my fingertips and study myself in the bathroom mirror. There seems to be a glow on my face that can't be attributable solely to Delhi's crisp winter air. The last time I glowed like this was when I was pregnant. It is an unadulterated shine that I recognize as stemming from a far deeper place, like happiness. Or love. Nat King Cole's sonorous voice fills the house and my heart. *The Very Thought of You* stirs something within me and makes me want to believe in love. It makes me want to waltz with Vasu in a grand ballroom.

The phone rings, interrupting my romantic reverie. It's Priya.

'Hey, stranger,' I greet her. Priya and I haven't spoken in ages. There is so much she doesn't know yet about Vasu and me. She will squeal with delight if I tell her about the little show we put up on Dad's Day.

'Hey, Ira. Have you dropped Abhi in school already?' Priya asks.

'Yes, I am at home now. What's up?'

'Can you please drop whatever you are doing and come over to my place? Like now?'

'Are you okay?' I yelp in concern. 'Hope Jo is fine?'

'Yes, we both are fine. It would be great if you could come now. I'll explain everything when you get here.' Priya hangs up on a mysterious note. Within minutes, I am out the door like a shot and turning the key in the ignition.

When Priya opens her apartment door, she takes a step back and studies me, her eyes shining bright. 'Wow, you look resplendent. Your chakras look super-positive.'

'Thanks, though you'll have to explain later what that means.' I drop my handbag on Priya's dining table and squeeze her arms affectionately. 'So, why did you call me?'

'How about some tea first?' she smiles, going into the kitchen.

We both lean against the cool kitchen countertop, watching the water come to a boil. Priya adds a spoonful of masala tea, a sprig of tulsi and crushed cardamom peels.

'It has been a month since I missed my period,' Priya says quietly, turning to face me. The mellow morning light pours in through the window and turns Priya's irises an even warmer shade of honey brown. She strains the tea and hands me a cup.

'Whoa, woman, and you tell me only now?' I give her a big hug.

'I never even realized it until recently...' Priya trails off.

'Have you guys...um...been at it seriously?' I ask.

Priya rolls her eyes. 'Oh yeah, like hormonal rabbits.'

'So you did go with Jonathan's decision then,' I say with a smile.

Priya shrugs nonchalantly. 'You could say I myself got a bit enthu about this mommy business somewhere in the middle, and stopped using contraceptives.'

'Oh, Pri! Let's run to the chemist and buy you a pregnancy kit.'

Priya pulls a face. 'Been there, done that.'

'What are you waiting for then?'

'I couldn't do this by myself. That's why I called you, you moron!'

Half an hour later, when the two pink lines show up on the pregnancy strip, there is that frozen minute of hushed euphoria before we scream, squeal and bring the roof down.

Vinnie calls me just as I am approaching Bumblebees to pick up Abhi. I take her call with a sense of trepidation. It is such a mood dampener after Priya's celebratory news, which I am yet to savour fully.

'Morning, Vinnie,' I answer cautiously.

'Ira, you won't believe what has happened, darling,' Vinnie booms.

I park the car and get out. 'What?' It can't be too bad if she calls me 'darling'. She has never used endearments before.

'Svetlana is staying with us!'

A gigantic wave of relief crashes over me. I lean against my car and exhale from my mouth like I am surfacing for air after remaining underwater for ages.

'That's brilliant, Vinnie!' Wow, did Chinmay actually pull off the impossible? Or did Vinnie succeed of her own accord?

'How...how did you finally manage to convince her, Vinnie?' I ask, a little awestruck by the news.

'I don't know, beats me!' Vinnie pauses and adds wryly, 'I just pray the lady was not blind drunk.'

'Did you better the offer by any chance?'

'No, not by a paisa, which is why it's a miracle, isn't it?' Vinnie chuckles. 'World Ink will survive, Ira. The show will go on. And best of all, I don't need my Valium any more.'

'I am so thrilled, Vinnie. Congratulations!'

'And to you too, Ira, to you too.'

The first thing I do when I go home is fish out Chinmay's visiting card that he had given Vasu and me. When I finally hang up after talking to him for about an hour and a half, I sit stunned for a long time at my study desk. The sun is slipping away; the room feels ice cold even though all the windows are shut. I wrap my shawl tighter around me, wondering about life's strange circumstances. If I had not run into Chinmay, Svetlana would have moved out of World Ink. It sounds like an impossible sequence of events—too good to be true—but that's exactly what has transpired. We read about life's miracles happening to other people, but when one happens to you, you question its plausibility.

Svetlana's family and Chinmay's had been neighbours and close family friends during their growing-up years in Pune. Their fathers were business partners in the auto parts outfit they ran. Svetlana was seven years older than Chinmay and fondly considered him her younger brother. Though Chinmay was not academically inclined, he was a favourite of Svetlana's father, who was well known in their business circles as a strict disciplinarian. Having no sons, her father indulged Chinmay and took great pains to groom him for the business—more than his own father did. Apparently, during her younger days, Svetlana had been a stunningly attractive woman. I can well believe that remembering her gorgeous face from my meeting with her. Her dark brown eyes framed by thick lashes, her generous mouth, flawless skin and a curvy figure do make her an attractive package in the publishing business. Her good looks also work to her profile's advantage as the bestselling author of erotica. It seems she had been such a good-looker that men were constantly wooing her, much to her conservative parents' distress. Chinmay was the first to know when she fell in love with a college batchmate who was considered to be a no-gooder and rumoured even to do drugs. But, despite Chinmay's repeated pleas to Svetlana to dump him, she continued her torrid affair with that man. When she had eventually expressed her desire to marry him, she met with stiff family opposition and her father's thunderous wrath. Torn between love and her family, Svetlana impulsively ran away from home and was betrothed to that man. For almost a year following that shameful episode, there was no news from her. Her father disowned her and vowed never to take her back if she were to re-establish ties with the family. The only person she kept in touch with was Chinmay, who knew Svetlana was leading a pathetic existence in one of Mumbai's dilapidated chawls. He secretly sent her money for her monthly expenses and kept persuading her to leave her no-good fiancé.

When she finally broke ties with that man and returned to her family home in Pune, her father stuck to his word and refused to take her back. Shame-faced, miserable and penniless, Svetlana gratefully took refuge in Chinmay's home for a few months. Despite being neighbours, Svetlana's father refused to have anything to do with a daughter who had brought disrepute to their well-known business family. Though he was livid with Chinmay for sheltering his daughter, Svetlana's father continued to mentor him for the business that he was to take over eventually. Gradually, over a period of time, due to Chinmay's and his family's constant prodding, Svetlana's father came round and spoke to her for the first time during that year's Diwali. Amid tears, apologies and drama, she was reconciled with her family and went back to her own home. Soon after that, she was spotted at a family gathering by her present father-in-law, the noted industrialist Lalram Swaroop, who went to her house to ask for her hand in marriage with his eldest son, the dashing, US-returned Anil Swaroop. After Svetlana married into wealth equal to that of Kubera, her past misdeeds were forgotten by her father and the community at large.

Chinmay and Svetlana had remained in touch over the years. Though he had never asked for any favour from her, he always knew that he held a special place in her heart and that she still valued his advice.

'How did you convince her, Chinmay?' I asked in an incredulous tone.

'I reasoned with her that she was already blessed by Goddess Lakshmi, so why was she being greedy? How was an extra crore going to add to her already overflowing bank accounts?' Chinmay told me. 'I am a businessman and my reputation matters a lot to me. That's how I can get new clients and build up my business. So I told Svetlana that she should reconsider her decision to leave World Ink after all that the publisher had done for her as an author. Since wealth is already on her side, she should prove her loyalty and stick with you guys.'

'Did she immediately agree with you, Chinmay?' I asked.

'She heard me out patiently and called me after a week,' said Chinmay.

'What did she say?'

He chuckled. 'Chinmay bhai, tune mera emotional athyachar kar diya.'

Thirty-six

'Papa!' Abhi throws back the blanket and leaps out of bed at seven in the morning.

I stiffen and ask him in a nonchalant tone, 'Who is Papa, Abhi?'

'Vasu Uncle.' Abhi replies groggily, rubbing his eyes. He dashes to the bathroom to pee. He must have had a dream. He emerges from the bathroom chanting Papa, Papa, trying out the word like a new sound. I feel my throat constrict, even though I know Abhi is completely unaware of the real meaning of Papa—a simple enough word that is so hard to explain to my child.

'It's Vasu Uncle, baby. Not Papa,' I correct him gently.

'Vasu Uncle Papa,' retorts Abhi. 'Bianca says Vasu Uncle is my Papa.' Well done, Ira, for muddling your child's mind. And thank you, Bianca, for poking your button nose in affairs that don't concern you.

I look down tenderly at Abhi's face as my mind battles with complex emotions beyond his comprehension. 'Bianca is wrong, baby, it is Vasu Uncle.' My tone is firm this time, as if that would make things easier. I rub my forehead, obviously not enjoying this heavy-duty conversation so early in the morning. I grab a towel and lead him back to the bathroom for a shower.

An hour later, Abhi is eating his banana porridge while I pack his lunch and check his schoolbag for missing stationery. To my great relief, he seems to have forgotten the Papa topic. He is bundled up in a navy blue turtleneck sweater and a light jacket. I pull on my cardigan and collect my handbag from the sofa.

Once inside the car, Abhi shoots me a thoughtful look in the rear-view mirror. 'Amma, it is Vasu Uncle Papa.' Groan.

After I drop Abhi off at the gate, a group of Bumblebees mothers emerges like winter nymphs from the morning mist as they make their way across the lawns. They are in jeans and tights, their long pullovers clinging suggestively to their curves. I know this is the group that has now started going to the nearby park. It's hard not to overhear their chit-chat during my daily drop and pick-up. Until recently, they were part of a Pilates class and, before that, power yoga. As more women materialize at the gate, I note the winter fashion they have endorsed for this season, putting a lot of pressure on plain-Jane mothers like me: knee-high boots, printed scarves, cashmere sweaters, leather jackets, knitted dresses, and liquid leggings. I drive away thinking I should seriously consider doing a PhD on women's wear after this eye-opening year at Bumblebees. I have never before obsessed over appearance and clothes as I have done in recent months. At the next traffic light, I check my cell phone for messages. Vasu has messaged that he will be dropping in this evening before he leaves for Manila tomorrow. Sometimes I think things are going too fast between Vasu and me. But as the light turns green, I feel it's another eleven painful hours till we meet at night.

Ever wondered what you should do when the man you think you are in love with is on his Blackberry in your living room, while you unobtrusively study his face as you put away the dishes? The child is asleep and it is just the two of you in the 2,000-square-foot carpeted area, your very own fiefdom in Delhi's concrete jungle. This is so perfect, I sigh to myself. The man is on the phone, the child is sleeping, and the woman is cleaning the mess. A perfect family scene played out in so many homes across the world. As if on cue, Vasu looks up and smiles at me. A warmth settles on my neck and travels down to my spine.

'Need help?' he calls out.

'Nope, all done,' I walk over to him with a tray containing two mugs of hot chocolate. I settle down beside him and put my legs up on the table.

'You know, of all the exotic countries I have visited, I still feel there is no place like home,' says Vasu.

'Your own home or your country?' I ask, trying to grasp the metaphor.

'Both, I guess.'

I take a sip of the hot chocolate. 'Does all this travelling get to you, Vasu?'

'Sometimes, when there are long hauls and no decent vegetarian fare.'

'What do you do when there is no vegetarian food?'

'I drive to the nearest supermarket and buy canned tomato soup and bread.' He rubs his chin at a memory. 'I was once served a raw bamboo specialty at a colleague's home in Bangkok. His family was so solicitous that I felt compelled to polish it off even though it was all I could do to keep from puking.'

I shrug. 'When I was new in America, for a long time I mistook pepperoni pizza to be vegetarian. I thought the red topping was tomato, sprinkled with pepper.'

'Rookie mistake,' Vasu grins. He brushes a strand of hair from my face. 'So, are you on a better wicket with the Bumblebees moms, now that your "husband" finally showed up from *Cali*?' He mimics the way Avantika says California.

I giggle. 'Oh God, Vasu, I have no clue as to what sort of person I am turning into these days. I wonder why the approval of these women should have mattered so much to me that I lied about my divorce?'

'Ira, just come clean with them about being a divorcee. Why do you need to lie and kill yourself over it?' Vasu raises his eyebrows. 'We are supposed to be living in modern times!'

I pull a face. 'Too late to turn back the clock. We just had Dad's Day, remember?' We laugh at the memory. Then I remember how we felt a sense of urgency at our touch, how we almost kissed in front of everybody. The memory is so intense that I need to close my eyes and lean back on the sofa.

'Ira,' Vasu says softly in the dimly lit room. 'I will miss you and Abhi when I am away.'

I remain silent for a long moment. 'Vasu, do you really care about Abhi?' I eventually ask, searching his face for telltale signs of doubts.

His eyes widen in surprise. 'Of course. Why else would I have played his dad the other day?' he asks in a wounded tone. 'I have started caring so much for the little fellow.'

I lean on him. 'It's…it's important for me to know…you do know Abhi is my life…' I don't want to put undue pressure on him by sharing what Abhi told me this morning.

'Of course I know, sweetheart.' Vasu pulls me closer and looks into my eyes. 'I think I am falling in love with you.'

I feel giddy hearing this, as if I were floating in a dream. 'Me too,' I say shyly.

His fingers trail my collarbone. Our lips lock in a kiss. 'I would like us to take this slowly,' he whispers against my hair when we finally pull apart. 'Is that fine with you?'

'Yes,' I whisper back and bury my face in his shirt, dampening it with my tears. 'Yes.'

Thirty-seven

The most anticipated and dreaded time of the year is upon us Bumblebees parents. Delhi schools have thrown open their doors for Nursery admissions, making us scuttle around like headless chickens. Everybody is so busy that the mothers don't get a breather for even a cheek kiss or a coffee break.

There are fifteen schools on my shortlist and I have started doing the rounds of each for admission forms. Between work commitments, home, Abhi and Nursery admissions, I find it tough to connect with my parents on Skype. So there is a flurry of emails exchanged between us. I am told that Anusha is coming along splendidly in her final trimester and that the baby kicks like Beckham. My parents ask me again if Abhi and I can make it to London for Christmas. It's a tempting thought but I have too much going on here—most of all, Vasu. If my parents get a whiff of our romance, they will waste no time in booking a wedding hall and the nadaswaram players. Besides, such matters of the heart are best discussed in person and not on the phone. I really need to have a long chat with my mother to clear my head.

'Ira!' Carol calls out to me as I am about to get into my car.

'Hey,' I say.

Carol seems to be back in form these days. She looks resplendent in a baby pink knitted dress. Her hair is pulled back from her face making her look young enough to pass off as her daughters' older sister. She comes up to my car and hugs me. 'I just wanted to thank you for your concern the other night.'

'Oh, it was nothing,' I reply. I guess Carol took my advice to heart since her Facebook posts are no longer rants about the percentage of housewives who fantasize about strangling their husbands or about having an affair with the neighbour. She has bounced back to her newswire-like posts: links to WHO guidelines for swine flu testing in infants and fifty ways to boost creativity in children.

Carol wears a sheepish expression. 'I guess I was going a little crazy till you stopped me from making a complete ass of myself.'

I shrug. 'Don't we all make asses of ourselves sometimes?' I ask rhetorically.

Carol beams. 'Just wanted to tell you that the girls and I are joining George for a fortnight in Sydney. He is at a client site for a month and what you suggested got me thinking…'

'Wow, that sounds great!'

Her forehead creases in worry: her Alpha Mom personality makes a fleeting appearance. 'But Anna and Saira will lag behind in their schoolwork. I will miss out on Shelly's classwork updates, the PTA meetings at Saira's school, after-school activities and—'

'Carol,' I gently interrupt her. 'Just go and have fun with your family. That's far more important than homework and PTA meetings.' God, how does the DNA of such women work? I would take the next flight to Sydney, if I could!

Carol lets out a sigh. 'You are so right, Ira. I wish I were as chilled-out as you. Sometimes I sweat the small stuff too much for my own good.'

A compliment? Since when did Carol and her ilk start giving me compliments?

We hug Bumblebees mothers'-style. 'Take care and have fun, Carol. I can bring you up to speed on classwork and school activities once you are back. No worries there. Anna is not yet on the fast-track course for Harvard.' We laugh.

Seeing Carol's retreating back, I am reminded of the first time I had got acquainted with her at Java Lava. She had been the epitome of confidence and self-assuredness back then. It's hard to believe that, after all these months, it is I who have been instrumental—in a teensy way—in making her a happier person. Told you, motherhood is a level playing field and, notwithstanding the Steve Maddens and Zaras, every mother is equally vulnerable to its highs and lows.

Thirty-eight

Vasu called from Manila, suggesting that we throw a surprise party for the new parents-to-be, Priya and Jonathan, during the Christmas holidays. We planned to invite our common college friends since it would also serve as a perfect excuse for a reunion of sorts for our batch. Priya dropped in the other day to tell me that Jonathan is so over the moon with the news of their impending parenthood that he has already ordered a fancy crib on Amazon, and has stripped their kitchen cabinets of alcohol bottles! Priya—who had carefully planned her life to the exclusion of babies—seems to be slowly coming round to the notion of motherhood. Unlike Jonathan, she doesn't wear her happiness on her sleeve. Knowing her as well as I do, I can sense that she is cautiously happy about the life stirring within her. She is worried about how a baby will impact her life and career; how she will keep her sanity intact, having heard horror stories of colic, dirty diapers and breastfeeding till the nipples are sore. But I instinctively know she is going to turn to mush once the baby starts kicking. I now know that the brouhaha over the umbilical cord is not misplaced. While most women are quick to stake claim to an intuitive maternal instinct, a few take slightly longer to recognize it.

This seems to be the week of happy tidings. I finally receive a reply from Mrs Hiroo Zardari's son, Jay, in Ireland. His email to his mother is brief but heartfelt. It talks about wading through a mid-life crisis and about his quest to 'find himself' in the wake of job pressures, minor marital discords (that have now been resolved), and Siddy's upbringing. He deeply regrets having neglected his own mother, a person whom he 'respects, adores and worships'. I click open the Zip drive he has attached. It contains several photos of him, his wife, and Siddy. Mrs Zardari is right: her grandson is growing up to be a very handsome young man with his light eyes, chestnut hair and Celtic colouring that he has inherited from his Irish mother. But the best gift that Jay has sent is a scanned drawing by Siddy of a grandmother and her toddler grandson in a garden blooming with flowers. The handwritten heading in pencil says: 'To my Sweet Grandma. With all my love—Siddy.'

I get the photos developed, enclose a printout of the email and Siddy's drawing, put everything in an envelope and Speed-Post it to Mrs Zardari's address. It is my early Christmas present to her.

Thirty-nine

Abhi is terribly excited today. All the children from Bumblebees are going to the Rail Museum for a day trip. This is his first outing by school bus and even I am hurrying through the morning drill with great excitement. I pack Smileys and jam sandwiches in his lunch box and tuck a small Tetra Pak of mango juice into the side pouch of his rucksack. The children have been instructed to wear their blue sports T-shirts and trackpants with the Bumblebees logo, which they wear every Thursday for their tae kwon do classes. I swathe Abhi in thermals before I help him on with the sports uniform.

When we reach the school, five buses are already parked along the main road, and the teachers are making the kids form a line to board them. Parents are taking pictures of their children on their phones and cameras, and I follow suit. I had already charged my camera last night to take photos of this momentous occasion. As I have been observing of late, the parenting journey is replete with small astonishing moments that slip away like chimera. I make Abhi pose with his friends and click away. Then I take some of Shelly and Abhi together. Back to shooting some more of Abhi. Then I request someone to take pictures of Abhi and me. The scene plays out like camera calls for movie stars at Cannes. When Abhi finally boards the bus and waves out to me, I can see he is rather relieved to get away from his trigger-happy mother.

As soon as the last bus has departed, someone taps me on my shoulder. I turn around to see Nikki in a chic all-black ensemble, like a wealthy widow in a Hollywood film. 'Ira, I want to talk to you,' she says in a conspiratorial tone, her slanted eyes furtively scanning our surroundings. 'Do you have time to do coffee with me at City Market?' She is wearing her sunglasses and she flicks her hair with her acrylic nails. I feel like an agent in a hi-concept thriller. Is this my cue to slip a packet of cocaine into Nikki's handbag? I am a little taken aback by her request because I am normally not her first choice to 'do' coffee with.

Nikki touches my arm. 'Please,' she says, her eyes gently pleading behind the honey-tinted glares.

Ten minutes later we are at Brew, the same coffee shop where I had hung out with Carol, Nikki, Hutoxi, Riya, Tina, and Jasmine a few months ago. We order two lattes (double skim, no sugar for her) and smile awkwardly at each other. Some colour seems to have returned to Nikki's cheeks and she no longer looks frightfully pale and sickly. She clears her throat and rests her hands on the table. 'I...I saw you at Priya's Delhi Power Girls class that day and have been meaning to talk to you about something...' She glances at the tables around us to check for eavesdroppers.

I nod encouragingly.

She takes a deep breath and says in a rush, 'Please, Ira. Keep whatever you saw that day confidential. Please don't tell anyone about the self-esteem therapy that I am undergoing...' she trails off and looks at me with a tinge of embarrassment. 'Since you are Priya's business partner in this, you...you might be aware of my...umm...issues.' I bite back a smile at being called a business partner in Delhi Power Girls. Trust Priya to land me in another sticky issue—as if I didn't have enough of my own, self-created mess to contend with!

I reach across the table and lightly squeeze Nikki's arm. 'Please don't worry, Nikki. Your secrets are safe with me. I am as concerned about your welfare as Priya is.'

Nikki smiles. 'Thanks, Ira. I have been so worried. You know how it is in a place like Bumblebees...if the other mothers get to know, they will laugh at me.'

I feel a pang of sadness swell inside me. Are all of us women cut from the same cloth? Whether it is Nikki, Carol or me, why do we feel pressured to please others of our gender? Why do we feel the urge to fit in? Why can't we be square pegs in round holes? Why should we allow life to be a cookie cutter, stamping out all of us in identical shapes? Why should we buckle under pressure and lie about our husbands, weight problems, career woes, bank balances, and so many other irksome life issues that make us who we are—flawed, imperfect and vulnerable women?

I sit up straight. 'I don't think anyone will laugh at you, Nikki. But call me if anyone does. I'll promptly send them to Priya for a dressing-down.'

We laugh and sip our lattes. 'May I ask you some personal questions, Nikki?' I venture.

'Sure,' she says.

'How did you meet Prince? Are things fine between you guys?' I ask with the confidence of a professional counsellor like Priya. If only Nikki knew the self-esteem issues I myself am trying to overcome.

Nikki leans back on her sofa. 'You know, Ira, I had wanted to be a Bollywood actor,' she confesses shyly. 'I won the Miss Chandigarh title and thought I would land in Mumbai and try my luck in the movies. Kya pata, Yash Chopra ne mujhe dekh ke ek role diya toh?' She giggles.

I am fascinated. 'Then?'

'Bas, kuch nahin. My parents didn't allow me to even participate in the Miss India contest that year. They got me married to Prince. He came from a very wealthy family and why would my parents give up such a big catch?' She pauses and looks into the distance. 'I was only nineteen then, and I had Bianca soon after my marriage.'

'So yours was an arranged marriage,' I say.

She shrugs. 'You can say love-cum-arranged. Prince would be so romantic those days...he would buy me flowers...call me perfect...' Her voice cracks. 'And now all I hear from him is how fat I have become, how my nails are not done, my hair is not coloured, my stretch marks are visible when I wear a sari…' Her eyes turn misty.

'You are anything *but* fat and ungroomed!' I exclaim. 'I think your husband needs glasses.'

Nikki shakes her head. 'You don't know the pressures of high society, darling. Prince is a man and can get away with a big tummy but I am supposed to be the gorgeous wife who is perfectly put together.'

'Is he physically abusive?' I add a bit too hastily, 'Sorry, I ask because I am concerned about you.'

She shrugs nonchalantly. 'He was, sometimes, but not now.'

I flinch. 'Is Priya's coaching helping you?'

'Very much. Now I know I need to stand up for my rights.'

Atta girl! I feel myself warming up to Nikki and her innate earthiness that only a small-town upbringing can lend to one's personality. 'Good, you must come to me if there are any problems. Promise?'

'Promise,' she grins through her tears. She delicately dabs her eyes with a tissue.

'And please don't starve yourself, Nikki!' I admonish.

She gives me a wan smile. 'I am slowly learning how to treat my body and soul, Ira.'

'I can see Priya's words have rubbed off on you,' I grin.

'Ira…can I ask you for another favour?' Nikki says shyly.

'Sure.'

'I...I want to be well-read like you. Can you suggest some good books for me? I have never read English novels in my life. Priya says knowledge should be my soul food.'

I am touched at the honesty of her statement. 'Of course, let's get you started right away.'

Nikki insists on settling my bill after which we head out to the most popular bookshop in City Market to feed Nikki's famished soul.

Forty

Getting your child into a decent school at the Nursery level is like an obstacle race where the hoops and jumps are invisible. The admission forms are daunting, with trick questions like the values you would like to pass on to your child; the role you expect the school to play; your views on disciplining your child; and so on, and so forth. The questions are seemingly innocuous but can zap even the Mensa champs, PhDs, and rocket scientists among parents. These days, the only buzz I hear at Bumblebees pertains to which schools parents are applying to, and the chances of their child making it to the formidable portals of the crème-de-la-crème of Delhi schools. Never before have we unearthed so much background information on our fellow parents without indulging in gossip. I now know where the moms and dads in Abhi's class are from; their professions, their education; and the categories they qualify for: alma mater, girl child, siblings, neighbourhood and so on. I am probably the only privileged one in Bumblebees who gets five valuable points for being a single parent—damn, I can't even boast about it! I silently thank Arun for facilitating in getting these additional points.

Nursery admissions bring out the survival spirit in the meekest amongst us. Parents who were hitherto considered laid-back now display a daring streak of competitiveness. The pressure of getting into a good school is so immense that rumour mills are abuzz with stories of what so-and-so is doing to get his or her child into XYZ school. The word 'donation' floats around like a wisp of smoke. The underhand admissions procedure of a particular school that counts amongst the oldest in the city is discussed in hushed tones by parents who are in the know. The word is that this school accepts 'donations' for its sports facility, library, and computer labs only in lakhs. While most of us are ready to resign ourselves to our fate, some of us seem to have Plan B ready in case our children don't make it to any school of their choice. One of the mothers is planning to take advantage of her daughter's US citizenship for getting through to the American School, if all else fails. Many others have decided to retain their children in Bumblebees for an additional year and retry at next year's Nursery mela. The slim minority who smugly state that they are confident of making it to at least one leading school are looked at with unmasked envy.

When I go to pick up Abhi this afternoon, my head is spinning with an information overload on my shortlisted schools. For the last ten days I have been carrying a big blue folder containing school forms, photostat copies of a million documents—my marksheets, proof of address, our passports,

Abhi's birth certificate, passport photographs and essential stationery. I am obsessed with this folder and lug it around lest I need to make an impromptu dash to one of the schools. I am so engrossed in my thoughts today that I don't immediately respond to Riya calling out to me.

'Ira, wait,' she says, running to me.

'Hi, Riya.'

'My mother-in-law is holding a jagran for the Nursery admissions tomorrow—we are going to pray for the success of all the children in our class. Please come; I am inviting everybody.' She pulls out her new iPhone and texts me her address and other details for the jagran.

'Thanks, I think a jagran is a great idea,' I say. If that fails, we should all stand on one leg in the Himalayas and meditate.

Avantika walks over and greets Riya, coolly ignoring me. 'I have parcelled the sari and choli to your address, sweetie,' she says. 'You can pay me tomorrow.'

'Great, I'll wear them for the jagran,' says Riya.

'You'll pay me using a credit card or by cash?'

'Cash.'

'Okay, the bill is inside the parcel.'

This is not the first time I have heard Avantika conduct her business dealings at the school gate. I think it's a little tasteless to discuss payment issues openly, especially where friends are concerned. Then again, I have often wondered whether Avantika views any of these women as her friends. She is first and foremost a businesswoman and the mothers at Bumblebees—whom she has painstakingly cultivated—are her clients.

Riya is back to gushing over Avantika's hair while the latter preens and accepts the compliment, as if it were her legitimate due. It occurs to me that I have never heard Avantika return any compliment to Riya. Seeing Riya's reverent expression, I want to shake her shoulders and tell her to tread carefully around women like Avantika who equate friendship with the potential it offers for business dealings.

Just then the gate opens and a commotion breaks out as parents and maids move as one body to pick up their wards. These days, everyone seems to be in a bit of a rush due to the ongoing Nursery admissions, and even the most civilized amongst us don't hesitate to elbow our way roughly to the gate to pick up our children. I reach through the crowd and grab Abhi's hand, his water bottle, and school bag. Shelly hands me two folders with Abhi's artwork to take home. Only an hour after we reach home do I realize with a jolt that my precious blue folder is missing. I must have dropped it at the gate and it could either be at the school's lost and found or trashed by the sweeper. I will have to wait patiently until tomorrow to find out.

Forty-one

The school office doesn't have my folder, and the sweeper blinks at me when I inquire about it. My heart sinks, thinking of all the schools I would need to revisit to get the brochures; the number of forms I would have to download and re-fill; of re-ordering passport photos, photocopying the documents...essentially, re-starting the entire process. I thank my lucky stars that there were no originals in the folder.

Urvi approaches me as I walk towards my car. 'What's happened? Why are you looking so dukhi?'

I tell her. 'Oh no, that is going to be a lot of hard work,' she exclaims.

'Tell me about it. How many schools are you applying to?'

'Thirty! I am applying everywhere...in Delhi, Noida and Gurgaon.' Her voice drops to a whisper, 'We are seeing if we can use our "pull" anywhere.' She covers her mouth and giggles. 'You know what I mean.'

I smile, though my insides are in a twist. God, I wish

I had been more careful with the folder yesterday. Where could it be?

From the corner of my eye I see Avantika approaching us. Her hair is pulled back in a severe ponytail and her face is slathered with foundation. She tilts her chin and smiles patronizingly at us. There is something she is clutching to her chest. *My blue folder.*

'Hey, Ira, I think you dropped this yesterday,' she hands me the folder, her eyes narrowed on me for a reaction. Act cool, Ira. Act cool.

I take the folder from her as nonchalantly as possible. 'Thanks.'

'I saw you drop it yesterday, but by the time I could pick it up, you were gone.'

Liar. If you had seen me drop it, you could have called out to me immediately.

I am sure this was the moment Avantika had been waiting for and, thanks to my carelessness, this opportunity had presented itself beautifully to her yesterday. She rocks back on her heels and studies my face. Her teeth gleam like she has just used a whitening product—boy, does she look like the cat that has swallowed a canary! And at that instant I just know she has the vital information that could possibly topple my world.

'Ciao,' she gives me a withering smile, turns on her heels and walks away.

'Badi banti hai,' smirks Urvi at Avantika's retreating back.

I take leave of Urvi and walk across the lawn. With shaking hands I open the folder and rummage through its contents. Everything seems to be in order. I gingerly take out the one document that contains the key information Avantika has been so desperately trying to dig her talons into. Abhi's birth certificate. There, in the cursive font—typical of American government authorities—are the names of Abhi's parents. And the father is certainly not Vasu.

When I go to pick up Abhi a few hours later, Nikki and Carol are engrossed in conversation. Earlier, they would have given me the dreaded Bumblebees once-over and dismissed me with a toss of their pretty heads. But today they acknowledge me with genuine smiles that reach up to their eyes. However, I can't bring myself to smile back. My nerves are taut with worry about Avantika's next move. What will she do? Will she call all the mothers from our class and let slip the fact that Vasu is not Abhi's real father? I can already envision the pitying glances the women will throw at me. They would titter:

'Poor, Ira, why did she have to lie to us about her husband?'

'Who then was that hot guy she claimed to be her husband on Dad's Day?'

'Must have booked his services from hire-a-husband.com!'

Someone giggles, then another, and the giggles grow louder and louder till I feel as if my head will explode.

'Ira?'

Carol and Nikki are standing beside me, looking at me curiously.

'What's happened? You don't look too well,' says Carol.

I smile feebly. 'Nothing, just worried about Abhi's admission.'

Carol sighs. 'I know, but thank God Anna has been assured of a seat at Loreto Convent School. In fact, I am pretty certain that's where I will put her.'

Nikki remains silent but it's a given that Bianca will get into the leading school that takes hefty 'donations'.

Carol touches my arm. 'Since I will be off to Sydney this weekend, I thought we should all do coffee tomorrow. Let's drop the kids and head out to Brew. You must come, Ira.'

Nikki chirps, 'Great idea. We are not left with too much time at Bumblebees anyway.'

I feel even more dejected when I hear that. Abhi will be off to a big school and our leisurely mornings on the Churchill Lane lawns will soon come to an end. I will miss so many things about the whole Bumblebees experience, not excluding the nebulous ties I have just started forging with some of the mothers. It is sort of depressing that just as I am getting to enter their gated community, it is time to bid them adieu.

'So, shall we all meet at Brew at, say, 10-ish?' asks Carol.

'Yes,' chirps Nikki.

'Sure,' I say, without actually meaning to join them there. I am in no mood to socialize when my mind is in extreme turmoil.

A few minutes later, just after Abhi and I are buckled into our car seats, my eyes lock with Nivedita's. She is seated behind the wheel of her Honda City that is parked next to mine. Her narrow eyes bore laser rays through me, making me shiver involuntarily. To my utter horror, she silently mouths, 'I know'. And, pouf! She is off like a shot before I can even blink.

'Just tell them, Ira,' urges Vasu that night on the phone from Manila. I have rattled away all that has happened with the blue folder and what Nivedita tried to tell me. 'You are not doing yourself any favour by carrying on with this lie. I think you are losing your mind over it.'

Easy for him to say! He doesn't have to face a room full of dolled-up women and confess to something as pitiful as lying about a non-existent husband.

'I'll mull over it,' I say, sitting on my bed and running a brush through my hair.

'I just don't get your Bumblebees moms,' says Vasu for the umpteenth time that night. 'Why should their standards be like the ISO for you? '

'I don't know, that's just the way all this has panned out,' I remark with a combination of shame and irritation.

'Did that woman really mouth "I know" to you?'

'Yes, Vasu! It can mean only one thing: that she has learnt from Avantika about my lie. They are thick as thieves, so she must know.'

There is a moment's pause before Vasu comes on the line

again. 'Wow! I mean, simply wow! It's creepy, like you are in the middle of *I Know What You Did Last Summer*. I never knew Abhi's school was such an exciting place for even the adults.'

'I am screwed if I confess to the women and I am screwed if I don't,' I groan. 'Can you imagine my plight?'

'Ira, there is a line from *Jerry Maguire* that has stayed with me,' Vasu intones sofly.

'"You had me at hello?"' I ask. How I love that line!

'No. "Single mother man, that's a sacred thing." '

Something lodges in my throat, making it difficult to breathe.

'Just talk to them, Ira. There is nothing to be ashamed about.'

Forty-two

I have dressed with care this morning. Black corduroy trousers paired with a navy blue turtleneck sweater. I throw on a black jacket, and my recently purchased black slip-ons to complete my look. If there is one thing I have learnt from the swish Bumblebees mothers, it is to pay more attention to my appearance. It's quite admirable that, even after subjecting their bodies to the demands of pregnancy, they have not neglected their figures and grooming. They may still consider me as frumpy as a cow, but only I know how many extra minutes I spend in front of the mirror and the interest I now show in the correct fit of clothes. Priya and I have gone shopping a couple of times and there is much I have learnt from her, of which the most important is, that the first rule of dressing to kill is to wear your confidence king-sized.

I hold Abhi tight, unwilling to let him go. His warm breath caresses my cheek that has turned stone-cold in the morning air. I adjust his red monkey cap, kiss him and send him inside the Bumblebees gate. He walks a little distance and turns to blow me the biggest kiss his little mouth can manage.

'Love you too, baby,' I whisper, my breath making smoke loops in the light fog that hangs over the city. My teeth chatter in the frigid late November air as I walk to City Market. It's going to be a red-letter day for me—I have decided to confess to my Big Lie to the mothers gathered at Brew. Though my main interaction has been only with a few of them, there are other mothers from Abhi's class to whom I have mentioned in passing about a husband. I feel faint imagining Avantika and Nivedita spilling the beans before I do, and I take quick strides to reach the sidewalks of City Market. Vasu is right, I should get this load off my chest if I want to enjoy the remaining months at Bumblebees. I must do this for my peace of mind and self-respect. There is no shame in being a single mother. And it is so important for me to beat Avantika and Nivedita at the game.

Carol, Nikki and Hutoxi have already occupied the most comfortable corner at Brew. They greet me cheerily when I walk in. 'Hey, Ira, sit here,' says Carol, patting the seat next to hers. Her phone beeps. 'Uh-oh, Riya and Nivedita won't be able to make it since they are at Avantika's place,' she says.

I struggle to contain my happiness and relief.

'They must be checking out the clearance items from the last season,' remarks Hutoxi, a little snidely.

'What about the others from our class?' asks Nikki.

'They should be here soon, I guess. I'd texted everyone,' shrugs Carol.

Hutoxi signals to the waiter to take our orders.

While everybody lapses into animated chit-chat, I am a bundle of nerves. I look around at these women who, I now know, are not living in picture-perfect worlds. But at least they have not stooped to fabricating a husband. My heart is hammering. I feel unnerved at the thought of coming clean before them. Will I fall from their hard-earned grace? Will they tell their kids to stop playing with Abhi because of his mother's disgraceful lie? I straighten my shoulders and sit erect—I *have* to do this, whatever the repercussions.

I take a deep breath. 'Ladies,' I say in a small voice. 'I...I have something to say...um...confess.' All eyes turn to me.

'I...it...' I grapple for the right words and feel the heat rising to my cheeks.

The women exchange puzzled looks and wait for me to continue.

Before I lose my remaining nerve, I let it all out in a torrent: 'I am a divorcee. I don't have a husband in America who is trying to get transferred to India. It's actually my ex who lives there.' My eyes dart from one woman to the other, 'I am a single mom; I am sorry I lied to you all.'

There is no immediate reaction and I mentally brace myself to hear their barbed comments. I check their faces for mocking expressions, but there aren't any. I am taken by surprise when Carol leans over and hugs me. 'That's perfectly fine, Ira. But why did you have to lie to us about this?'

I shrug helplessly. 'I...I...didn't want to feel like a pariah in Bumblebees. You all seemed like such happily married women and I...I...too wanted to project the same image about myself. I was obviously not thinking clearly.'

'My dear, you didn't have to lie,' says Nikki. 'I think it's great you are managing as a single mom.' I shakily smile at her in gratitude.

'Yes, absolutely. It must be tough being a single parent, doing everything yourself,' shudders Carol. We exchange knowing looks.

Hutoxi's melancholic eyes are fixed on me. 'Ira, divorce can happen to the best of us. My sister is a single mother with two kids. It was tough at first when she had to fend for them, but now she is in a much happier zone. The older one is already in college.'

'Oh, I have quite a few of my friends from IIM who are divorced,' adds Carol breezily. 'It's common these days.'

I let out a small sigh of relief. I didn't know it is so cool to be a divorcee these days.

Nikki tilts her head thoughtfully. 'Then who was that man who came with you on Dad's Day? Prince was all praise for him.'

I catch the teasing expressions around me and sheepishly answer. 'After I had let slip this lie, I didn't know how to get out of the sticky situation. Like they say, one lie begets another, and before I knew it, I had roped in my close friend, Vasu, to act as my husband and Abhi's father for Dad's Day.'

There is a moment of awkward silence before Carol

speaks. 'But why did you feel pressurized to go to such lengths? Did you really think we would have sneered at your divorced status?'

The waiter arrives and serves us our orders.

I finally find my voice, 'To be very honest, I caved under pressure mainly because of Avantika.'

Hutoxi looks up from her coffee and frowns. 'Why?'

I shake my head. 'That woman seems to have some sort of vendetta going against me.' I tell them about the challenges Avantika constantly throws at me, having smelt something fishy about my marital status. I also tell them about how she had got hold of my folder and pieced together the puzzle about who my husband actually was—and leaked everything to Nivedita.

'Wow, is Avantika really up to all this?' asks Hutoxi in an incredulous tone. Carol and Nikki look equally intrigued.

I nod wordlessly.

'You know, Avantika is so full of herself that these days I just ignore her when she boasts about her business,' says Carol in a dismissive tone.

I am surprised to hear this from her since I had always considered her to be close to Avantika.

'Oh, it's always about her stupid saris and cholis,' adds Nikki. 'She is either trying to sell me something or make contacts through me.'

'I know!' chime Carol and Hutoxi.

We all laugh. It's refreshing to know I am not the only one who is not on Avantika's team.

'What about the millions of emails we receive?' Carol sniggers. 'They are downright annoying!'

Hutoxi leans forward conspiratorially, 'I am guessing you guys don't know about the skeletons in Avantika's closet.'

Suspense hangs like a heavy cloud in the air as we stare at her blankly.

'Her marriage to Promod is such a sham,' she states in a flat tone.

'How do you know?' asks Carol.

'Sweetie, she and I mingle in the same party circles and, somehow, such news gets around. Harbhajan knows someone who has the insider perspective on Avantika's marriage.'

'Sham in what sense?' I ask, my heart thumping. Is this why Avantika always tries to flirt with Vasu? A woman who is truly in love with her husband would not indulge in such behaviour.

Hutoxi wags an admonishing finger at us. 'Okay, so don't quote me on this, but word is that Avantika and Promod routinely...ahem..."see" other people.'

A stunned silence falls over us. I have read about swinging couples in Delhi, Noida and other places, but it's absolutely shocking to learn that Avantika—however loathsome she may be—indulges in it.

'Seriously?' Carol claps a hand to her mouth. 'Are they cool about what the other is doing?'

Hutoxi shrugs. 'Of course they are, why else are they still'—she makes quote marks in the air—'"happily" married?'

When the bill arrives, I am surprised that everyone

pays her individual share without arriving at complicated mathematical equations. I guess our brains are still processing what Hutoxi has just disclosed. I feel a lightness in my step as I walk with the others to Bumblebees. I can't believe I have finally got the load off my chest about something that has been rankling in me through the school year. But Hutoxi's scoop on Avantika has left me astounded. Never before have I felt so relieved and so shaken at the same time.

Forty-three

Priya is lying on my couch, lazily flipping channels. 'No way did Vasu pose as your husband!' she says, stopping at a Seinfeld re-run.

I can't wipe the smug grin off my face. 'That's exactly what he did, Pri.' Then I tell her about how I had been so bold as to confess before the Bumblebees mothers and about the newfound bonding among us.

She throws a cushion at me. 'Get out! I can't believe you didn't tell me all this sooner.'

I wear an apologetic grin. 'There was too much happening at the same time…'

'But this is just great. Told you, things would turn out fine with these women.' Priya grins. 'Jo and I have an ongoing bet about whether you and Vasu will marry in the next year or not. He says you'll marry after a year and I say you'll marry before that. I have ten thousand rupees riding on this, so you'd better not disappoint me, lady.'

'See? This is exactly why I didn't tell you.' I throw the cushion back at her.

There is a soft glow on Priya's face. She won't admit it yet—not even to herself—but the pregnancy has made her a happier person.

'So, are you guys dating?' she asks, propping an elbow on a cushion.

I look at her uncertainly. 'Looks like we are getting there, though I have no clue where we are headed. Honest.'

'Bullshit,' says Priya.

'What is that supposed to mean?' I ask.

'You analyse too much, Ira. Get on with it; go with what the Universe is telling you to do.'

'Which is...?'

Priya sits up with a small jerk. 'Marry Vasu, of course!'

I pull a rueful face. 'The M word scares the hell out of me, Pri. You know that.'

Priya reaches out and squeezes my hand. 'You have got to let go of your insecurities.' Her face deadpans. 'Heck, girl, make Vasu your *real* husband.'

Vasu calls the following day, announcing his return to Delhi.

'Hey, want to catch a movie tonight?' he asks.

'Which one?' I ask.

'Maybe the new Steve Martin film?'

The idea is tempting, starved as I am for a movie outing. And I adore Steve Martin. But what will I do with Abhi?

'Ira?'

'Um...maybe not tonight, Vasu. I don't want to take Abhi for an adult movie.'

'Abhi can come; it's not at all violent. I've read the reviews.'

'But it will still have some adult content, I'm sure. Besides, I don't believe he will sit through the entire movie,' I say.

'Then let's watch the new *Batman*. Abhi will like that.'

'Vasu!' I say with a giggle. 'I don't believe you know what a barely three-year-old should be watching.'

'Ira, even women love *Batman*,' replies Vasu exasperatedly.

'But Vasu, there is time enough for Abhi to join *The Dark Knight* fan club. For now, he is only allowed to watch kiddy stuff.'

Vasu sighs. 'All right, maybe you have a point there. Let's do this some other day.'

I feel a pang, knowing he was really looking forward to a movie.

'Hang on,' I say, before the line disconnects. 'Maybe I can check with Priya if she can watch Abhi for a couple of hours?'

'You sure?'

I hesitate for a microsecond, 'Absolutely. Let me call you back.'

Fifteen minutes later, I call Vasu to confirm our movie outing, or 'date' as a jubilant Priya had corrected me.

When I meet Vasu outside the theatre, he pulls me into a bear hug. God, I'm surprised at how much I have missed him, his scent and his touch. He hands me a big bag of goodies. It has soft toys and chocolates for Abhi and some perfume bottles for me.

'Thanks, Vasu,' I give him a peck on his cheek. 'I'll keep this in my car and come.'

When I return, he flashes two tickets at me.

I crinkle my nose. '*Batman*?'

'Steve Martin,' Vasu grins and leads me by my arm inside the Cineplex.

There are some moments in life that one is absolutely prepared for, like, say, a job interview. But then there are several others that often leave you stumped—even if you had secretly hoped for that very moment to occur in your life. So when, in the darkened movie hall, Vasu tenderly wraps his arm around me and leans towards me for a kiss, I stiffen at his touch. I feel frozen to my seat. Something holds me back from reciprocating to his overtures. It's like a floodgate of bad memories from a failed marriage has been thrown open, Arun's callous remarks poisonously floating between Vasu and me. I try to surrender to Vasu's kiss but, to my horror, find myself roughly brushing off his arm and clumsily rising to my feet. The bucket of popcorn we are sharing topples and spills on the floor, my blurred vision making me stumble on the steps leading to the exit door. As the hot tears stream down my face, I know I am terrified to take my relationship with Vasu to the next level. A little shiver travels to the base of my spine. What if this, too, doesn't work out?

Forty-four

I groggily get Abhi ready for school the next morning, trying not to dwell on my spectacular performance at the theatre. I barely slept at night, since I was constantly checking my phone for messages from Vasu. But shouldn't I be the one calling him to apologize?

'Amma,' says Abhi, snapping me back to the present. 'Don-waan jacket!' He wriggles out of his jacket and flings it on the floor. He squeals and runs all over the house. I pick up the jacket and chase after him to make him wear it. I scoop him up and point at the mist outside. 'See how cold it is? You have to wear your jacket, baby.' He sticks out his tongue and reluctantly allows me to bundle him up.

As we make our way to Bumblebees, I try to calm the thumping of my heart. What could be the reason for not hearing from Vasu? He could be busy, or he may have lost his phone, or he could be on a flight to Haiti. I feel sick thinking that he may never talk to me again. I will myself not to cry as I pull over at the Bumblebees car park. I want my mother now. Like, *right now*.

I decide to walk with Abhi to his class; it might help me clear my thoughts. It's freezing today—the snowfall raging in the Himalayas has hit the northern belt—and a heavy fog clouds our vision even at 8.30 am. I dig my hands deep into my jacket pockets as we take quick strides on the damp grass. A sense of déjà vu hits me when I see a group of mothers gathered at the entrance to Abhi's class. Carol, Nikki, Hutoxi, Avantika, Urvi, and Nivedita are huddled together in conversation. This is how it had all started at the orientation, I think with a wry smile. Abhi hangs his school bag on one of the hooks on the wall and runs to join his friends on the swings.

'Hiya, Ira,' says Avantika, waving her red fingertips in the air.

'Hi, Avantika,' I say. I take in her zebra-print dress, scarlet lips and sharply out-lined eyes. Her hair that has been teased into a volume looks more messy than stylish. She reminds me of someone…Cruella de Vil, minus the streaked hair and fur.

'Ira, Nivedita and I are captioning the photos from Dad's Day for the school noticeboard,' says Avantika. She pauses and gives me a withering smile. 'We need some of the dads' names who won the races. Your *husband's* name is Vasu, right?'

Her emphasis on the word 'husband' sounds like a snake's hiss. Nivedita sidles over to Avantika, her pen poised over her notepad. They wait for me to respond, their eyes running over me languidly, their lips twitching in mirthful anticipation.

I think of all the times these women have tried to snub

me, ridicule me and pry into my private life. I feel like yelling at them to shut up, but bite my tongue instead. Vasu's words come floating back to me: *Single mother man, that's a sacred thing*.

I tilt my chin mutinously and remark in a clipped tone, 'I don't have a husband, Avantika; I am a divorcee and a single mom.'

A hushed silence befalls the mommy gang. From the corner of one eye, I see Carol flashing me a thumbs up. Urvi stares at me in surprise. I fleetingly wonder how she will regard me henceforth. I shrug. Whatever! At least, I am no longer entangled in my own web of lies.

My gaze goes back to Avantika and Nivedita. Their jaws have dropped almost to the ground. They would never have expected me to confess before everybody. *Bravo, Ira*! Avantika, especially, looks flustered. 'But who is Vasu who came with you on Dad's Day?' she asks me with a challenge in her tone.

'Oh, Vasu? Just a friend,' I reply brightly.

Avantika frowns. 'Bu…but…you…you said he is—'

Carol taps Avantika lightly on her shoulder. 'You heard her, Avantika. Vasu is her friend.'

Avantika's eyes bore through Carol like a high-power drill. She is not used to being snubbed by the other mothers, especially Carol, the queen bee of our mommy gang.

'Is there any more information you require for the captions?' I ask innocently. Her face reddens like the Himachali apples the season has brought. She lowers her glares, presses her mouth in a tight smile, and strides off in a huff. Nivedita snaps shut her notepad and follows on Avantika's heels.

Avantika shoots me an icy glare over her shoulder. 'Liar,' she says, before vanishing into the morning fog.

Carol, Nikki, and Hutoxi join me as I double up with laughter. Seeing us laughing, Urvi also wears a broad grin, though I don't blame her for looking a little confused. Riya saunters in, her fingers thumb-dancing on her iPhone as usual. 'What's so funny?' she blinks in confusion. Thinking of her reverential disposition toward Avantika makes me laugh even harder. If only the poor girl knew what her role model was up to in her 'swinging' private life!

Forty-five

It's been a week since I met Vasu and I haven't had the nerve to call him. This is turning into a bad dream. Did I really brush him off and run away from the theatre like a woman possessed? If not for all the work that has piled up, I would have crumpled into a nervous wreck by now. Vinnie and I have been busy gearing up for the launch of my non-fiction imprint in January. There are marketing budgets to be finalized; press releases to be written; publicity tie-ups to be arranged; guest lists to be prepared; and a host of other things to sort out before the books hit the market. To my pleasant surprise, I can sense a newfound trust Vinnie has in me after the Svetlana coup—even though she is clueless about Chinmay's role in making this happen. She has been giving me additional responsibilities which, of course, translate into longer working hours. But I am happy to be swamped with work—this helps me keep my mind free of Vasu and going wild with anxiety.

It's a Saturday evening and I have been sitting at my desk and working on a book pitch for a few hours now.

I yawn and stretch my limbs. I need to get away from work and do something fun with Abhi this weekend. He is sprawled out on our bed, leafing through some books from the *Pepper* series. To my amazement, he has memorized all the lines in these books, even though he has yet to start reading. I really do want to cultivate a reading habit in him. I sometimes worry that this generation of Xbox kids will grow up never appreciating books and libraries.

I am startled when my cell phone rings. I'm a little disappointed that it's Priya. Will I ever hear from Vasu again?

'Hey, what's up?' I ask listlessly.

'Ira, how soon can you make it to my place?' she says.

I panic, hoping all is well with her baby. Then I remember getting a similar SOS call from her on the day we confirmed her pregnancy.

'Is all well, Pri? I told you not to strain yourself!'

'Oh, things are fabulous. This is not about the baby, silly.'

I exhale in relief. 'Why do you want me to come then?'

'I am going on a business trip to Mumbai to meet with a potential celebrity client. Wanted your help in putting together my wardrobe.'

I giggle, 'I am hardly a fashionista. Why would *you* need my help?'

Priya clucks her tongue impatiently. 'Oof, are you coming to help the pregnant lady or not?'

Forty minutes later, Abhi gingerly tip-toes and rings the doorbell outside Priya's apartment. Expecting Priya, I am poised to give her a hug when the door cracks open. Instead, I almost fall into Vasu's waiting arms.

Forty-six

'Vasu?' I stare at him in disbelief and joy, gently stepping back to study his handsome face in the saffron light of dusk.

He grins. 'Last I checked, that was my name.' His eyes are warm as he looks at me. My throat feels tight. *How much I have missed him.*

He picks up Abhi and kisses him. 'How are you, champ?'

'Fine. Uncle, you know, I am Santa's reindeer,' says Abhi.

'Abhi is one of the reindeer for his school Christmas programme,' I explain.

'Wow, is your name Rudolph by any chance?' says Vasu.

'No, it's Abhi!'

'Hmm...but I think you have a red nose.'

Abhi giggles. 'No, *you* have a red nose.' He wriggles out of Vasu's hands and runs to the toy corner in the lobby area. He pulls out a bucket of Lego blocks. Priya has thoughtfully created a toy corner for Abhi and stacked the cane shelves with age-appropriate puzzles, blocks, books, and toys for his entertainment.

'Priya?' I walk around the apartment, searching for her. Neither she nor Jo seems to be home. I look bewilderedly at Vasu. 'She just called asking me to come over immediately. Do you know where she is?'

Vasu clears his throat. 'Priya and Jo have stepped out. They...um...wanted to give us some privacy,' he says.

I raise my eyebrows in surprise as understanding dawns on me. 'Really? Wait till I get her,' I mutter in a mock-annoyed tone.

Vasu wears a boyish grin, 'Actually, it was my idea this time.'

I look at him questioningly.

'After seeing you flee from me like I were Satan himself, I wasn't sure if you ever wanted to see me again,' he says, running his fingers through his hair. He wears such a lost-puppy expression that I laugh.

I clasp his hand firmly in mine. 'I am so sorry for running away like that, Vasu. I...my mind was a little muddled up that night.'

'A little?' he asks and we laugh.

We go to the living room and sit on the couch. The light is fading outside and I switch on the side-table lamps. I love winter evenings; the world seems perfect in the cosy, warm glow of Priya's immaculately kept living room.

'So tell me, Ira. What is it that's holding you back from committing to me?' Vasu looks at me earnestly. 'I wanted to have a frank conversation with you before I left.'

My heart lurches. 'Where are you going?'

'I'm going for ten days to the World Bank's Washington, DC office.' Catching my sullen expression he adds, 'Only ten days, sweetheart. I'll be back to help you organize the surprise party for Priya and Jo.'

My face lights up at the thought. I want to pull out all the stops and make this the most special party ever for my friend.

Vasu takes my hand in his. 'So what is it that's holding you back from committing to me?' he repeats his question.

I bite my lip, trying to pin down my buzzing thoughts. I want to talk to him about having financial independence and the liberty to exercise my choice, voice my opinions, if we were to be in a serious relationship. But I decide these heavy discussions can be had another day.

I take a deep breath, 'I am absolutely terrified of things not working out for me again. You could say I have become a bit paranoid after my failed marriage. What if we were to break up, Vasu? Where would that leave me and Abhi?' I meet his gaze and blink. 'And you?'

Vasu's dark expressive eyes are fixed on me. 'I love you, Ira,' he whispers. 'There is no question of us breaking up... because, we were meant to be.' He says it with so much conviction that it sends a current through my body. I bury my face in his chest and hear the rhythmic beating of his heart. 'God, I love you too, Vasu,' I feverishly whisper back, my hand resting on his chest. 'I do...I do...even if it seems like I am running away from you.'

'Well, you did run away the last time,' he says with a twinkle in his eyes.

'True, guilty as charged,' I smile. Then I look at him with some apprehension. 'Vasu, I want to take this slow and easy… don't want to rush into anything, even though I am bonkers about you.'

Vasu cocks an eyebrow at me. 'Really? Am I that irresistible?'

I give his arm a light rap. 'Don't fish for compliments, mister.'

'Ira, I would marry you today, if I had your consent,' he says in a matter-of-fact tone. I see honesty and love in his eyes, and a wave of guilt washes over me. I want to cry with happiness. When I had tearfully wound up my life in the US and taken the sixteen-hour trans-Atlantic flight to India with only fatigue and a sense of loss over my marriage pounding in my veins, I would never have thought that I would find the love of my life.

'I…I am sorry for being so ambivalent, Vasu. I—'

He puts his finger on my lips. 'Don't be sorry. I respect what you have gone through earlier, and would like you to take this one step at a time.' His eyes flicker with passion. 'But I do hope to marry you one day and become a real father to Abhi.' He wags his finger with a deadpan expression, 'Not a fake dad for his school functions.' I flush and we laugh.

Vasu leans over and tenderly presses his lips to mine. I savour the kiss like it were the first spring shower. When his fingers trail dangerously close to my neckline, I pull away with a giggle, 'All hanky-panky will have to wait. There is a kid in our midst.'

Vasu rises to his feet. 'I have a surprise for you and Abhi,' he says. He goes away and returns with his guitar. Abhi comes charging behind him. 'Gittaarr, gittaarr!' he cries happily. 'I am a rock star!' he shouts. He hops on the couch and flails his arms in Bon Jovi style. I wonder where he has learnt all this from. Maybe I have watched the *Rockstar* promos one time too often on TV?

When Vasu sits on the sofa and strums the opening riff of *Hotel California*, I feel the goosebumps on my arms. It's like the clock has been rewound and I'm listening to him on our college campus again. Hearing Vasu lend his deep vocals to this classic rock number has us mesmerized. The evening wears on with Vasu playing popular Hindi and English numbers, and even nursery rhymes at Abhi's request.

'What is the number you said you'd dedicate to us?' I ask when Vasu takes a break.

'*Lady* by Kenny Rogers,' he says and proceeds to play the song for me.

Whenever my eyes meet Vasu's over the melodious notes he is strumming, I can't help feeling that all is okay with this tiny world that we are trying to create: Papa Bear, Mama Bear, and Baby Bear.

Forty-seven

I feel guilty about keeping my parents and Anusha in the dark about Vasu. 'Amma, I want to tell you something when you and Appa return to India,' I tell my mother. We have just got on to Skype.

'What? Hope all is well?' she asks with concern.

'Of course, Amma, don't worry. But it's something I can discuss with you only in person.' I smile to myself thinking how ballistic with joy my parents will be when they learn about Vasu. But I don't want to raise any hopes. I deliberate over telling Anusha, but decide that my mother should hear it first.

'Ira, why don't you try and join us for New Year?' my father joins the conversation. 'We would like you to be present to welcome Anusha's baby. You know your mother and I are longing to see Abhi.'

'I too would love to come, Appa, but work is very tight. Sorry,' I reply. And I can't bear to be away from Vasu. Of course I don't say this out loud!

My mother cajoles, 'Think about coming here for a short break, Ira. Maybe we can all fly back to India together?'

'Sure, Amma, let me think about it,' I say cheerily to humour her.

Abhi comes on the line and regales my parents, Anusha and Venkat with all that occupies his world.

'Is your mom strict, Abhi?' Venkat asks in a teasing tone before we disconnect.

Abhi crinkles his nose in thought. 'Hmm...*sometimes*, when I am out of control,' he says in all seriousness. We all laugh.

I feel happiness swelling in me seeing the sunny day outside. It's a welcome respite after the freezing spell we've been having in recent weeks. Today is the Bumblebees annual Christmas carnival and Abhi nudged me awake at 6 o'clock to help him wear the reindeer costume the school has given. I look at the clock. It's 8.15. Vasu should be here any time now to pick us up. Priya and Jo are also coming for the programme. I hug myself with joy. I feel blessed to have such great friends who are my extended family in Delhi. My face grows warm thinking of Vasu and the way he makes me feel: special, beautiful and loved. My family will never understand why I should dither over marrying such a great guy. Sometimes even I feel I am taking a very cautious approach with regard to Vasu. But, like they say, once bitten, twice shy.

Abhi is chewing on his cheese toast, the reindeer horns bobbing on his head. He looks incredibly cute in his brown jumpsuit and the reindeer horns' headband. I must have taken at least fifty photos of him.

I give myself a long look in the full-length mirror in the bedroom. I run the brush one last time through my shoulder-length hair that I have left untied. I have chosen a flowing red-and-black mirror-work Gurjari skirt and teamed it with a black turtleneck sweater, over which I'm wearing a maroon quilted Nehru jacket. In my ears dangle the red jhumkas Priya had gifted me after a weekend trip to Jaipur with Jo. They have been going on short babymoons, wanting to spend quality time together before the baby arrives. Vasu and I have been working hard at organizing the surprise party for them at my place and have managed to get confirmation from twenty-odd friends from college, which is not a bad number for my jet-setting generation of professionals. What I am most looking forward to is Vasu playing the guitar that evening.

When the doorbell rings, I retouch my lipstick and rush to open the door.

'Hey, gorgeous,' says Vasu, hugging me. He looks groovy in his khaki Dockers and a navy blue blazer. 'Where is our little reindeer?'

Abhi comes running into Vasu's open arms, 'Here I am!'

We hurriedly leave the house, wanting to beat the rush hour traffic.

I have never seen Bumblebees wear such a celebratory look. The atmosphere is rife with triple the merriment that had prevailed on orientation day. A huge man dressed like Santa is milling about, distributing candies to the children. Rows and rows of chairs have been arranged on the school lawns, facing a make-shift stage where the kids will soon perform. The clientele of Bumblebees being what it is, the sophisticated crowd of parents and grandparents has turned out in their most elegant winter wear. Needless to say, the Bumblebees mothers have taken extra care to outrival each other today in the wardrobe department. Urvi is in dazzling Indian wear that looks like an Anokhi find. I spot a beaming Carol with her family at a distance. She is attired in a smart leather jacket, denims and knee-length boots. Her hair has been streaked a honey brown and goes well with her bronzed skin—looks like she has acquired a nice tan on the beaches of Australia. Our eyes meet and we wave to each other. Nikki comes over and gives me a hug. She is wearing a plaid miniskirt and a short suede jacket over black leggings. She approves of Vasu with a covert wink and a thumbs up. I am relieved to note she looks so much more filled out these days. I carefully take in Prince's plaited gold chains and the protective manner in which he has his arm wrapped around Nikki. I can only hope this man is treating his wife well.

While Vasu goes to find seats for us, I walk up to Mrs Sippy and exchange pleasantries with her. She is as elegant as ever and asks me about my experience with the Nursery admissions. A teacher comes on stage to request everybody to take their seats. I walk between the rows of chairs to where Vasu is seated, third row from the front. I am touched to see that he has brought his camcorder along. I give his arm a tight squeeze and whisper 'Love you' into his ear. He takes my hand and kisses it in response. My eyes search the crowd for Priya and Jo. 'Where are you?' I text Priya. 'Seated right at the back', she texts back. I am relieved that she won't be standing in the aisles for the entire show like so many latecomers.

Someone taps me from behind. It's Mrs Hiroo Zardari looking the most cheerful that I have ever seen her so far. 'I knew our Abhi would be performing and didn't want to miss it for the world,' she says. Her wrinkled face breaks out into a broad grin. Her bony hand rests on my shoulder. 'I can never thank you enough, my dear, for connecting me with my son and grandson.'

I shake my head. 'Not at all, Aunty. It was all my pleasure,' I assure her. She excitedly tells me that Jay and Siddy are visiting her in January and she will invite me home when they are here.

Just then the first batch of students comes out to perform and the chatter in the audience ceases. As the children take their positions on stage, I feel a mellow sense of calm settling on me. When Abhi and I were new to Bumblebees, I remember feeling lost and alienated in this plush playschool that looked like an entirely new world to me. It is hard to believe that along the way, I have somehow managed to forge genuine friendships with some of the Bumblebees mothers who used to intimidate me not so long ago. I cast a sideways glance at Vasu's handsome profile. And who would have thought

I would find Mr Right within months of my journey as Independent Career Woman / Tough Single Mother in India? Yes, life has come up smelling of roses, after all.

When Abhi comes on stage with his friends, Vasu and I cheer loudly with the other class parents. Abhi is wearing light make-up and has whiskers drawn on his face. My heart swells with pride when he does his little solo number with confidence and style, and the audience applauds his performance. Vasu's camcorder is trained on Abhi till we see the last of his short furry tail vanishing down the exit steps.

An hour later, when the programme ends, the crowd scatters in the school grounds. Priya and Jo join Vasu and me, and we all march to Abhi's class to find him. I lift Abhi and give him a big kiss. Vasu puts his arms around both of us. Just then Priya's camera flashes. She gives me a radiant smile and shouts, 'Picture-perfect family', to the amusement of everybody around.

We all thank Shelly for doing a great job with the kids and start making our way to the gate. I can sense someone's frosty gaze on me and swivel to see who it is. Avantika. She gives me a dismissive once-over and looks at Vasu with an expression that is clearly one of unbridled desire. There is unmasked envy in her eyes seeing Vasu and me together. How did *he* pick *you?* she seems to ask. I smile, remembering being dropped from Avantika's Facebook list within minutes of my snubbing her the other day. I did a small jig that day knowing I would no longer be bombarded with her crazy promotional emails. I throw Avantika a snickering look and toss my hair with attitude, like I've seen her do umpteen times.

The melodious strains of 'Joy to the World' float towards us as Vasu, Abhi and I make our way out of the Bumblebees gate. I lift Abhi and smother him with kisses. 'Told you, baby, we'd make it.' Abhi flings his arms around me and kisses me back with happiness.

Acknowledgements

I would like to express my sincere gratitude to the many people who saw me through this book:

First and foremost, I would like to thank my beautiful Amma for being the outstanding human being and mother that she is. She has always been my first reader and the biggest champion of my writing. Her remarkable courage and grace are traits I wish I had inherited. My deepest gratitude to her for so lovingly raising her grandson whenever his mother would escape to the fictional world that had become her alternate reality. It is only because of my mother's generous ways that I was able to write the book, and I can't thank her enough for everything she has done for me. Amma, I salute you.

To my loving Appa—a man-in-a-million—for being the other pillar of strength for me. His constant encouragement, pep talk and advice greatly fuelled my writing process. I shall be eternally indebted to him for, among other things, all the impromptu dictations he had given me during my school years and for filling our home with such stellar works of literature.

I am so grateful to my parents for pushing me to achieve when on most days I was ready to give up. This book happened only because of them.

Aparna and Sai: What can I say? Their several acts of generosity, love and kindness fill my heart with gratitude. I wish to thank them for sharing their beautiful Himalayan abode with me—now I too can say that I retreated to the hills to write and recharge my batteries! Thanks also for having Antariksh over for play dates to help me reach the finish line.

My sincere thanks to Mama and Mami for their steadfast support and encouragement. Mahesh and Gayatri, thanks so much for being there for me.

My deepest thanks to Milee Ashwarya for so enthusiastically believing in my work from the word go. Heartfelt thanks to my editor, Trisha Bora, for her patience and support through the period it took me to complete the book. She and Milee were truly understanding of the demands on my time, and I wish all authors get to enjoy this kind of support from their publishing house.

A huge thank you to the extremely talented Roopa Sachidanand for designing such a gorgeous book jacket. You were meant for this book.

I am truly grateful to my distinguished colleagues at work for their kind support and encouragement: Mr R.K. Mehra, David Davidar, Ravi Singh and Kapish Mehra. Thank you for so generously allowing me to play the dual role of an author and editor.

And finally, the real star behind *Mom in the City* is

Antariksh, my deeply affectionate, funny and precocious little boy. Thank you, baby, for putting up with my long hours on the computer; for displaying so much kindness, patience and wisdom far beyond your years. Your hugs, laugh, and kisses are what kept me going. I love you so much, my darling son. A sweeter child I could not have asked for, so Thank You God.

A Note on the Author

Photo: Katharina George

Kausalya Saptharishi works in the publishing industry in India. She holds an MA in Journalism from the University of Colorado at Boulder. She is the proud mother of a sprightly six-year-old boy with whom she is rediscovering the small and beautiful moments of life. Her first novel was *The TamBrahm Bride*. She can be reached at: Kausalya.Saptharishi@gmail.com